最專業的職場會話，從此擺脫中式英文，
口說能力三級跳，倍增職場即戰力！

User's Guide 使用說明

Point ❶

76篇上班族一定會用到的情境主題

所有貼近上班族生活和工作方面的各種話題，本書全部收錄，讓你花時間學習的內容，保證能夠運用在職場上，確實達到即學即用。

Contents 目錄

002／ 使用說明　004／ 前言

Part 1 初入公司

014／ Unit 01 · Can you tell me something about my job?
你能跟我說明一下我的工作內容嗎？

017／ Unit 02 · This is your first day in our company.
這是妳第一天在公司上班。

020／ Unit 03 · How about my salary?
那我的薪水怎麼樣呢？

023／ Unit 04 · Today we will have a new colleague.
今天我們來了一位新同事。

026／ Unit 05 · Oh, it's time to have lunch. 喔，該吃午飯了

029／ Unit 06 · There are so many documents to deal with.
有好多檔案必須處理

032／ Unit 07 · How do you find your job? 妳的工作怎麼樣呢？

035／ Unit 08 · Wanna go home together? 要一起回家嗎？

Part 2 加薪與升遷

040／ Unit 09 · If there's any possibility for a salary raise.
是否有加薪的機會。

043／ Unit 10 · I decided to give you a salary increase.
我決定調整你的薪資。

046／ Unit 11 · I decided to promote you as the Sales Manager.
我決定將你升職為業務經理

049／ Unit 12 · With greater power, comes the greater responsibility. 能力越強，責任越大。

005

Unit 01

Can you tell me something about my job?

你能跟我說明一下我的工作內容嗎？

職場會話跟著說！ 🎧 Track 001

John: Please sit down. Nice to meet you, Ms. Penn. I am in charge of this section. You can call me John. And are you satisfied with our company at the present time? Tea?

Megan: No, thanks. The personnel manager just now gave me a cup of tea. This company and this job, both are satisfying. Mr. Hann, no, John, can you tell me something about my job? I am eager to know about it. Please call me Megan, too!

John: In our company, we expect our new staff can work from the bottom and work up later on. Maybe a lot of difficulties are in front of you. Can you make it without complaining?

Megan: I get it. I really appreciate you and this chance. I think it's fair for everybody to work from the bottom. I will take advantage of this opportunity to gain experiences. I believe time will tell.

John: That's good. I believe you can make it. Please try your best when you work. Remember: No pains, no gains.

約翰：請坐，很高興見到妳，潘小姐，我是負責這個部門的人。妳可以叫我約翰。妳對我們公司目前感到滿意嗎？喝茶嗎？

梅根：不用了，謝謝。剛才人事主管已經給我倒過一杯茶了。這個公司和這份工作，我都很滿意。韓先生，不，約翰，你能跟我說明一下我的工作內容嗎？我很想知道。也請叫我梅根好了！

約翰：在我們公司裡，我們希望新進職員都能從基層做起，往後再慢慢升職。或許在妳面前還有很多困難。妳能不抱怨地做到嗎？

梅根：我明白了。我真的很感謝你，也感謝這次機會。我覺得每個人從基層做起都是公平的。我會利用這次機會來累積經驗。我相信時間會證明一切。

約翰：很好，我相信你能做到這一點。你在工作的時候盡力。記住：一分耕耘，一分收穫。

014

Point ❷

不怕說錯話，不怕沒話題！

在「職場會話跟著說！」這個單元中，教你最正確、最道地、最實用的會話該怎麼說，單字該怎麼使用。害怕多說多錯的「話題終結者」有福了！這裡將為你示範延續話題的技巧和說法，讓你可以輕鬆的用英文與人暢所欲言，聽到成串的對話不再心生畏懼，也不再為了擠出一句回應而手足無措。

Point ③

文法解析讓你跟
中式英文說bye bye！

在口說會話時，身為華人很容易就掉入「中文思考」的模式，忘了英文的架構和整體思考邏輯是與中文相異的，進而掉入「中式英文」的陷阱。本書精心挑選出在每篇會話當中最可能出錯的語句進行分析，讓你掌握正確的文法，不再為中式英文所困擾。

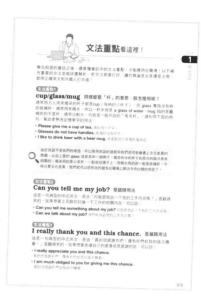

Point ④

單字大集合，
重要單字全都會

在每一單元的最後都有「會話單字懂多少？」的部分，學習完前面的會話與文法，透過寫題目的方式充分了解自己的學習程度，並利用解答迅速找出自己有哪些單字誤解了原意，進而加深對單字的印象、鞏固記憶，達到真正的高效率學習。

Preface 前言

　　在過往人們不認為「英文好」可以提升自己的職場競爭力，然而這個觀念現今已被完全地顛覆了！在地球村時代，全球商務往來頻繁，除了具備專業能力，英文更是上班族征戰職場的「語言護照」，所有待遇好、高薪的工作，除了專業技能外，大多需要具備良好的外語能力。

　　因此，把英文視為自己在職場上的「必備能力」，而非「加分工具」，是目前保有未來競爭力的最大關鍵。

　　本書以「實用性」為主要的出發點，讓有心加強英語能力的上班族可以將書中學到的句子與單字，實際應用在職場生活上，其中以簡短會話描繪出各式切合職場的情境，讓上班族可以根據所需環境做出最適當的應答，同步矯正自己的「中式英文」，從此說英文輕鬆流利、不再出糗！

　　一開始本書利用「職場會話跟著說！」的單元，帶出可能在職場上會遇到的各種情境，並為所有上班族示範該情境最正確的會話說法，以及延續話題的技巧，讓你不但會說還能說更多！接著在「文法重點看這裡！」中，把一些最容易混淆的單字，以及大家常誤用的中式英文做最全面的解析以及示範用法，鎖定細節、抓住差異，學好英文很容易！最後的「會話單字懂多少？」，則是將會話主題與文法重點相關的單字提取出來，彙整成題目做自我檢測，單字是學習語言的重要基石，懂得掌握並運用詞彙，讓英文能力向前邁進一大步！

　　希望可以勉勵所有想在職場上出頭天的上班族們，機會是留給準備好的人，只要願意努力充實自己的實力，就一定會有成功的機會，大家一起加油！

Contents 目錄

002／ 使用説明　　004／ 前言

Part 1 初入公司

014／ **Unit 01** Can you tell me something about my job?
你能跟我説明一下我的工作內容嗎？

017／ **Unit 02** This is your first day in our company.
這是妳第一天在公司上班。

020／ **Unit 03** How about my salary?
那我的薪水怎麼樣呢？

023／ **Unit 04** Today we will have a new colleague.
今天我們來了一位新同事。

026／ **Unit 05** Oh, it's time to have lunch. 噢，該吃午飯了。

029／ **Unit 06** There are so many documents to deal with.
有好多檔案必須處理。

032／ **Unit 07** How do you find your job? 妳的工作怎麼樣呢？

035／ **Unit 08** Wanna go home together? 要一起回家嗎？

Part 2 加薪與升遷

040／ **Unit 09** If there's any possibility for a salary raise.
是否有加薪的機會。

043／ **Unit 10** I decided to give you a salary increase.
我決定調整你的薪資。

046／ **Unit 11** I decided to promote you as the Sales Manager.
我決定將你升職為業務經理。

049／ **Unit 12** With greater power, comes the greater responsibility. 能力越強，責任越大。

052/ **Unit 13** ► **Stanley has been promoted as the Sales Manager.** 史丹利升職為業務經理了。

055/ **Unit 14** ► **We are going to hold a party in our company tonight.** 我們公司晚上要舉辦一個派對。

058/ **Unit 15** ► **Albert, could you explain to Simon about his daily routine first?**
艾伯特,請先告訴賽門他每天的例行公事。

061/ **Unit 16** ► **We should now make certain arrangements for your duties.** 所以現在我們必須進行分工。

064/ **Unit 17** ► **We shall discuss about the annual sales target of our department.** 我們要討論本部門年度的銷售目標。

Part **3** 通訊軟體談公事

068/ **Unit 18** ► **May I pass you to our colleague responsible for after-sale services?**
讓我把您的電話轉給負責售後服務的同事好嗎?

071/ **Unit 19** ► **Would you like to leave a message?**
你要留言給他嗎?

074/ **Unit 20** ► **Now it's time we visited our customers.**
現在是我們拜訪客戶的時候了。

077/ **Unit 21** ► **I am sure you will be interested in our products, too.** 我保證您對我們的產品也會很感興趣的。

080/ **Unit 22** ► **I have to inform all the employees in time.**
我得及時通知各位同仁。

083/ **Unit 23** ► **We must find the underlying problem in ourselves and its solution.**
我們必須找出我們自身隱藏的問題和它的解決辦法。

086/ **Unit 24** ► **Only by multiplying our efforts can we succeed in difficulties.**
只有再加倍努力,我們才能擺脫困境,取得成功。

089/ **Unit 25** ► **I want to adjust my former plan.**
我想調整一下我之前的計畫。

092／ **Unit 26** ▶ I will ask you to carry out the market survey first.
我要妳們先進行一次市場調查。

095／ **Unit 27** ▶ Now please allow me to draw a conclusion to this conference. 現在讓我對這場會議做個總結。

Part **4** 工作問題排除

100／ **Unit 28** ▶ It seems you make mistakes in the order sheet as well as the contract. 好像是訂單及合約出了錯。

103／ **Unit 29** ▶ I will ask Steven for more materials.
我等會就叫史蒂芬給我更多的資料。

106／ **Unit 30** ▶ Could you do me a favor? 妳能幫我一個忙嗎？

109／ **Unit 31** ▶ Cross the bridge when you come to it.
船到橋頭自然直。

112／ **Unit 32** ▶ I heard that you performed very well in this program. 我聽說妳在這次的工作項目中表現突出。

Part **5** 信件往來

116／ **Unit 33** ▶ Thank you for your attention and looking forward to your prompt reply.
謝謝您的關注，我們將等待您的回覆。

119／ **Unit 34** ▶ If you are interested in any of these items, please contact us.
如果您對其中任何一樣產品感興趣，敬請告知。

122／ **Unit 35** ▶ But I am afraid that we still need a further discussion. 但是，我想我們還是需要進一步的商談。

125／ **Unit 36** ▶ We would like to invite you to our anniversary celebration.
我們敬請您屆時參加我們周年慶典。

128／ **Unit 37** ▶ We are so glad to receive your letter.
很高興收到您的來信。

Part 6 簡報製作

132／ **Unit 38** ► I need you to brief me on our new item.
我要妳先向我做個新產品的簡報。

135／ **Unit 39** ► Did you work on all the papers and documents we need for tomorrow's brainstorm meeting?
明天集思會議需要的報告和檔案你都弄好了嗎？

138／ **Unit 40** ► But these figures do not support Max's argument.
但是這些數據並無法支持邁斯的論點。

141／ **Unit 41** ► And I'll make sure all the presentation slides are ready on the computer.
我也會確定電腦上的簡報投影片檔案都準備就緒。

144／ **Unit 42** ► My presentation contains two main sections: sales and distribution channels.
我的簡報包含兩個主要部分，就是銷售數字和通路。

147／ **Unit 43** ► The statistics show that sales could stand out in the third quarter even more.
統計資料顯示，銷售數字在第三季將會有更傑出的表現。

150／ **Unit 44** ► Well, we are going to make a product presentation to Top Craft Co.
我們要向頂力公司做產品簡報。

153／ **Unit 45** ► Honestly, what you mentioned last time will be a real challenge for our company. 老實說，您上次提的方案，對我們公司將會是個很大的挑戰。

156／ **Unit 46** ► I'm so honored that you joined me for the presentation.
非常榮幸你們能來參加這場產品說明會。

159／ **Unit 47** ► Therefore, this product is just right for your needs.
因此，這個產品完全符合你們的需求。

Part **7** 行銷活動

164/ **Unit 48** ► **Today we're deciding which items will be the key products that we are going to promote this quarter.** 今天我們要決定這季的重點促銷商品。

167/ **Unit 49** ► **Everyone of us will get a new assignment today.** 每個組員今天都會分配到新任務。

170/ **Unit 50** ► **I've sorted out all the materials we need and sifted three great ways of marketing.** 我已經整理出所需的資料，並篩選出三種很棒的行銷方式。

173/ **Unit 51** ► **They've promised to support our plan no matter how we would market our items.** 他們已經承諾不管我們的行銷方式為何都會贊助我們。

176/ **Unit 52** ► **We definitely need to choose internet as a means of marketing.** 我們一定要選擇網路作為行銷的工具。

179/ **Unit 53** ► **Renee, did you talk to our suppliers about our promotion details?** 芮妮，妳跟廠商談過促銷細節了嗎？

182/ **Unit 54** ► **What are we gonna do with the prices?** 我們要如何決定價格呢？

185/ **Unit 55** ► **I'm calling again to discuss the exhibitions with Mr. Martin.** 我又打來想跟馬丁先生討論展示會的事。

188/ **Unit 56** ► **Not selling like hot cakes. They are selling like crazy!** 何止賣得非常好，簡直是賣翻了！

191/ **Unit 57** ► **Dan, did you inform APR Co. that we are having a promotion for CB series?** 阿丹，你有通知APR公司我們現在CB系列有優惠的訊息嗎？

Part 8 報價與協調

196／ **Unit 58** ► She wants us to provide pricing and samples for their approval ASAP.
她要我們盡快提供報價和樣品讓她們審核。

199／ **Unit 59** ► She thinks both our pricing and minimum order quantity are too high.
她說我們報的價格和最低訂購量都太高了。

202／ **Unit 60** ► However, our supplier insists on increasing MOQ to 1000 dozen.
但是，我們的廠商堅持一定要將最低訂購量調到1000打。

205／ **Unit 61** ► Will we make any money on this order if we agree to her price?
如果我們接受她的價格，我們還有利潤嗎？

208／ **Unit 62** ► After negotiating with our supplier, we now can offer you $15.00 per dozen. 在跟廠商協商之後，現在我們可以提供妳一打15美元的價格。

211／ **Unit 63** ► I'd like to know what would be your production lead time for a new order of 10K forks.
我想知道10萬支叉子從下單到出貨要多少時間。

214／ **Unit 64** ► We will send the signed contract over and proceed with your order in no time. 我們馬上會簽好合約寄過去，然後立刻處理您的訂單。

217／ **Unit 65** ► It's a bit late since it's supposed be made a month ago.
這筆款項有點遲了，應該一個月以前就要付了。

220／ **Unit 66** ► I'm sorry for the defective goods.
對於瑕疵品我們深感抱歉。

Part 9 展覽

224／ **Unit 67** You will be responsible for the exhibition this year.
妳將負責今年的展覽事宜。

227／ **Unit 68** Dan and I will work on the design of our booth.
阿丹和我會負責設計我們的攤位。

230／ **Unit 69** I've also got the information about move-in and move-out hours and the show hours.
我手上也有進出場時間及展示時間的資料。

233／ **Unit 70** By the way, when is the application deadline?
對了，參展報名截止是什麼時候？

236／ **Unit 71** Actually, we went online and collected lots of fair related materials.
其實，我們上網收集了很多展覽相關資料。

239／ **Unit 72** The main point of our show is to promote our latest products into the global market.
我們展覽的重點就是要把最新的產品推到國際市場。

242／ **Unit 73** We are not far from the fair. 我們離展場並不遠。

245／ **Unit 74** Dan, what do you think of our exhibition so far?
阿丹，你覺得到目前為止我們展覽辦得如何？

248／ **Unit 75** Maybe we should buy some creative products for our RD team.
也許我們該幫研發團隊帶些有創意的產品回去。

251／ **Unit 76** We will inform you of the shipping details before we ship the goods. 我們出貨前還會再通知妳出貨明細。

Part **1**

初入公司

Can you tell me something about my job?

你能跟我說明一下我的工作內容嗎？

 職場會話跟著說！ Track 001

John: Please sit down. Nice to meet you, Ms. Penn. I am in charge of this section. You can call me John. And are you satisfied with our company at the present time? Tea?

約翰：請坐！很高興見到妳，潘小姐。我是這個部門的負責人，妳可以叫我約翰。妳對我們公司目前還滿意吧？需要喝茶嗎？

Megan: No, thanks. The personnel manager just now gave me a cup of tea. This company and this job, both are satisfying. Mr. Hann, no, John, can you tell me something about my job? I am eager to know about it. Please call me Megan, too!

梅根：不用了，謝謝。剛才人事主管已經為我倒過一杯茶了。這個公司和這份工作都很讓人滿意。韓先生，喔不，是約翰，你能跟我說明一下我的工作內容嗎？我非常想要快點瞭解。也請你稱呼我梅根就好了！

John: In our company, we expect our new staff can work from the bottom and work up later on. Maybe a lot of difficulties are in front of you. Can you make it without complaining?

約翰：在我們這個公司，我們希望我們的新員工能從底層做起，然後再逐漸地往上升遷。可能妳會面臨到很多工作上的困難！妳能毫無怨言，做好分內的工作嗎？

Megan: I get it. I really appreciate you and this chance. I think it's fair for everybody to work from the bottom. I will take advantage of this opportunity to gain experiences. I believe time will tell.

梅根：我明白。真的很感謝你們，還有你們給我的這次機會。從底層做起對誰都是公平的。我會好好利用這次機會，獲得工作經驗。我相信時間會證明一切的。

John: That's good. I believe you can make it. Please try your best when you work. Remember: No pains, no gains.

約翰：很好。我相信妳能做到這一點。請努力工作吧！記住：要怎麼收穫，先怎麼栽！

文法重點看這裡！

學完前面的會話之後，還要懂會話中的文法重點，才能應用在職場！以下補充重要的文法並做詳盡解析，把文法根基打好，讓你無論是出差還是洽商，都用正確英文和外國人打交道！

文法重點1

cup/glass/mug 同樣都是「杯」的意思，該怎麼用呢？

通常西方人用來喝茶的杯子都是cup（有柄的小杯子），而 glass 專指沒有柄的玻璃杯，通常用來喝水，所以一杯水就是 a glass of water。mug 指的是圓桶狀的平底杯，通常比較大，也就是一般所説的「馬克杯」。請利用下面的例句，幫助更熟悉記憶單字的用法：

- **Please give me a cup of tea.** 請給我一杯茶。
- **Glasses do not have handles.** 玻璃杯沒有把手。
- **I like to drink beer with a beer mug.** 我喜歡用大啤酒杯喝啤酒。

由於英語不是我們的母語，所以使用英語的過程中我們很可能會遇上文化差異的問題。比如上面的 glass 就是其中一個例子。喝茶和水的杯子在西方的區分是很明顯的。喝茶用的是小茶杯，一般放在碟子上，而喝水用的則一般是玻璃杯。平時注意文化差異，我們就可以很有效的避免在職場上鬧出令你出糗的笑話了。

文法重點2

Can you tell me my job? 是錯誤用法

這是一句典型的中式英文，是由「你能跟我説一下我的工作內容嗎？」直翻過來的。如果想要上司跟你討論一下工作的相關內容，可以說：

- **Can you tell me something about my job?** 你能跟我説一下我的工作內容嗎？
- **Can we talk about my job?** 我們能談談我的工作內容嗎？

文法重點3

I really thank you and this chance. 是錯誤用法

這是一句典型的中式英文，是由「真的很感謝你們，還有你們給我的這次機會。」直翻過來的。如果想要表達自己的感激或是感謝的話，可以說：

- **I really appreciate you and this chance.**
  真的很感謝你們，還有你們給我的這次機會。
- **I am much obliged to you for giving me this chance.**
  真的很感謝你們給我這次機會。

會話單字懂多少？

讀過前面的內容後，你是不是都懂得這些單字了呢？下列題目中的單字都是與會話及文法相關的單字，測驗看看自己會了多少吧！

( ) ❶ staff： (A) 開始 (B) 員工 (C) 稅收

( ) ❷ supervisor： (A) 超級明星 (B) 建議人 (C) 主管

( ) ❸ excuse： (A) 藉口 (B) 慢跑 (C) 參加

( ) ❹ charge： (A) 圖表 (B) 負責 (C) 飛標

( ) ❺ section： (A) 部門 (B) 分割 (C) 設置

( ) ❻ satisfy： (A) 坐下 (B) 輕鬆 (C) 滿意

( ) ❼ bottom： (A) 底部 (B) 借取 (C) 墳墓

( ) ❽ handle： (A) 手 (B) 把手 (C) 懶散

( ) ❾ mug： (A) 馬克杯 (B) 泥土 (C) 偷運

( ) ❿ personnel： (A) 人員 (B) 人力 (C) 人才

( ) ⓫ manager： (A) 控制 (B) 經理 (C) 生氣

( ) ⓬ complain： (A) 抱怨 (B) 完全 (C) 競爭

( ) ⓭ appreciate： (A) 合適 (B) 感謝 (C) 估計

( ) ⓮ advantage： (A) 優勢 (B) 進步 (C) 劣勢

( ) ⓯ opportunity： (A) 港口 (B) 機會 (C) 反對

答案： 1. (B) 2. (C) 3. (A) 4. (B) 5. (A) 6. (C) 7. (A) 8. (B) 9. (A)
10. (A) 11. (B) 12. (A) 13. (B) 14. (A) 15. (B)

This is your first day in our company.

這是妳第一天在公司上班。

職場會話跟著說！ 🎧 Track **002**

Tony: Hi, Megan, have you finished the talk with John already? Are you available now? If so, let me describe your work duties, OK?

東尼：嗨，梅根，妳和約翰已經談完了嗎？妳現在有空嗎？如果現在有空的話，就讓我幫妳介紹一下工作內容，可以嗎？

Megan: Yeah, we just talked about my future job. And the supervisor hoped that I can make progress by degrees in my work. I am free now. And what am I expected to do?

梅根：是的，我們剛剛談了一下我的工作。主管希望我能在工作中逐步進步。我現在沒事了，我要做些什麼工作呢？

Tony: As a newcomer, you are going to be responsible for some basic tasks first, including certain routine duties like answering the telephone, typing... Later, you will be assigned to the sales department. There you can learn much about the workings of our company and its sales quickly.

東尼：身為一個新員工，妳必須要先負責一些基本的工作，包括一些每天的例行公事；比如說接電話啦，打字之類的。日後，你會被分配到銷售部去。在那裡，妳可以瞭解到很多關於我們公司營運以及銷售方面的情況。

Megan: I see. It must be a challenging job. But it's not a surprise to me. That's to be expected. I can deal with it as well as I can. And what about now? What should I do? Er...if I have some problems, may I speak out directly?

梅根：我明白了。這一定是一個充滿挑戰性的工作。但是這並不會讓我太吃驚，也是意料之中的事情。我會盡我所能把它做好。那麼現在呢？我應該做什麼？呢……如果我遇到問題的話，我能直接說出來嗎？

Tony: For this is your first day in our company, you can begin with our products. Before you do your job, it's necessary for you to be familiar with our own products. Then you can get down to your work smoothly. Don't hesitate to tell us if you have a problem.

東尼：由於這是妳第一天在公司上班，妳可以先從產品開始。在妳開始工作前，有必要先熟悉一下我們自己的產品，然後就可以比較順利地開始工作了。有問題就請妳發問！

文法重點看這裡！

學完前面的會話之後，還要懂會話中的文法重點，才能應用在職場！以下補充重要的文法並做詳盡解析，把文法根基打好，讓你無論是出差還是洽商，都用正確英文和外國人打交道！

文法重點1

say/speak/state 同樣都是「說」，該怎麼用呢？

以上三者都可以用來表示「口語表達」，但如果是「說的內容是一般生活上的內容」通常是用 say；而「說某種語言」則是用 speak，例如：speak English（說英語），state 較 say 和 speak 更為正式，且含有「權威性，武斷」的意味，state 也可以用來指某人明確的立場或對事物的觀感。另外，say 和 state 也可以用在書面表達方面，如 the book said that（書上說⋯⋯）。請利用下面的例句，幫助更熟悉記憶單字的用法：

- **Kenneth said that he didn't want to go to the party.**
  肯尼斯說他不要去參加派對。
- **The two friends had not spoken to each other in two years.**
  這兩個朋友彼此之間已經兩年沒有說話了。
- **The witness stated that he saw the accused at the scene of the crime.**
  目擊者陳述他看到了被告出現在犯罪現場。

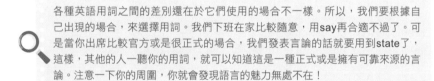

各種英語用詞之間的差別還在於它們使用的場合不一樣。所以，我們要根據自己出現的場合，來選擇用詞。我們下班在家比較隨意，用say再合適不過了。可是當你出席比較官方或是很正式的場合，我們發表言論的話就要用到state了，這樣，其他的人一聽你的用詞，就可以知道這是一種正式或是擁有可靠來源的言論。注意一下你的周圍，你就會發現語言的魅力無處不在！

文法重點2

I have nothing now! 是錯誤用法

這是一句典型的中式英文，是由「我沒事了。」直翻過來的。如果想要表述自己現在有空，可以說：

- **I am free now.** 我現在有空。
- **I am available now.** 我現在有空。

會話單字懂多少？

讀過前面的內容後，你是不是都懂得這些單字了呢？下列題目中的單字都是與會話及文法相關的單字，測驗看看自己會了多少吧！

( ) ❶ available： (A) 便利的 (B) 有空的 (C) 多樣的

( ) ❷ describe： (A) 描述 (B) 增加 (C) 印刷

( ) ❸ responsible： (A) 反映 (B) 負責的 (C) 思考

( ) ❹ assign： (A) 謀殺 (B) 指派 (C) 符號

( ) ❺ department： (A) 部門 (B) 離別 (C) 寓所

( ) ❻ necessary： (A) 薪水 (B) 有必要的 (C) 評估

( ) ❼ familiar： (A) 名譽 (B) 家庭 (C) 熟悉的

( ) ❽ smoothly： (A) 牙齒 (B) 流暢地 (C) 推進

( ) ❾ hesitate： (A) 表達 (B) 遲疑 (C) 情況

( ) ❿ witness： (A) 目擊 (B) 智慧 (C) 邪惡

( ) ⓫ accuse： (A) 控告 (B) 理由 (C) 接受

( ) ⓬ progress： (A) 進步 (B) 草 (C) 節目

( ) ⓭ degree： (A) 程度 (B) 同意 (C) 減少

( ) ⓮ deal： (A) 處理 (B) 昂貴 (C) 分發

( ) ⓯ instruction： (A) 阻礙 (B) 指導 (C) 興趣

答案： 1. (B) 2. (A) 3. (B) 4. (B) 5. (A) 6. (B) 7. (C) 8. (B) 9. (B)
10. (A) 11. (A) 12. (A) 13. (A) 14. (A) 15. (B)

How about my salary?

那我的薪水怎麼樣呢？

 職場會話跟著說！ 🎧 Track 003

Megan: Tony, how about my salary? You have decided to meet all my requirements? I hope you can consider it carefully. I think a good company will ensure its staff a good salary. In return, the staff can work harder and harder for the company.

梅根：東尼，那我的薪水怎麼樣呢？你決定答應我所提出的薪資嗎？我希望你能認真考慮一下。我認為一間好的公司能保證給它的員工一份好的薪水。相對地，它的員工也會更賣力的為公司工作。

Tony: Yes, you are one hundred percent right. Our company provides every employee here with a good welfare, in order to let them concentrate on their work. So don't worry about that. We agree to all of them. Congratulations!

東尼：是的，妳說的完全正確。我們公司給每一個員工都提供了一個相當好的福利政策，就是要讓大家能專心工作。因此，妳不用擔心這個了，我們決定同意妳提出的薪水，恭喜了！

Megan: Wow, really thank you. Plus, when can I get my salary then? And also, do you mind telling me something else, like attendance record, holiday, and how to ask for leave?

梅根：哇，真的太感謝了！另外，我們是什麼時候領薪水呢？您不介意告訴我一下別的事情吧？比如出缺勤應注意的事項、放假，還有該如何請假之類的事情。

Tony: All new staff members are likely to ask the same questions. Haha...I can understand that. Er...on the 20th day of every month, you can get your salary on time. And you are required to work for eight hours per day, from nine a.m. to six p.m. Every month you have three days off, except the weekend and some important holidays.

東尼：所有的新員工似乎都會問同樣的問題。哈哈……我能明白。每個月的20號可以領到薪水。妳需要每天工作八小時，早上九點上班，下午六點下班。除重大節日和週末外，每月還有三天假。

Megan: Okay. That's good. I get it. I have no question to ask. And do you have anything else to tell me, Tony?

梅根：好的，太好了。明白了。我沒有問題了。你還有什麼事情要跟我說嗎，東尼？

文法重點看這裡！

學完前面的會話之後，還要懂會話中的文法重點，才能應用在職場！以下補充重要的文法並做詳盡解析，把文法根基打好，讓你無論是出差還是洽商，都用正確英文和外國人打交道！

文法重點1

salary/wage/fee 同樣都有「薪水」的意思，該怎麼用呢？

salary 在西方國家通常是指「有專門技能的人員、企業管理人員或經理人員」所領取的薪水，一般是月薪或是年薪；而 wage 在西方常指「勞動者」所領取的薪水，一般指週薪或時薪、日薪；fee則是指一次付清的固定報酬，指「自由職業者，如律師、醫生、會計師」收取的各種費用。請利用下面的例句，幫助更熟悉記憶單字的用法：

- **As a manager, he earns a huge salary every year.**
  身為一名經理人，他每年都獲得很高的薪資。
- **My wages are 200 dollars an hour.**
  我的時薪是二百元。
- **The layewr charged an enormous fee in the divorce case.**
  那名律師在離婚案中索取了昂貴的費用。

　　人類的語言源遠流長，它是伴隨著人類的發展而發展，進步而進步的。所以，語言就會反映發展中的各種現象。在人類歷史上，我們有過腦力勞動和體力勞動的分工，正因為如此，我們的薪水階級也因此而不同。體力勞動者的工資被叫做 wage，而腦力勞動者的工資則是 salary 這個單字。語言和社會是緊密相連的，我們可以從社會中找尋語言的意義所在。

文法重點2

How is my wage? 是錯誤用法

這是一句典型的中式英文，是由「那我的薪水怎麼樣？」直翻過來的。如果想要說詢問自己的薪水怎麼樣，可以說：

- **What about my wage?**
  那我的薪水怎麼樣？
- **How about my wage?**
  那我的薪水怎麼樣？

會話單字懂多少？

讀過前面的內容後,你是不是都懂得這些單字了呢?下列題目中的單字都是與會話及文法相關的單字,測驗看看自己會了多少吧!

( ) ❶ wage: (A) 水 (B) 龐大 (C) 薪酬

( ) ❷ employee: (A) 員工 (B) 雇傭 (C) 空曠

( ) ❸ welfare: (A) 健康 (B) 收費 (C) 福利

( ) ❹ concentrate: (A) 集中 (B) 關心 (C) 會議

( ) ❺ enjoy: (A) 快樂 (B) 享受 (C) 拆封

( ) ❻ salary: (A) 沙拉 (B) 薪水 (C) 春天

( ) ❼ fee: (A) 費用 (B) 感覺 (C) 腳部

( ) ❽ divorce: (A) 聲音 (B) 離婚 (C) 分開

( ) ❾ ensure: (A) 確保 (B) 說明 (C) 保險

( ) ❿ return: (A) 歸還 (B) 轉彎 (C) 放鬆

( ) ⓫ percent: (A) 禮物 (B) 百分比 (C) 美分

( ) ⓬ congratulations: (A) 祝賀 (B) 議會 (C) 感激

( ) ⓭ attendance: (A) 跳舞 (B) 出席 (C) 照顧

( ) ⓮ leave: (A) 請假 (B) 葉子 (C) 草原

( ) ⓯ except: (A) 興奮 (B) 除了 (C) 接受

答案: 1. (C) 2. (A) 3. (C) 4. (A) 5. (B) 6. (B) 7. (A) 8. (B) 9. (A)
10. (A) 11. (B) 12. (A) 13. (B) 14. (A) 15. (B)

Unit 04

Today we will have a new colleague.

今天我們來了一位新同事。

 職場會話跟著說！ Track 004

Fank: Hello, everybody, let me have your attention, please. Today we will have a new colleague. Megan, could you introduce yourself to us first?

法蘭克：大家好，請注意了。今天我們來了一位新同事。梅根，妳先為我們做個自我介紹好嗎？

Megan: Hello, everyone, nice to meet you. My name is Megan. I am a newcomer in our company. I must say I feel so honored to work with you. I hope we can be friends in the near future.

梅根：大家好，很高興見到你們。我叫梅根，是新來的。我想說我感到很榮幸能與你們一起工作。希望在不久的將來，我們能成為朋友。

Frank: Certainly we can. And Megan, come on, tell us more about you. Your hobby, your personality, or even your ambition, your ideas, if you don't mind? Everything is OK here.

法蘭克：當然了。梅根，快點告訴我們更多關於妳的事吧？比如妳的愛好，妳的個性，甚至是妳的志向、想法，如果妳不介意的話？在這裡，講什麼都可以的。

Megan: I am trying to make my dream come true. And this company gives me a precious chance. I won't let it go. I hope I can make some achievements here and make progress with all of you together. So, you can see that I am a determined person.

梅根：我在努力實現自己的夢想。這個公司給了我一個寶貴的機會，我會牢牢把它抓住。我希望我能在這裡做出一點成就，與諸位共同進步。因此，你們也可以看出，我是一個有決心的人。

Frank: You know, a person with perseverance is always welcomed here.

法蘭克：我們這裡歡迎有毅力的人。

文法重點看這裡！

學完前面的會話之後，還要懂會話中的文法重點，才能應用在職場！以下補充重要的文法並做詳盡解析，把文法根基打好，讓你無論是出差還是洽商，都用正確英文和外國人打交道！

文法重點1

aid/assist/help 都有「幫忙」的意思

assist 是「以助手的方式來協助」。aid 則是比較積極的救助，如公益團體對弱勢團體的救助就用 aid。help 的用途最廣，大部分的情況都可以用 help 來代替 aid 和 assist。help 通常和 with 連用，例如 help me with the luggage（幫我提行李）。

請利用下面的例句，幫助更熟悉記憶單字的用法：

- **She came to the gentleman's aid.** 她來援助那位先生。
- **She assisted the hostess with preparing snacks.** 她協助女主人準備點心。
- **She helps with housework at home.** 她在家時會幫忙做家事。

> 上面的 assist 的意思是以助手的形式去幫助他人完成某樣事情。如果是剛來的新人，我們是不可能要求別人做自己的助手的。所以新人萬萬不能對前輩說you can assist me（你可以幫我忙），而是要用give me a hand（幫幫我）。

文法重點2

hope 的用法

hope 作為動詞，後面如果要接另一個動作，需要使用 hope to do sth. 的結構。

- **I hope to fly into the blue sky like a bird.** 我希望像鳥兒一樣飛向藍天。

也可以用 that 接一個句子（that 可以省略）。

- **I hope that I can grow up quickly.** 我希望我能快快長大。

> I just hope do something here.是一個錯誤示範！hope和do兩個動詞不可以直接連用，應該插入to或者改用that子句，如：
> - **I just hope to do something here.** 我只是希望能在這裡做點什麼。
> - **I just hope that I can do something here.**
>   我只是希望我可以在這裡做點什麼。

會話單字懂多少？

讀過前面的內容後，你是不是都懂得這些單字了呢？下列題目中的單字都是與會話及文法相關的單字，測驗看看自己會了多少吧！

( ) **❶ attention**： (A) 注意 (B) 參加 (C) 努力

( ) **❷ colleague**： (A) 大學 (B) 同事 (C) 團隊

( ) **❸ introduce**： (A) 興趣 (B) 導入 (C) 介紹

( ) **❹ hobby**： (A) 愛好 (B) 曲棍球 (C) 照顧

( ) **❺ personality**： (A) 人性 (B) 個性 (C) 素質

( ) **❻ ambition**： (A) 範圍 (B) 軌道 (C) 志向

( ) **❼ expectation**： (A) 期望 (B) 過期 (C) 專家

( ) **❽ assist**： (A) 扶住 (B) 堅持 (C) 協助

( ) **❾ snack**： (A) 抓 (B) 蛇 (C) 點心

( ) **❿ honor**： (A) 榮幸 (B) 磨刀石 (C) 線索

( ) **⓫ precious**： (A) 寶貴 (B) 謹慎 (C) 預言

( ) **⓬ achievement**： (A) 承認 (B) 成就 (C) 創造

( ) **⓭ determine**： (A) 決定 (B) 減少 (C) 指責

( ) **⓮ perseverance**： (A) 保留 (B) 毅力 (C) 儲備

( ) **⓯ experience**： (A) 希望 (B) 經驗 (C) 實驗

答案：1. (A) 2. (B) 3. (C) 4. (A) 5. (B) 6. (C) 7. (A) 8. (C) 9. (C)
　　　10. (A) 11. (A) 12. (B) 13. (A) 14. (B) 15. (B)

Oh, it's time to have lunch.

噢，該吃午飯了。

Megan: Oh, it's time to have lunch. But I don't know where the restaurant is. Excuse me, may I ask where I can have my lunch?

梅根：噢，該吃午飯了。但是我不知道餐廳在哪裡。不好意思，請問我可以去哪裡吃午餐啊？

Sarah: Tony didn't tell you yet? You can follow me then, and I'll treat you to lunch, my new colleague. My name is Sarah, nice to meet you!

莎拉：難道東尼還沒告訴妳嗎？那妳跟著我吧，我就順便請我的新同事吃個飯吧。我叫莎拉，很高興認識妳！

Megan: Thank you very much, Sarah. I need to get familiar with these trifles, so that I won't waste too much time on them and bother you guys, either.

梅根：非常謝謝妳，莎拉！我覺得我該熟悉一下這些事，以便日後在這些事情上不會浪費太多時間，還麻煩了妳們。

Sarah: It doesn't matter. Have you known of your work now? I believe you will get used to it very soon. Don't feel too ashamed to ask for help.

莎拉：沒關係。妳現在知道妳的工作內容了嗎？我相信妳很快就會上手的。如果有什麼需要幫忙的，請不要不好意思說出來喔。

Megan: That's very kind. I have already roughly known of my job. Thank you for your concern.

梅根：妳真是太好了！我已經大致知道我的工作內容了。謝謝妳的關心！

文法重點看這裡！

學完前面的會話之後，還要懂會話中的文法重點，才能應用在職場！以下補充重要的文法並做詳盡解析，把文法根基打好，讓你無論是出差還是洽商，都用正確英文和外國人打交道！

文法重點1

also/too/either 同樣都有「也」的意思，該怎麼用呢？

三者都有「也」的意思，但只有 either 用於否定句，或句子中含有否定的意味。而 also 和 too 的差別在於：also 放在主要動詞之前或動詞之後，too 只能放在句中及句末。請利用下面的例句，幫助更熟悉記憶單字的用法：

- **He teaches English, I also teach that language.** 他教英語，我也教英語。
- **You like tomatoes, I like them too.** 你喜歡吃番茄，我也喜歡。
- **My father doesn't like such music, I don't either.**
  我爸爸不喜歡這種音樂，我也是。

文法重點2

waste 的用法

當 waste 作動詞用的時候，可以表達浪費時間，精力的意思。而 lose 則沒有，僅表示失去，丟失的意思。這時，waste 常和 on 搭配使用，例如：

- **He wastes so much time on this project.** 他在這個計畫上浪費太多時間了。

也可以作名詞來用，表達同樣的意思，例如：

- **The manager thinks it's a waste of time.** 經理認為這是在浪費時間。

I won't lose my time on it.是一個錯誤示範！lose意為「失去；迷失；輸了」，這句話的正確説法為：
- **I won't waste my time on it.** 我不會在這件事上浪費時間。

文法重點3

Hi, what place can I have my lunch? 是錯誤用法

這是一句典型的中式英文，是由「嗨，請問我可以到什麼地方吃午餐呢？」直翻過來的。如果想要打擾一下他人詢問某事，可以説：

- **Excuse me, may I ask where I can have my lunch?**
  不好意思，請問我可以去哪裡吃午餐呢？
- **Please, could you tell me where to have lunch?**
  可以請你告訴我哪裡可以吃午餐嗎？

會話單字懂多少？

讀過前面的內容後，你是不是都懂得這些單字了呢？下列題目中的單字都是與會話及文法相關的單字，測驗看看自己會了多少吧！

( ) ❶ restaurant： (A) 休息 (B) 餐廳 (C) 標準

( ) ❷ yet： (A) 是 (B) 還 (C) 吃

( ) ❸ dinner： (A) 禮貌 (B) 校長 (C) 正餐

( ) ❹ bother： (A) 哥哥 (B) 麻煩 (C) 借取

( ) ❺ pleasure： (A) 請求 (B) 確定 (C) 快樂

( ) ❻ tomato： (A) 番茄 (B) 明天 (C) 墳墓

( ) ❼ either： (A) 枯萎 (B) 也 (C) 其他

( ) ❽ project： (A) 工程 (B) 期許 (C) 注射

( ) ❾ disturb： (A) 辭退 (B) 打擾 (C) 丟失

( ) ❿ follow： (A) 跟隨 (B) 荒蕪的 (C) 傻瓜

( ) ⓫ trifle： (A) 瑣事 (B) 換班 (C) 文件

( ) ⓬ waste： (A) 粘貼 (B) 智慧 (C) 浪費

( ) ⓭ ashamed： (A) 害羞的 (B) 粉塵 (C) 痛苦的

( ) ⓮ roughly： (A) 勉強地 (B) 一般地 (C) 大致地

( ) ⓯ concern： (A) 關心 (B) 審批 (C) 音樂會

答案： 1. (B) 2. (B) 3. (C) 4. (B) 5. (C) 6. (A) 7. (B) 8. (A) 9. (B)
10. (A) 11. (A) 12. (C) 13. (A) 14. (C) 15. (A)

There are so many documents to deal with.

有好多檔案必須處理。

 職場會話跟著說！ 🎧 Track **006**

Sarah: Megan, there are so many documents for me to deal with. I am afraid I can't submit them to our supervisor in time. Could you help me?

莎拉：梅根，我現在手頭上有好多檔案必須處理。我怕我來不及交給主管。妳能幫我一下嗎？

Megan: No problem. I have finished my own work now. Tell me, what can I help you?

梅根：沒問題。我已經把我自己的事做完了。跟我說吧，我能幫妳做點什麼呢？

Sarah: Thanks. You can help me design a form by using Excel, then input data into it, and lastly print the form and give it to me, OK? Here are the files.

莎拉：謝謝妳了。我需要妳幫我用Excel 設計一個表格，然後輸入資料，最後把這個表格列印出來交給我，好嗎？檔案在這裡。

Megan: Okay. And can you tell me which items are required? Shall I need to highlight them with color, so that you can get it more conveniently and quickly?

梅根：好的。妳能告訴我哪些項目是妳需要的嗎？我需要用顏色把它們區分開來，讓妳看起來更方便、更快速一點嗎？

Sarah: One in this file, one in this, two in that... You can do it like that. All the data in these items mentioned must be input. Each heading of the items should be colored and all the headings should be put in the same row.

莎拉：有一個項目在這個檔案裡，一個在另一個檔案，還有兩個在這個檔案裡……妳可以按照這樣來做。我剛剛所提到的這些項目中的所有資料，都必須輸入進去。項目的標題都要用顏色標示出來，而所有的標題都保持在同一行裡。

Megan: OK, I see. I'll make sure all the items are contained. By the way, what about its specification when I print it? Do you need to use the continuous forms paper?

梅根：好的，我明白了。我會確保所有的項目都包括進來。順便問一下，列印表格時，要使用什麼規格呢？需要用連續列印紙嗎？

Sarah: Just the normal style.

莎拉：普通樣式就行了。

文法重點看這裡！

學完前面的會話之後，還要懂會話中的文法重點，才能應用在職場！以下補充重要的文法並做詳盡解析，把文法根基打好，讓你無論是出差還是洽商，都用正確英文和外國人打交道！

文法重點1

choose/select/pick 同樣都有「選」的意思，該怎麼用呢？

select含有「選拔」的意思，強調在特定的範圍內進行精心的比較和淘汰，並以客觀為標準進行選擇。而 choose 是最常見的一般用詞，指一般的「選擇」，含有憑個人判斷作出選擇的意思。pick則是從許多物件中進行挑選。請利用下面的例句，幫助你更熟悉記憶單字的用法：

- **There are plenty of restaurants to choose from.** 有許多餐館供你選擇。
- **Pick a number from one to twenty.** 請從一到二十中挑選一個數字。
- **He hasn't been selected for the team.** 他未能選進那個隊伍。

文法重點2

require 的用法

require作為動詞，意思是「要求」或「需求」。

- **I add all the items that you require.** 我加入所有你要求的元素了。

而一個物件作主語或是主語是被動物件時，常用被動態表示。例如：
- **All the items required are included.** 所有需求都包含在裡面了。

And which items are you require? 是一個錯誤示範！這句犯了動詞使用上的錯誤，正確的說法為：
- **Which items do you require?** 哪些項目是你需要的？
- **Which items are required?** 哪些項目是你需要的？

文法重點3

It's out of the question. 是錯誤用法

這是一句典型的中式英文，是由「這是沒有問題的。」直翻過來的，英文意思卻是「這是不可能的。」。如果想要表達某事沒有任何問題，可以說：

- **It's out of question.** 這是沒有問題的。
- **No problem!** 沒問題！

會話單字懂多少？

讀過前面的內容後，你是不是都懂得這些單字了呢？下列題目中的單字都是與會話及文法相關的單字，測驗看看自己會了多少吧！

( ) ❶ successful： (A) 繼承 (B) 成功的 (C) 可進入的

( ) ❷ document： (A) 文件 (B) 公司 (C) 妥協

( ) ❸ design： (A) 標記 (B) 決定 (C) 設計

( ) ❹ form： (A) 來自 (B) 表格 (C) 為了

( ) ❺ data： (A) 逗號 (B) 約會 (C) 資料

( ) ❻ file： (A) 解雇 (B) 檔案 (C) 火苗

( ) ❼ mention： (A) 提到 (B) 介意 (C) 修補

( ) ❽ select： (A) 愚蠢 (B) 演講 (C) 選擇

( ) ❾ submit： (A) 提交 (B) 減去 (C) 次要

( ) ❿ highlight： (A) 燈光 (B) 醒目 (C) 高尚的

( ) ⓫ conveniently： (A) 方便 (B) 交談 (C) 傳遞

( ) ⓬ heading： (A) 標題 (B) 頭上 (C) 閱讀

( ) ⓭ contain： (A) 棉花 (B) 阻止 (C) 包括

( ) ⓮ specification： (A) 期望 (B) 規格 (C) 特殊

( ) ⓯ continuous： (A) 減少 (B) 緊張 (C) 持續

答案： 1. (B) 2. (A) 3. (C) 4. (B) 5. (C) 6. (B) 7. (A) 8. (C) 9. (A)
10. (B) 11. (A) 12. (A) 13. (C) 14. (B) 15. (C)

How do you find your job?

妳的工作怎麼樣呢？

 職場會話跟著說！ Track 007

Daniel: Hi, Megan, take a seat! How do you find your job?

丹尼爾：嗨，梅根，請坐！妳的工作怎麼樣呢？

Megan: Great! In the morning, Tony told me about my work. After lunch, I began my work. Especially, during the fifteen minutes' break, I printed a data table for Sarah.

梅根：很好啊！早上東尼有告訴我工作的內容。午餐後我就開始工作了。特別是在中間十五分鐘休息的空檔，我還幫莎拉列印了一個資料表格。

Daniel: Good job! It seems you are busy with your work now. Are you accustomed to it?

丹尼爾：妳表現得很好！看來現在工作開始忙起來了。還習慣嗎？

Megan: I think I learned a lot from that. I am familiar with our products, the management system as well as file manipulation. All in all, owing to my colleagues' help, I've successfully completed my task.

梅根：我想我學到了很多東西。我熟悉了產品、管理系統還有檔案處理。總之，多虧了同事們的幫助，我才得以完成了自己的任務。

Daniel: I must praise you for your modesty and diligence. These can help you go further in your career.

丹尼爾：我真是必須稱讚一下妳的勤奮和謙虛呢！這些絕對能幫助妳在職業生涯中走得更遠。

Megan: Thanks for your compliment. There are still plenty more to learn.

梅根：謝謝您的誇獎。還有很多需要學習的呢！

文法重點看這裡！

學完前面的會話之後，還要懂會話中的文法重點，才能應用在職場！以下補充重要的文法並做詳盡解析，把文法根基打好，讓你無論是出差還是洽商，都用正確英文和外國人打交道！

文法重點1

break/pause/interval 同樣都有「停」的意思，該怎麼用呢？

pause 指的是短暫的停頓，原先的狀態並沒有改變，例如音響上的暫停鍵就是 pause，原先播放的音樂還是停留在原來的地方。而 break 則強調中斷，改變了原先的狀態，至於中斷的時間則可長可短。interval 是指兩件事情之間的時間間隔，也指兩幕或兩場戲之間的休息時間。請利用下面的例句，幫助更熟悉記憶單字的用法：

- **Let's take a break and have our lunch.** 停下來吃飯吧！
- **The speaker had to pause as he had forgotten what he was going to say.** 演講者不得不停頓一下，因為他忘了他要說的話。
- **He came at intervals of about a month.** 他每隔一個月左右來一次。

關於「休息時間」在英語中有各種不同的說法，平時上班、上學、開會時有休息時間（break）。表演演出有幕間休息時間（interval），台上發言人講話也會有個停頓（pause），請好好分辨並使用吧！

文法重點2

how 的用法

當我們要用 how 來引導一個感歎句的時候，後面直接加上形容詞，然後再接名詞，例如：

- **How beautiful the girl is!** 這個女孩好漂亮！
- **How beautiful a girl!** 這個女孩好漂亮！

也可以用 what，但是用法有些不同，也可以直接接名詞。例如：

- **What a beautiful girl!** 好一個漂亮的女孩！

How busy day! 是一個錯誤示範！這句話的正確說法為：
- **How busy a day!** 真是忙碌的一天！
- **How busy the day is!** 真是忙碌的一天！
- **What a busy day!** 真是忙碌的一天！

會話單字懂多少？

讀過前面的內容後，你是不是都懂得這些單字了呢？下列題目中的單字都是與會話及文法相關的單字，測驗看看自己會了多少吧！

( ) ❶ find： (A) 良好 (B) 結實 (C) 找到

( ) ❷ pause： (A) 停止 (B) 鼓掌 (C) 驕傲

( ) ❸ accustom： (A) 習俗 (B) 習慣 (C) 控告

( ) ❹ modest： (A) 謙虛 (B) 模式 (C) 模特兒

( ) ❺ diligence：(A) 紳士 (B) 勤奮 (C) 挖掘

( ) ❻ quality： (A) 能力 (B) 數量 (C) 品質

( ) ❼ excellent： (A) 驅逐 (B) 優秀 (C) 顧客

( ) ❽ forget： (A) 拋棄 (B) 保護 (C) 忘記

( ) ❾ interval： (A) 間隔 (B) 內部 (C) 網路

( ) ❿ especially： (A) 昂貴 (B) 尤其 (C) 偵察

( ) ⓫ manipulation： (A) 消滅 (B) 處理 (C) 污染

( ) ⓬ owe： (A) 賒欠 (B) 擁有 (C) 悲哀

( ) ⓭ complete： (A) 刪除 (B) 完成 (C) 恭維

( ) ⓮ career： (A) 關心 (B) 拿起 (C) 職業

( ) ⓯ compliment： (A) 奉承 (B) 完成 (C) 遵守

答案： 1. (C) 2. (A) 3. (B) 4. (A) 5. (B) 6. (C) 7. (B) 8. (C) 9. (A)
10. (B) 11. (B) 12. (A) 13. (B) 14. (C) 15. (A)

Unit 08

Wanna go home together?

要一起回家嗎？

職場會話跟著說！ 🎧 Track **008**

Sarah: Ah...at last, I have delivered my documents to our supervisor. Now it's time to go back home! My brain is buzzing! Hi, Megan, where do you live? Wanna go home together?

莎拉：啊！終於把檔案交給主管了！現在該回家了！腦袋都嗡嗡響了。嗨，梅根，妳住哪裡啊？要一起回家嗎？

Megan: Okay, I live in the 7th Building, Rainbow Garden, DaAn District. Are you going my way?

梅根：好啊，我住在大安區彩虹花園第七棟。我們順路嗎？

Sarah: Really? I live in the Star Building, just next to the Rainbow Garden. Haha...fabulous! A big discovery, isn't it?

莎拉：真的嗎？我住在明星公寓，就在彩虹花園的旁邊。哈哈……好極了！一個大發現，不是嗎？

Megan: We became neighbors then! Can you give me a ride?

梅根：我們成了鄰居了！那妳可以載我一程嗎？

Sarah: Sure! Let's go.

莎拉：好啊！走吧！

Megan: What fresh air outside! Sarah, will you cook after work? I am so tired that I even don't want to move my legs.

梅根：外頭空氣真清新！莎拉，回家還要做飯嗎？我累得連腳都不想動了呢。

Sarah: You don't move your legs, the car does! Haha... That's because it's the first day you get to work. It will be all right tomorrow! I don't want to cook, either. Do you know the KFC nearby?

莎拉：妳本來就沒動腳啊，是車子在動呢！哈哈……這是因為妳第一天剛上班，明天就會沒事的！我也不想做飯了。妳知道附近的那間肯德基嗎？

Megan: Oh, you mean the one at the corner of the main street? Yeah, we can go there. It's my turn to buy you dinner.

梅根：哦，妳是指在大馬路上轉角那間？知道啊，我們可以去那裡吃。這次我請客。

文法重點 看這裡！

學完前面的會話之後，還要懂會話中的文法重點，才能應用在職場！以下補充重要的文法並做詳盡解析，把文法根基打好，讓你無論是出差還是洽商，都用正確英文和外國人打交道！

文法重點1
air/gas/atmosphere 同樣都有「氣」的意思，該怎麼用呢？

gas 是可流動的微小分子，並能夠四處擴散，即所謂的「氣體」，也可以指「瓦斯」。air指的是圍繞在我們周圍的，供我們呼吸的空氣，是多種氣體（gas）的混合物；atmosphere 則是指圍繞在地球外的氣層或「氣氛」。請利用下面的例句，幫助更熟悉記憶單字的用法：

- **The room was so stuffy that it felt like there was no air.**
  屋子裡很不通風，感覺好像沒有空氣。
- **Did you remember to switch off the gas?** 你有記得關掉瓦斯嗎？
- **Despite the argument which took place earlier, the atmosphere was amicable.** 儘管先前發生了爭執，氣氛還是友善的。

atmosphere 和 air 都可以用來形容團體互動中所產生的感受或情緒上的緊張，air 也可以形容某人所流露出來的態度，如：
- **She carried an air of superiority.** 她有一種優越感。

文法重點2
in the corner 的用法

當我們要表達某一事物內部的角落，用 in the corner 例如：
- **You can find a flag in the corner of the classroom.**
  你可以在教室的角落找到旗子。

而表達在某一條路外面的轉角，則用 at the corner 例如：
- **There is a stall at the corner of the street.** 這條路的轉角有一個攤子。

文法重點3
We go the same way? 是錯誤用法

這是一句典型的中式英文，是由「我們順路嗎？」直翻過來的。如果想要表達是否同路，可以說：
- **Are you going my way?** 我們順路嗎？

會話單字懂多少？

讀過前面的內容後，你是不是都懂得這些單字了呢？下列題目中的單字都是與會話及文法相關的單字，測驗看看自己會了多少吧！

( )❶ deliver： (A) 遞交 (B) 肝臟 (C) 撤銷

( )❷ district： (A) 歸還 (B) 區域 (C) 嚴格

( )❸ neighbor： (A) 鄰居 (B) 居住區 (C) 馬嘶聲

( )❹ atmosphere： (A) 疆域 (B) 蚊子 (C) 氣氛

( )❺ tired： (A) 嘗試 (B) 勞累 (C) 無聊

( )❻ corner： (A) 松樹 (B) 玉米 (C) 拐角

( )❼ stuffy： (A) 通風不良的 (B) 僵硬的 (C) 職員的

( )❽ switch： (A) 無恥 (B) 開關 (C) 巫婆

( )❾ argument： (A) 爭論 (B) 熱烈 (C) 裝飾

( )❿ amicable： (A) 陰險 (B) 友好 (C) 軟弱

( )⓫ flag： (A) 拍打 (B) 落後 (C) 旗幟

( )⓬ stall： (A) 安裝 (B) 攤子 (C) 叫停

( )⓭ buzz： (A) 公車 (B) 扣子 (C) 嗡嗡響

( )⓮ discovery： (A) 發現 (B) 折扣 (C) 封面

( )⓯ fresh： (A) 匆忙 (B) 新鮮 (C) 臉紅

答案： 1. (A) 2. (B) 3. (A) 4. (C) 5. (B) 6. (C) 7. (A) 8. (B) 9. (A)
10. (B) 11. (C) 12. (B) 13. (C) 14. (A) 15. (B)

Part **2**

加薪與升遷

If there's any possibility for a salary raise.

是否有加薪的機會。

 職場會話跟著說！ Track 009

Kevin: Good morning, Mr. Thomas. Do you have time now?	凱文：早安，湯瑪士先生，請問你現在有空嗎？
Mr. Thomas: Sure. Sit down. What is it?	湯瑪士先生：有啊，坐吧！你想說什麼？
Kevin: I would like to discuss with you about my job.	凱文：我想跟你談談我的工作。
Mr. Thomas: Is there any problem?	湯瑪士先生：工作上遇到問題了嗎？
Kevin: No, not at all. Well, I've been working really hard during the probation period and I would like to know if I'm qualified for this position and if there's any possibility for a salary raise.	凱文：不，工作完全沒有問題。是這樣的，試用期間我非常地努力，所以想知道我的能力是否符合此職務的要求，以及是否有加薪的機會。
Mr. Thomas: I know you've been working really hard these three months and you have certain abilities that are required by our company. Furthermore, I can see that you do fit in with the company. I will sure put your request into consideration.	湯瑪士先生：我知道這三個月來你非常努力，而且你的能力也符合本公司的要求。不僅如此，我覺得你適應得不錯。我會認真考慮你的請求。

文法重點看這裡！

學完前面的會話之後，還要懂會話中的文法重點，才能應用在職場！以下補充重要的文法並做詳盡解析，把文法根基打好，讓你無論是出差還是洽商，都用正確英文和外國人打交道！

文法重點1

Do you have time? 的用法

若要問對方而「是否有空」，有以下說法：

- **Do you have time now? We should have a short meeting with the contractor.** 你有空嗎？我們應該跟承包商開會討論一下。
- **Do you have a minute?** 你有空嗎？
- **Are you available tonight? There's a ballet show tonight, would you like to come along?** 你今晚有空嗎？今晚有一場芭蕾舞表演，要一起去嗎？

Do you have the time?是要詢問他人「是否知道時間」，其用法與 What time is it?相同：

- **Do you have the time?** 現在幾點了？

文法重點2

discuss 的用法

Discuss後面可以直接接要討論的主題，也可以用with來帶出一起討論的對象，並用about帶出要討論的事。例如：

- **I would like to discuss the test.** 我想討論考試。
- **I would like to discuss with you about my job.** 我想跟你談談我的工作。

文法重點3

「have / has been+現在分詞」 的用法

現在完成進行式，用於表示某件事從過去到現在一直持續進行中，其句型為「has / have been +現在分詞」，要注意的是 been 後面一定得用現在分詞：

- **That part-timer has been giving away fliers for four hours.**
  那位工讀生在那裡發傳單已經發了四個小時。
- **The technicians have been fixing the escalator for two hours.**
  技師們從兩個小時以前就開始修理手扶梯。

會話單字懂多少？

讀過前面的內容後，你是不是都懂得這些單字了呢？下列題目中的單字都是與會話及文法相關的單字，測驗看看自己會了多少吧！

( )❶ probation：(A) 預防 (B) 試用期 (C) 探查

( )❷ period：(A) 期間 (B) 凝視 (C) 優先

( )❸ salary：(A) 薪資 (B) 銷售 (C) 沙拉

( )❹ raise：(A) 比賽 (B) 種族 (C) 增加

( )❺ position：(A) 職務 (B) 郵局 (C) 決定

( )❻ confidence：(A) 困惑 (B) 充公 (C) 自信

( )❼ request：(A) 要求 (B) 必需品 (C) 消遣

( )❽ contractor：(A) 承包商 (B) 聯絡人 (C) 叛徒

( )❾ ballet：(A) 子彈 (B) 芭蕾 (C) 談判

( )❿ part-timer：(A) 工讀生 (B) 全職 (C) 分擔者

( )⓫ flier：(A) 騙子 (B) 飛魚 (C) 傳單

( )⓬ technician：(A) 建築師 (B) 老師 (C) 技師

( )⓭ escalator：(A) 電扶梯 (B) 階梯 (C) 電梯

( )⓮ possibility：(A) 可能性 (B) 地位 (C) 持有人

( )⓯ furthermore：(A) 因此 (B) 此外 (C) 由於

答案： 1. (B) 2. (A) 3. (A) 4. (C) 5. (A) 6. (C) 7. (A) 8. (A) 9. (B)
10. (A) 11. (C) 12. (C) 13. (A) 14. (A) 15. (B)

I decided to give you a salary increase.

我決定調整你的薪資。

職場會話跟著說！  Track **010**

Mr. Thomas: Kevin, I would like to have a word with you. Have a seat.

湯瑪士先生：凱文，我想跟你談談，請坐。

Kevin: Thank you.

凱文：謝謝。

Mr. Thomas: After our last discussion, I decided to give you a salary increase. Starting next month, there will be a NT$3,000 raise to your salary. Although your first raise might not sound considerable, but the company believes that with your ability, sooner or later you will have a better raise.

湯瑪士先生：經過我們上一次的面談，我決定調整你的薪資。下個月開始，你的薪資將調漲台幣三千元。或許第一次的調薪金額不盡理想，但公司相信依你的能力，很快就會有更好的調漲幅度。

Kevin: Thank you very much, Mr. Thomas. As a newcomer of the company, I understand that you have your consideration and I am satisfied with the raise.

凱文：謝謝你，湯瑪士先生。我是公司的新進員工，因此瞭解你有你的考量。我對此次的加薪感到很滿意。

Mr. Thomas: I think you deserved this.

湯瑪士先生：我認為這是你應得的。

Kevin: I will continue to do my best and contribute to the company.

凱文：我會繼續努力，為公司盡一份心力。

文法重點看這裡！

學完前面的會話之後，還要懂會話中的文法重點，才能應用在職場！以下補充重要的文法並做詳盡解析，把文法根基打好，讓你無論是出差還是洽商，都用正確英文和外國人打交道！

文法重點1
do/work/make 同樣都是「做」，該怎麼用呢？

do 實際強調「做」的動作，帶有「實行」、「完成」的意味；work 本身有很多意思，但若要用來 指「做」時，則有讓某樣東西得以「運作」的意思；make 指的是「製造」或做某個舉動的意思。請利用下面的例句，幫助更熟悉記憶單字的用法：

- **You ought to do the research by yourself.** 你必須自己完成這份研究。
- **We don't know how to work that projector.**
  我們不知道如何使用這台投影機。
- **Please stop making unrealistic promises.** 請不要作出不切實際的承諾。

 請注意，若要說到把事情做到最好，只能使用「do my best」、「try my best」。

文法重點2
Thanks very much. 是錯誤用法

Thanks. 是較為口語的說法，後面不可接 very much。要向他人表示感謝，還有以下用法：

- **Thanks for the coffee and croissant.** 謝謝你的咖啡和可頌麵包。
- **Thank you very much for your participation.** 非常感謝你的參與。
- **I appreciate your patience.** 感謝你的耐心等候。

文法重點3
many 和 much 的用法

當所指的事物為可數名詞時，得用 many；所指對象是不可數名詞時，就用 much。

- **How many reporters attended the press conference?**
  有多少位記者來參加記者會？
- **I don't have much time left.** 我沒有多少時間了。

會話單字懂多少？

讀過前面的內容後，你是不是都懂得這些單字了呢？下列題目中的單字都是與會話及文法相關的單字，測驗看看自己會了多少吧！

( ) ❶ increase： (A) 減少 (B) 增加 (C) 控告

( ) ❷ considerable： (A) 相當的 (B) 保存 (C) 保守

( ) ❸ newcomer： (A) 新人 (B) 收入 (C) 新聞播報員

( ) ❹ satisfy： (A) 公認 (B) 滿意 (C) 諷刺

( ) ❺ contribute： (A) 貢獻 (B) 分佈 (C) 合約

( ) ❻ research： (A) 搜查 (B) 收據 (C) 調查

( ) ❼ projector： (A) 投影機 (B) 印表機 (C) 傳真機

( ) ❽ unrealistic： (A) 不切實際 (B) 現實 (C) 難以辨認

( ) ❾ promise： (A) 隱瞞 (B) 預告 (C) 承諾

( ) ❿ croissant： (A) 可頌 (B) 十字架 (C) 貝果

( ) ⓫ participation： (A) 分開 (B) 參與 (C) 預期

( ) ⓬ patience： (A) 耐心 (B) 病人 (C) 貴族

( ) ⓭ reporter： (A) 記者 (B) 歌手 (C) 畫家

( ) ⓮ press： (A) 稱讚 (B) 新聞媒體 (C) 沮喪

( ) ⓯ conference： (A) 參考 (B) 招認 (C) 會議

答案： 1. (B) 2. (A) 3. (A) 4. (B) 5. (A) 6. (C) 7. (A) 8. (A) 9. (C)
10. (A) 11. (B) 12. (A) 13. (A) 14. (B) 15. (C)

I decided to promote you as the Sales Manager.

我決定將你升職為業務經理。

職場會話跟著說！ 🎧 Track 011

Mr. Thomas: Stanley, recently I did a careful estimation on your performance of work. I am satisfied with your capability, efficiency and decisiveness.

湯瑪士先生：史丹利，最近我仔細評估了你工作上的表現。你的能力、工作效率與果斷性令我非常滿意。

Stanley: I am flattered by your praise.

史丹利：對於你的稱讚，我感到受寵若驚。

Mr. Thomas: As a result, I decided to promote you as the Sales Manager.

湯瑪士先生：因此我決定將你升職為業務經理。

Stanley: You can be assured that I acquired all the requirements for this job. I am well familiar with the department's duty and goals.

史丹利：我向你保證我具備這份工作所需的條件。我也非常熟悉此部門的職責與目標。

Mr. Thomas: I am glad to hear that. Nevertheless, we need to discuss about your new responsibilities. Are you clear about your duties as a Sales Manager?

湯瑪士先生：很高興聽你這麼説。不過，我們必須先討論你的工作內容。你瞭解業務經理的職責嗎？

Stanley: Yes. A Sales Manager should make great efforts to achieve a higher goal himself. Other than that, he should help the department to define its goals and assist each individual to achieve their personal target. As a leader of the team, he should also keep the team motivated and inspired.

史丹利：是的。一位業務經理必須盡力達成更高的目標。除此之外，他也必須協助訂定部門目標，並協助每位業務達成其個人目標。身為團隊領導人，業務經理也得激發團隊的動力與靈感。

文法重點看這裡！

學完前面的會話之後，還要懂會話中的文法重點，才能應用在職場！以下補充重要的文法並做詳盡解析，把文法根基打好，讓你無論是出差還是洽商，都用正確英文和外國人打交道！

文法重點1

I sure you. 是錯誤用法

sure 不是動詞，而是形容詞，因此不得直接置於受詞前面。要向他人作出保證，可使用assure、guarantee或ensure：

- **I can assure you of his ability.** 我向你保證他的能力。
- **The manufacturer guarantees that their products are safe and edible.** 該製造商保證他們的產品安全可食用。
- **I can ensure that the problem will be solved.** 我保證將有辦法解決問題。

文法重點2

require/acquire/enquire 該怎麼用呢？

這三個單字看似類似，發音也頗雷同，一不小心就會造成混淆。require 指「需要」或「要求」，通常後面接動作；acquire有「取得」的意思；enquire則是指「詢問、查詢」。請利用下面的例句，幫助更熟悉記憶單字的用法：

- **Employers are required not to be late for work.** 公司要求員工不得遲到。
- **I have just acquired my supervisor's permission.** 我剛剛取得主管的允許。
- **She enquired about the next train to Kaohsiung.** 她詢問有關下一班開往高雄的火車班次。

> I required all the requirements for this job. 是錯誤示範！搞混了require和acquire 兩個單字的用法，正確的句子應該是：
> **I acquired all the requirements for this job.** 我具備這份工作所需的條件。

文法重點3

more high 或 higher 誰正確？

常見的形容詞比較級有兩種方式：「more + 形容詞」或者「形容詞-er」，high 這個字屬於單音節，因此它的比較級屬於後者。

- **My team scored higher than his.** 我們隊伍贏得的分數他們的高。

會話單字懂多少？

讀過前面的內容後，你是不是都懂得這些單字了呢？下列題目中的單字都是與會話及文法相關的單字，測驗看看自己會了多少吧！

( ) ❶ estimation： (A) 疏遠 (B) 決定 (C) 評估

( ) ❷ capability： (A) 能力 (B) 能源 (C) 容量

( ) ❸ efficiency： (A) 效率 (B) 熱情 (C) 經歷

( ) ❹ admiration： (A) 欽佩 (B) 討厭 (C) 管理

( ) ❺ acquire： (A) 取得 (B) 認識 (C) 通曉

( ) ❻ decisiveness： (A) 成果 (B) 果斷 (C) 果樹

( ) ❼ flattered： (A) 受寵若驚 (B) 扁平 (C) 跟蹌

( ) ❽ assure： (A) 疑慮 (B) 保證 (C) 估計

( ) ❾ effort： (A) 負擔 (B) 努力 (C) 實施

( ) ❿ define： (A) 界定 (B) 緊縮 (C) 提煉

( ) ⓫ assist： (A) 反抗 (B) 堅持 (C) 協助

( ) ⓬ individual： (A) 團體的 (B) 個人的 (C) 家庭的

( ) ⓭ target： (A) 忘記 (B) 尖酸 (C) 目標

( ) ⓮ motivated： (A) 有積極性的 (B) 多元的 (C) 有主題的

( ) ⓯ inspired： (A) 注意的 (B) 有靈感的 (C) 可解決的

答案： 1. (C) 2. (A) 3. (A) 4. (A) 5. (A) 6. (B) 7. (A) 8. (B) 9. (B)
10. (A) 11. (C) 12. (B) 13. (C) 14. (A) 15. (B)

Unit 12

With greater power, comes the greater responsibility.

能力越強，責任越大。

 職場會話跟著說！ 🎧Track **012**

Mr. Thomas: Well begun is half done. Let's start talking about the company's expectation on you and the Sales Department.	**湯瑪士先生**：好的開始是成功的一半。不如我們來談談公司對你與業務部門的期望吧！
Stanley: I will try my best and I promise won't let you down.	**史丹利**：我會盡最大的努力，也向你保證一定不會讓你失望。
Mr. Thomas: Well, actions speak louder than words. Please put in mind that you should be responsible for every decision you make.	**湯瑪士先生**：行動勝於言辭。請記住，你必須為你所做的每一項決策負責。
Stanley: Yes. I understand. With greater power, comes the greater responsibility.	**史丹利**：是的，我瞭解。能力越強，責任越大。
Mr. Thomas: Good. The company hopes that sales of this year should have a raise of at least 5%. In addition to this, I observed that some of the employees in the Sales Department seemed to lose interest. I hope you can inspire them with new stimulations.	**湯瑪士先生**：很好。公司希望今年的銷售成績得以提升百分之五。與此同時，我注意到某幾位業務部同仁似乎提不起勁了，我希望你能激勵他們。
Stanley: I got it. I will start to work on a new sales plan right away. I will have a meeting with the co-workers.	**史丹利**：我明白。我會馬上著手擬定一個新的業務計畫書。上任後，我們內部也將進行業務會議。
Mr. Thomas: OK. I expect to see a new and energetic team.	**湯瑪士先生**：好的。我期待能看到一個全新、充滿幹勁的團隊。

文法重點看這裡！

學完前面的會話之後，還要懂會話中的文法重點，才能應用在職場！以下補充重要的文法並做詳盡解析，把文法根基打好，讓你無論是出差還是洽商，都用正確英文和外國人打交道！

文法重點1

won't / wouldn't 該怎麼區分呢？

兩者在拼法上略為雷同，因此有時會產生混淆。won't 是 will not 的縮寫，屬於未來式；而 wouldn't 則是 would not 的縮寫，would not 是過去式：

- **I won't give up.** 我絕不放棄。
- **I wouldn't lie to you if I knew you care.**
  早知道你在意的話，我就不會隱瞞你。

文法重點2

disappointed 的用法

disappointed是形容詞，後面必須接at、that、with，指「失望的」、「沮喪的」：

- **She was disappointed at our work.**
  她對我們的工作表現很失望。
- **They are disappointed that I won't attend their cocktail party.**
  我無法出席雞尾酒派對，讓他們很失望。

 要用英文表達「使失望」除了disappoint外，還可以用let ... down。如：
  - **I won't let you down.** 我不會讓你失望。

文法重點3

raise 的用法

raise既是動詞也是名詞，作為動詞意思為「舉高；提升；增加」，作為名詞時代表「加薪；提升；增加」。用法如下：

- **Please raise your hand.**
  請舉起你的手。
- **This year should have a raise of at least 5%.**
  今年至少要提升百分之五。

會話單字懂多少？

讀過前面的內容後，你是不是都懂得這些單字了呢？下列題目中的單字都是與會話及文法相關的單字，測驗看看自己會了多少吧！

( )❶ expectation： (A) 期望 (B) 流放 (C) 展開

( )❷ strategy： (A) 海峽 (B) 數據 (C) 策略

( )❸ confuse： (A) 困惑 (B) 充公 (C) 拒絕

( )❹ action： (A) 行為 (B) 行動 (C) 保護

( )❺ haste： (A) 濃霧 (B) 急忙 (C) 大麻

( )❻ waste： (A) 嘗試 (B) 等待 (C) 浪費

( )❼ slang： (A) 俚語 (B) 動詞 (C) 名辭

( )❽ cocktail： (A) 公雞 (B) 雞尾酒 (C) 果汁

( )❾ delay： (A) 延遲 (B) 交易 (C) 接力

( )❿ divorce： (A) 草皮 (B) 離婚 (C) 貢獻

( )⓫ least： (A) 最大的 (B) 最少的 (C) 最多的

( )⓬ addition： (A) 扣除 (B) 發行數 (C) 附加

( )⓭ observe： (A) 觀察 (B) 忽略 (C) 重視

( )⓮ co-worker： (A) 屬下 (B) 伴侶 (C) 同事

( )⓯ energetic： (A) 疲憊的 (B) 無精打采的 (C) 精力旺盛的

答案： 1. (A) 2. (C) 3. (A) 4. (B) 5. (B) 6. (C) 7. (A) 8. (B) 9. (A)
10. (B) 11. (B) 12. (C) 13. (A) 14. (C) 15. (C)

Stanley has been promoted as the Sales Manager.

史丹利升職為業務經理了。

 職場會話跟著說！ 🎧Track 013

Irene: I'm in a hurry. Let's grab something to eat.	愛琳：時間不多了，我們買點東西果腹吧！
Sabrina: Sure.	莎賓娜：好啊。
Irene: Have you seen the announcement on the bulletin board?	愛琳：你看到公布欄上的公告了嗎？
Sabrina: No. Why?	莎賓娜：沒有，怎麼了？
Irene: Stanley has been promoted as the Sales Manager.	愛琳：史丹利升職為業務經理了。
Sabrina: That's wonderful. Good for him!	莎賓娜：太好了。幹得好！
Irene: I know. He works really hard. Besides, his great personality earned him good reputation.	愛琳：沒錯。他真的很賣力，而且他的個性不差，所以也擁有好人緣。
Sabrina: As his colleague and friend, I'm glad he is making progress.	莎賓娜：身為他的同事與朋友，看到他的進步讓我感到很開心。
Irene: Let's throw a party for him. What do you say?	愛琳：我們幫他辦一場派對吧！妳覺得呢？
Sabrina: That's a terrific idea.	莎賓娜：這是個好主意！

文法重點 看這裡！

學完前面的會話之後，還要懂會話中的文法重點，才能應用在職場！以下補充重要的文法並做詳盡解析，把文法根基打好，讓你無論是出差還是洽商，都用正確英文和外國人打交道！

文法重點1
drop by/drop off/drop behind 該怎麼用呢？

drop by 指的是「順道拜訪」的意思；drop off 則有「讓……下車」的意思，需搭配受詞使用；當進度落後時，可說 drop behind。

- **She dropped by on her way home from the law firm.**
  她從法律事務所回來的路上順道過來了。
- **Please drop me off at the MRT station.**
  請在捷運站讓我下車。
- **The progress at the construction site has been dropping behind in the last few weeks.**
  工地進度在過去的幾個星期落後了。

文法重點2
promote 的用法

promote 除了有「推銷、宣傳」的意思外，亦可指「升遷」，兩者用法略有不同：

- **They are promoting their latest product.**
  他們在促銷最新的產品。
- **He has been promoted as the new manager.**
  他升職成為新任經理。

文法重點3
hurry 的用法

hurry除了有「匆忙」的意思外，亦可指「催促」，兩者用法有不同：

- **I'm not in any hurry.**
  我沒有在趕時間。
- **Hurry up, or we will miss the train.**
  快一點，不然我們會錯過火車。

會話單字懂多少？

讀過前面的內容後，你是不是都懂得這些單字了呢？下列題目中的單字都是與會話及文法相關的單字，測驗看看自己會了多少吧！

( ) ❶ hurry： (A) 趕時間 (B) 放鬆 (C) 害怕

( ) ❷ grab： (A) 抓取 (B) 祝福 (C) 分級

( ) ❸ announcement： (A) 廢除 (B) 困擾 (C) 通知

( ) ❹ bulletin： (A) 公告 (B) 子彈 (C) 鬥牛

( ) ❺ promote： (A) 升遷 (B) 催促 (C) 產品

( ) ❻ product： (A) 預言 (B) 奇蹟 (C) 產品

( ) ❼ drop： (A) 抬高 (B) 丟下 (C) 撿起

( ) ❽ law： (A) 草坪 (B) 低的 (C) 法律

( ) ❾ firm： (A) 公司 (B) 學校 (C) 影片

( ) ❿ MRT station： (A) 機場 (B) 捷運站 (C) 公車站

( ) ⓫ construction：(A) 解釋 (B) 健身 (C) 建設

( ) ⓬ site： (A) 地點 (B) 引用 (C) 情境喜劇

( ) ⓭ earn： (A) 耳朵 (B) 賺得 (C) 渴望

( ) ⓮ reputation：(A) 名譽 (B) 代表 (C) 歸還

( ) ⓯ terrific： (A) 非常好的 (B) 緊急的 (C) 友善的

答案： 1. (A) 2. (A) 3. (C) 4. (A) 5. (A) 6. (C) 7. (B) 8. (C) 9. (A)
10. (B) 11. (C) 12. (A) 13. (B) 14. (A) 15. (A)

Unit 14

We are going to hold a party in our company tonight.

我們公司晚上要舉辦一個派對。

 職場會話跟著說！ 🎧Track 014

Stanley: Hey, Cesar, we are going to hold a party in our company tonight. Would you like to join us?	史丹利：嗨，凱薩，我們公司晚上要舉辦一個派對，你要不要來參加啊？
Cesar: Oh, really? What's the party for? A donation or to celebrate someone's promotion?	凱薩：喔，真的嗎？派對的主題是什麼？募款或是慶祝某人的升職嗎？
Stanley: Are you a fortune teller or something? I will be promoted as the Sales Manager next month.	史丹利：你是算命師嗎？你完全猜中了耶！下個月我將升職為業務經理。
Cesar: Congratulations. I think you deserved that. You tried really hard to increase a 40% earning for your company this year. It's a great achievement.	凱薩：恭喜你！我覺得這是你應得的，今年你很努力地把你們公司的業績增加了40%，那是個很了不起的成就。
Stanley: Thanks. In fact, I am just a workaholic. I'll see you tonight.	史丹利：謝了。老實說，我只是一個工作狂。那麼就今天晚上見。
Cesar: Can I bring my wife and daughter along? I'm afraid that I will feel bored.	凱薩：我能帶老婆和女兒出席嗎？我怕我會很無聊。
Stanley: Sure.	史丹利：沒問題。
Cesar: OK. I'll be there, see you then.	凱薩：好的，我會去的，到時候見！

文法重點看這裡！

學完前面的會話之後，還要懂會話中的文法重點，才能應用在職場！以下補充重要的文法並做詳盡解析，把文法根基打好，讓你無論是出差還是洽商，都用正確英文和外國人打交道！

文法重點1
bring/take/carry 同樣都是「帶」，該怎麼用呢？

請注意，以說話人為中心的「來」必須用bring，以說話人為中心的「去」必須用take；而carry不含方向，只表示「拿、帶」。請利用下面的例句，幫助更熟悉記憶單字的用法：

- **Next time when you come to a party, don't forget to bring more friends with you.** 下次參加派對時，別忘了多帶一些朋友過來！
- **Please remember to take your coat before you leave the party.**
  離開派對之前，別忘了把外套帶走。
- **Is this a theme party? I saw many waitresses carrying Jack-o'-lanterns.**
  這是主題派對嗎？我看到好多女服務生拿著南瓜燈籠。

文法重點2
afraid 的用法

當afraid 作為形容詞使用時，可以在句型中加入that 後接子句，例如：

- **I'm afraid that I will feel bored there.** 我怕在那裡我會覺得無聊。

> 若是後面想接名詞或是動名詞，則必須加入「of」，例如：
> - **I'm afraid of being bored there.** 我怕在那裡會很無聊。

文法重點3
My English is so poor. 是錯誤用法

這是一句典型的中式英文，由「我的英文真爛。」直譯。如果想要強調自己的英文不好，可以說：

- **My poor English.** 我的爛英文。
- **I don't speak English very well.** 我的英文說得不好。
- **I can speak a little English.** 我能稍微說點英文。

會話單字懂多少？

讀過前面的內容後，你是不是都懂得這些單字了呢？下列題目中的單字都是與會話及文法相關的單字，測驗看看自己會了多少吧！

( )❶ hold： (A) 舉辦 (B) 挑釁 (C) 宣佈

( )❷ join： (A) 滲透 (B) 慢跑 (C) 參加

( )❸ carry： (A) 領取 (B) 攜帶 (C) 照顧

( )❹ mention： (A) 慈悲 (B) 提及 (C) 懷念

( )❺ coat： (A) 外套 (B) 羊 (C) 目標

( )❻ waitress： (A) 女服務生 (B) 女主人 (C) 女歌手

( )❼ Jack-o'-lantern： (A) 桌燈 (B) 南瓜燈籠 (C) 聖誕節

( )❽ donation： (A) 捐款 (B) 募集 (C) 招待

( )❾ celebrate： (A) 名人 (B) 慶祝 (C) 紀念日

( )❿ promotion： (A) 升職 (B) 提案 (C) 動機

( )⓫ fortune： (A) 命運 (B) 叉子 (C) 打鬥

( )⓬ deserve： (A) 值得 (B) 點心 (C) 沙漠

( )⓭ earnings： (A) 支出 (B) 收入 (C) 費用

( )⓮ achievement： (A) 成就 (B) 節目 (C) 祖母

( )⓯ workaholic： (A) 懶惰蟲 (B) 工作狂 (C) 酒鬼

答案：1. (A) 2. (C) 3. (B) 4. (B) 5. (A) 6. (A) 7. (B) 8. (A) 9. (B)
10. (A) 11. (A) 12. (A) 13. (B) 14. (A) 15. (B)

Albert, could you explain to Simon about his daily routine first?

艾伯特，請先告訴賽門他每天的例行公事。

 職場會話跟著說！ 🎧 Track 015

Rachel: Listen, everyone. I have a short announcement here. We have a new recruit today. Simon, would you like to introduce yourself?	瑞秋：請大家注意，我有事情要宣布。今天我們部門來了一位新人。賽門，能否請你做個自我介紹？
Simon: Hello, my name is Simon. I graduated from the Fu Jen Catholic University, and I major in Mass Communication.	賽門：大家好，我叫賽門。畢業於天主教輔仁大學，主修大眾傳播學系。
Albert: I'm Albert, the Specialist. Welcome to the Public Relations Department.	艾伯特：我是艾伯特，是這裡的專員。歡迎加入公關部門。
Sally: My name is Sally. I graduated from the Fu Jen as well.	莎莉：我叫莎莉。我也是輔仁大學畢業的。
Simon: What a coincidence! It's nice to meet you.	賽門：好巧喔！很高興認識你們。
Rachel: Starting today, Simon will be assisting Albert with his new project.	瑞秋：從今天開始，賽門將協助艾伯特執行他的新企劃案。
Albert: That's fabulous. I really need someone to give me a hand.	艾伯特：太好了！我非常希望有人能對我伸出援手。
Rachel: Albert, could you explain to Simon about his daily routine first? And then you can proceed with your project.	瑞秋：艾伯特，請先告訴賽門他每天的例行公事。之後你們就能著手進行你的企劃。

文法重點看這裡！

學完前面的會話之後，還要懂會話中的文法重點，才能應用在職場！以下補充重要的文法並做詳盡解析，把文法根基打好，讓你無論是出差還是洽商，都用正確英文和外國人打交道！

文法重點1
It's nice to meet you./It's nice meeting you.
該怎麼用？

nice 本身為形容詞，因此nice to 後面必須接原形動詞；若nice 單獨存在，則後面必須接動名詞（原形動詞+ing），所謂的動名詞即指其同時具備動詞與名詞的特性。請參考下面的例句：

- **It's nice to see you. / It's nice seeing you.**
  很高興見到你。

- **It's nice to hear from you. / It's nice hearing from you.**
  很高興收到你的消息。

文法重點2
major in/major 的用法

要形容主修的科系時，major 可以以名詞、形容詞和動詞三種方式呈現。當名詞用時，major 前面必須接所有格：

- **Diplomacy was her major.** 她主修外交。

major 當形容詞時，即是指「主修的」，因此後面必須接名詞：
- **His major subject is International Trade.** 他主修的科目是國際貿易。

當動詞用時，則得用major in：
- **Kelly majors in Philosophy.** 凱莉主修哲學系。

文法重點3
Coincidence! 是錯誤用法

在街上碰到相識的人，或是生活中遇到巧合的事，我們會說「好巧喔！」，然而英文裡不能直接這麼說，因為coincidence 無法單獨成立一個句子。英文裡，可以用：

- **What a coincidence!** 好巧喔！
- **What a surprise!** 這真是一個驚喜！

會話單字懂多少？

讀過前面的內容後，你是不是都懂得這些單字了呢？下列題目中的單字都是與會話及文法相關的單字，測驗看看自己會了多少吧！

( ) ❶ Catholic： (A) 佛教 (B) 天主教 (C) 印度教

( ) ❷ specialist： (A) 專員 (B) 教職員 (C) 接待員

( ) ❸ public： (A) 大眾 (B) 酒吧 (C) 出版

( ) ❹ relation： (A) 觀眾 (B) 關係 (C) 親戚

( ) ❺ coincidence： (A) 巧合 (B) 硬幣 (C) 交通事故

( ) ❻ fabulous： (A) 難過的 (B) 恐怖的 (C) 極好的

( ) ❼ silly： (A) 愚蠢 (B) 開心 (C) 氣憤

( ) ❽ diplomacy： (A) 懇求 (B) 畢業文憑 (C) 外交

( ) ❾ trade： (A) 貿易 (B) 管理 (C) 政治

( ) ❿ philosophy： (A) 文學 (B) 哲學 (C) 經濟學

( ) ⓫ recruit： (A) 新人 (B) 新婚 (C) 離職

( ) ⓬ mass： (A) 大眾 (B) 大廳 (C) 面具

( ) ⓭ routine： (A) 道路 (B) 根部 (C) 例行公事

( ) ⓮ proceed： (A) 成功 (B) 著手 (C) 聲明

( ) ⓯ project： (A) 專案企劃 (B) 主修 (C) 抗議

答案：1. (B) 2. (A) 3. (A) 4. (B) 5. (A) 6. (C) 7. (A) 8. (C) 9. (A)
10. (B) 11. (A) 12. (A) 13. (C) 14. (B) 15. (A)

We should now make certain arrangements for your duties.

所以現在我們必須進行分工。

職場會話跟著說！ Track 016

Rachel: As you all know, our client, Royal Company Limited, is planning to hold a product release press conference next month. They're impressed with our proposal and decided that we shall organize the activity.

瑞秋：我想你們都知道，我們的客戶皇家有限公司，將於下個月舉辦產品發表記者會。他們對於我們的提案留下極好的印象，因此決定由我們負責規劃這次的活動。

Sally: That's terrific! We did everything we can on this proposal, it's lucky that we didn't waste our breath on the presentation.

莎莉：太好了！我們花了很多心力準備這個提案，還好我們的報告沒有白費口舌。

Simon: Congratulations, Albert.

賽門：恭喜你，艾伯特！

Albert: Well, you reap what you sow.

艾伯特：投入多少心血，你就獲得多少成就。

Rachel: Our first progress meeting with them will be next Wednesday. We should now make certain arrangements for your duties. Albert, you will be in charge of invitations and brochures. Simon, please send an invitation to every journalists and reporters on our contact list. Give them a call and confirm their participation.

瑞秋：下週三將向他們做第一次進度報告，所以現在我們必須進行分工。艾伯特，你負責邀請函和小冊子；賽門，請將邀請函寄給通訊錄上的媒體與記者們，並致電確認他們是否會出席。

Simon: OK. Should I prepare name tags for each of them?

賽門：好的。我該替他們準備名牌嗎？

Rachel: Absolutely. You're getting into the swing of things.

瑞秋：一點也沒錯。你越來越進入狀況了！

文法重點看這裡！

學完前面的會話之後，還要懂會話中的文法重點，才能應用在職場！以下補充重要的文法並做詳盡解析，把文法根基打好，讓你無論是出差還是洽商，都用正確英文和外國人打交道！

文法重點1
should/ought to/must 同樣都是「應該」，該怎麼用呢？

should 和ought to 兩者所指的「應該」，帶有較多義務、職責的意味；而 must 則是語帶命令：

- **You should have the quotation send to our client by today.**
  你必須在今天之內把報價寄給客戶。
- **As a secretary, you ought to arrange a reasonable schedule for your boss.** 身為秘書，妳應當適度地安排老闆的行程。
- **You must be there by noon.**
  你必須在中午以前抵達那裡。

文法重點2
do everything we can 的用法

do everything we can 意思是「想盡一切辦法」，後面不需再加do：

- **He did everything he can to get this job.**
  為了得到這份工作，他想盡一切辦法。
- **I will do everything I can to make her sign the contract.**
  我會想盡一切辦法讓她簽下這份合約。

文法重點3
Congratulation! 是錯誤用法

用congratulation 祝賀他人時，必須記得加上「s」，否則就是錯誤的用法。要祝賀他人，可參考以下說法：

- **Congratulations on your relocation!**
  恭喜你喬遷新居！
- **Congratulations! You did a wonderful job.**
  恭喜！你做得很完美！

會話單字懂多少？

讀過前面的內容後，你是不是都懂得這些單字了呢？下列題目中的單字都是與會話及文法相關的單字，測驗看看自己會了多少吧！

( ) ❶ limit： (A) 限制 (B) 線條 (C) 跛腳

( ) ❷ release： (A) 發財 (B) 發跡 (C) 發行

( ) ❸ organize： (A) 有機 (B) 安排 (C) 參加

( ) ❹ presentation： (A) 現在 (B) 禮物 (C) 報告

( ) ❺ reap： (A) 收割 (B) 撕裂 (C) 嘲笑

( ) ❻ sow： (A) 販售 (B) 播種 (C) 看見

( ) ❼ brochure： (A) 烤肉 (B) 小冊子 (C) 花椰菜

( ) ❽ journalist： (A) 新聞工作者 (B) 旅客 (C) 專員

( ) ❾ name tag： (A) 名冊 (B) 名牌 (C) 名單

( ) ❿ quotation： (A) 報價單 (B) 訂購單 (C) 收據

( ) ⓫ secretary： (A) 會計 (B) 秘書 (C) 售貨員

( ) ⓬ noon： (A) 月亮 (B) 早上 (C) 中午

( ) ⓭ relocation： (A) 喬遷 (B) 位置 (C) 反抗

( ) ⓮ venue： (A) 場地 (B) 金星 (C) 大街

( ) ⓯ issue： (A) 面紙 (B) 問題 (C) 孤立

答案：1. (A) 2. (C) 3. (B) 4. (C) 5. (A) 6. (B) 7. (B) 8. (A) 9. (B)
10. (A) 11. (B) 12. (C) 13. (A) 14. (A) 15. (B)

We shall discuss about the annual sales target of our department.

我們要討論本部門年度的銷售目標。

 職場會話跟著說！ Track 017

Stanley: Good morning, everyone. Let's start our meeting now. We shall discuss about the annual sales target of our department. Polly, please keep track of today's meeting and send it to everyone by today.

史丹利：各位，早安，開始開會吧！我們要討論本部門年度的銷售目標。波莉，請做會議紀錄，並於今天以內寄給所有人。

Polly: OK. I will post it on the internet as well.

波莉：好的。我也會把它張貼在網路上。

Stanley: Thank you. You're very thoughtful. Let's get into the subject matter now. The company hopes that sales of this year should be raised.

史丹利：謝謝，妳考慮得很周到。我們進入正題吧！公司希望本年度的銷售成績能夠提升。

Raymond: How?

雷蒙：該怎麼做呢？

Stanley: I did some analysis on all the factors and I've come up with some solutions. In the following months, I expect each of you to have at least five new clients every month. Is there any problem?

史丹利：我分析了某些因素，也整理出一些方案。接下來的幾個月裡，我希望大家每個月務必開發至少五名客戶。有問題嗎？

Nancy: No. We will try our best to achieve the goal!

南茜：沒問題。我們會盡最大的努力達成目標！

文法重點看這裡!

學完前面的會話之後,還要懂會話中的文法重點,才能應用在職場!以下補充重要的文法並做詳盡解析,把文法根基打好,讓你無論是出差還是洽商,都用正確英文和外國人打交道!

文法重點1
stick/paste/post 同樣都是「貼」,該怎麼用呢?

stick 可指「張貼」或「黏貼」;paste 有「黏貼」的意思,而會用電腦的人也知道paste 這個功能,就是將某段被剪下的文字或圖案貼上;僅有post可表示將文章張貼至網路上:

- **Who stuck those posters in the elevator?** 電梯裡那些海報是誰貼上的?
- **Don't paste anything on the wall. The glue will leave dirt on it.**
  不要在牆壁上貼東西,漿糊會弄髒牆壁。
- **She posts her diaries on her blog.** 她在部落格上張貼日記。

文法重點2
How 的用法

當How置於句首,用來詢問「怎麼、如何」時,後面不能接to。how 除了可單獨形成一個疑問句時,還可用於以下問句:

- **How do you know Janice from the Human Resource Department?**
  你怎麼會認識人事部的珍妮絲?

若要在陳述句裡表示「知道某件事如何做」,就能用how to:
- **He doesn't know how to operate that machine.**
  他不知道該怎麼操作這台機器。

文法重點3
My wrong. 是錯誤用法

此句話是「我的錯。」的英文直譯,並不正確,建議可以說:

- **It's my mistake.** 這是我的錯。
- **It's my fault.** 這是我的錯。

會話單字懂多少？

讀過前面的內容後，你是不是都懂得這些單字了呢？下列題目中的單字都是與會話及文法相關的單字，測驗看看自己會了多少吧！

( ) ❶ track： (A) 哄騙 (B) 追蹤 (C) 折磨

( ) ❷ update： (A) 更新 (B) 上傳 (C) 落後

( ) ❸ subject： (A) 拒絕 (B) 物件 (C) 主題

( ) ❹ matter： (A) 事情 (B) 數學 (C) 地毯

( ) ❺ factor： (A) 演員 (B) 事實 (C) 因素

( ) ❻ solution： (A) 稀釋 (B) 解決 (C) 幻覺

( ) ❼ post： (A) 張貼 (B) 郵局 (C) 烘烤

( ) ❽ poster： (A) 主持人 (B) 龍蝦 (C) 海報

( ) ❾ elevator： (A) 電梯 (B) 評估 (C) 樓梯

( ) ❿ diary： (A) 乳製品 (B) 日曆 (C) 日記

( ) ⓫ blog： (A) 積木 (B) 部落格 (C) 笨蛋

( ) ⓬ resource： (A) 資源 (B) 獲得 (C) 醬料

( ) ⓭ operate： (A) 分離 (B) 開啟 (C) 操作

( ) ⓮ fault： (A) 信仰 (B) 錯誤 (C) 秋天

( ) ⓯ thoughtful： (A) 奴隸 (B) 粗心 (C) 貼心

答案：1. (B) 2. (A) 3. (C) 4. (A) 5. (C) 6. (B) 7. (A) 8. (C) 9. (A)
10. (C) 11. (B) 12. (A) 13. (C) 14. (B) 15. (C)

Part 3

通訊軟體談公事

May I pass you to our colleague responsible for after-sale services?

讓我把您的電話轉給負責售後服務的同事好嗎？

 職場會話跟著說！ 🎧Track **018**

Megan: Hello, Blue Sky Corporation. Who's calling, please? How can I help you?	梅根：你好，這裡是藍天公司。請問您是哪位？有什麼可以幫忙的嗎？
Jason: What on earth have you sold to me?! There are serious problems in your products. I want a full refund for my loss. I hope you can give me an answer immediately. Or I will sue you.	傑森：妳們到底賣了什麼給我？！產品存在這麼嚴重的問題。我要求對我的損失進行全額退款。希望妳們立即給我答覆，否則我就要告妳們。
Megan: Sir, don't worry. We will try our best to solve your problem. If grave problems indeed exist in the products, we will refund your money at once. We are a company with a high reputation in this trade, so you can trust us absolutely!	梅根：先生，請別著急。我們會盡力解決您的問題的。如果產品確實存在嚴重問題，我們馬上給您退款。我們在這一行業中信譽良好，所以您完全可以相信我們。
Jason: Really? Then how do you solve my problem? I hope you can reply to me quickly!	傑森：真的嗎？那麼妳們要怎麼解決我的問題？我希望妳們儘快答覆我。
Megan: Ok, no problem. And may I pass you to our colleague responsible for after-sale services? He is the person in charge.	梅根：好的，沒問題。讓我把您的電話轉給負責售後服務的同事好嗎？他是這方面的負責人。

文法重點看這裡！

學完前面的會話之後，還要懂會話中的文法重點，才能應用在職場！以下補充重要的文法並做詳盡解析，把文法根基打好，讓你無論是出差還是洽商，都用正確英文和外國人打交道！

文法重點1

fame/reputation/honor
同樣都有「名聲」的意思，該怎麼用呢？

fame 強調高知名度，非常出名，通常指眾所周知的好名聲。honor 是別人賦予的好名聲，通常是因為自己作了值得頌揚的好事而獲得的名聲。而 reputation 強調一般人心目中的觀感。請利用下面的例句，幫助更熟悉記憶單字的用法：

* **He has a good fame in his village.** 在村子裡，他名聲很好。
* **He has a reputation for greediness.** 他有一個貪婪的壞名聲。
* **As a soldier, you should fight for the honor of your country.**
  身為一名士兵，你應該為國家的榮譽而戰。

 fame 和 honor 通常是較為正向的字。其中 honor 常指國家民族的榮譽。reputation 代表的也許是好的觀感，也許是不好的觀感，是較為中性的字。

文法重點2

Who are you? 是錯誤用法

這是一句典型的中式英文，是由「你是誰？」直翻過來的。如果想要在電話中禮貌的詢問對方是誰，可以說：

* **Who's calling, please?** 請問你是……？
* **May I have your name, please?** 請告訴我你的名字。

文法重點3

He is picking the phone at the moment.
是錯誤用法

這是一句典型的中式英文，是由「他現在正在接電話。」直翻過來的。如果想要表達某人正在接電話，可以說：

* **He is on the phone now.** 他正在講電話。
* **He is on another line at the moment.** 他此刻在跟其他人講電話。

會話單字懂多少？

讀過前面的內容後，你是不是都懂得這些單字了呢？下列題目中的單字都是與會話及文法相關的單字，測驗看看自己會了多少吧！

( )❶ corporation： (A) 農作物 (B) 操作 (C)公司

( )❷ sell： (A) 貝殼 (B) 出售 (C) 地獄

( )❸ serious： (A) 系列 (B) 嚴格 (C) 嚴重

( )❹ refund： (A) 退款 (B) 發現 (C) 資金

( )❺ loss： (A) 馬虎 (B) 損失 (C) 震盪

( )❻ solve： (A) 離開 (B) 袖口 (C) 解決

( )❼ honor： (A) 乾燥 (B) 榮譽 (C) 富裕

( )❽ trade： (A) 褪色 (B) 潮汐 (C) 行業

( )❾ reply： (A) 回覆 (B) 申請 (C) 負責

( )❿ fame： (A) 臭名 (B) 名望 (C) 名字

( )⓫ reputation： (A) 逐退 (B) 反駁 (C) 名譽

( )⓬ sue： (A) 燃料 (B) 她 (C) 控告

( )⓭ trust： (A) 扔出 (B) 信任 (C) 拋棄

( )⓮ absolutely： (A) 完全 (B) 吸收 (C) 解決

( )⓯ extension： (A) 邊界 (B) 緊張 (C) 擴充

答案：1. (C) 2. (B) 3. (C) 4. (A) 5. (B) 6. (C) 7. (B) 8. (C) 9. (A)
10. (B) 11. (C) 12. (C) 13. (B) 14. (A) 15. (C)

Unit 19

Would you like to leave a message?

你要留言給他嗎？

職場會話跟著說！ 🎧 Track 019

Steven: Excuse me, may I speak to Ben? I can't get through to him.

史蒂芬：打擾了，我想要找班。我打不通他的電話。

Megan: You have dialed the wrong number! But I can try to get him on the phone. May I have your name, please?

梅根：你打錯電話了。但是，我可以試著幫你轉接給他。請問你貴姓大名？

Steven: Thank you very much. This is Steven of the Market Department.

史蒂芬：非常感謝。我是市場部的史蒂芬。

Megan: Please hold on for a while, allow me to find out... I am sorry, but Ben is out. Would you like to leave a message?

梅根：請稍等，允許我去找一下……很抱歉，班不在公司。你要留言給他嗎？

Steven: Please tell Ben that our goods have reached the customs. We need a truck to transport the goods. And also when he dispatches the truck, please ask him to let the driver bring the receipt here. That's all.

史蒂芬：請告訴班，我們的貨物已經到達海關了。我們需要一輛車來運送。還請告訴他派車來的時候，請讓司機把收據也一起帶過來。就這樣！

Megan: Ok, I have written them down. You mean our goods are inspected in customs? This is an important matter! I will tell him as soon as possible.

梅根：好的，我把它們都記下來了。你是說我們的貨物在海關受檢嗎？這可是大事啊！我會儘快告訴他的。

文法重點看這裡！

學完前面的會話之後，還要懂會話中的文法重點，才能應用在職場！以下補充重要的文法並做詳盡解析，把文法根基打好，讓你無論是出差還是洽商，都用正確英文和外國人打交道！

文法重點1

inspect/examine/investigate
同樣都有「檢查」的意思，該怎麼用呢？

investigate一般用於調查，inspect 表示視察、察看，examine 指仔細地查看或對細節做澈底的研究。請利用下面的例句，幫助更熟悉記憶單字的用法：

- **The police examined my bag when I entered the country.**
  我入境時，員警仔細檢查了我的包包。
- **They inspected the goods in the shop.** 他們檢查了商店裡的商品。
- **He was investigated and found guilty.** 他被調查後發現有罪。

 investigate多用於調查疑雲重重的案件或事件，例如警探偵察案件即是用這個單字。inspect重點放在事物的優劣或是否符合標準。examine則可用於身體檢查。

文法重點2

You have called the wrong place! 是錯誤用法

這是一句典型的中式英文，是由「你打錯地方了。」直翻過來的。如果想要表達對方打錯了，可以說：

- **You have dialed the wrong number.** 你撥錯號碼了。
- **You have the wrong number.** 你的電話號碼是錯誤的
- **You have telephoned the wrong person.** 你打電話給錯誤的人了。

文法重點3

This is a big thing! 是錯誤用法

這是一句典型的中式英文，是由「這可是一件大事啊！」直翻過來的。如果想要說某件事情很重要，可以說：

- **This is an important matter.** 這是重要的事。
- **This is a serious matter.** 這是嚴重的事。

會話單字懂多少？

讀過前面的內容後，你是不是都懂得這些單字了呢？下列題目中的單字都是與會話及文法相關的單字，測驗看看自己會了多少吧！

( )❶ through： (A) 儘管 (B) 通過 (C) 粗糙

( )❷ market： (A) 判決 (B) 標記 (C) 市場

( )❸ message： (A) 聖賢 (B) 消息 (C) 凌亂

( )❹ alright： (A) 好的 (B) 輕鬆 (C) 航班

( )❺ reach： (A) 反應 (B) 桃子 (C) 到達

( )❻ customs： (A) 顧客 (B) 海關 (C) 陣容

( )❼ truck： (A) 卡車 (B) 象牙 (C) 褶皺

( )❽ transport： (A) 轉換 (B) 運送 (C) 港口

( )❾ investigate： (A) 調查 (B) 投資 (C) 衡量

( )❿ examine： (A) 煤礦 (B) 考試 (C) 檢查

( )⓫ inspect： (A) 視察 (B) 預料 (C) 昆蟲

( )⓬ dial： (A) 最後 (B) 鑽孔 (C) 撥打

( )⓭ allow： (A) 允許 (B) 箭頭 (C) 低矮

( )⓮ dispatch： (A) 解散 (B) 分派 (C) 路途

( )⓯ receipt： (A) 吸收 (B) 接待 (C) 收據

答案：1. (B) 2. (C) 3. (B) 4. (A) 5. (C) 6. (B) 7. (A) 8. (B) 9. (A) 10. (C) 11. (A) 12. (C) 13. (A) 14. (B) 15. (C)

Now it's time we visited our customers.

現在是我們拜訪客戶的時候了。

職場會話跟著說！ Track 020

Megan: Hello, Mr. James, This is Megan from Blue Sky Corp. Excuse my troubling you. You bought our products last year. Now it's time we visited our customers and knew about their workings. Are they still in good condition now?

梅根：您好，詹姆斯先生，我是藍天公司的梅根。恕我打擾。你在去年的時候購買我們的產品。現在是我們拜訪客戶，瞭解使用情況的時候了。他們現在是否狀況良好呢？

James: Yeah, exactly! I bought all of them last year. En...they work very well. At present, they are still in good state.

詹姆斯：是的，沒錯。我就是去年購買的。嗯……都運作的不錯！目前，狀況良好！

Megan: That's it! All of them have first class quality and performance. Besides, we adopt advanced technology. Now we have developed new products. They are much better than what you have bought.

梅根：這就對了！它們的品質和性能都是一流的。另外，還採用了先進技術。現在，我們還開發了新產品。它們更好了。

James: Your company is developing so fast, so is ours. Maybe later on I will plan to buy more.

詹姆斯：你們公司發展真快啊，我們也是。也許以後我們還要計畫買更多呢。

Megan: That's great! Thanks for your support. If any, please remember to call us. I am afraid I have to say goodbye now! See you soon, Mr. James!

梅根：太好了！謝謝你們的支持。如果有需要的話，記得聯繫我們哦。我想我現在該告辭了！再見了，詹姆斯先生！

文法重點看這裡！

學完前面的會話之後，還要懂會話中的文法重點，才能應用在職場！以下補充重要的文法並做詳盡解析，把文法根基打好，讓你無論是出差還是洽商，都用正確英文和外國人打交道！

文法重點1

condition/situation/status
同樣都有「情況」的意思，該怎麼用呢？

condition 主要是指物體，生物和環境的狀態，也有「條件」的意思。situation 主要是形容事情或事件的狀態。status 和situation 一樣，都是形容事情的狀態，而不是形容事情或人物。另外，status 也有「地位」的意思。請利用下面的例句，幫助更熟悉記憶單字的用法：

- **Mary said she would only accept the offer under one condition.**
  瑪莉說她只有在一種情況下才會接受這項提議。
- **He was in a rather difficult situation at the time.**
  他那時是處在一種很艱難的情況。
- **She has a high status job.** 她職位很高。

文法重點2

It's time 接子句的用法

當It's time 接子句的時候，我們需要在子句中採用過去時態。例如：

- **It's time we went to our hometown.** 是時候讓我們回家鄉了。

It's time 後面還可以接to do sth。例如：
- **It's time to go home.** 該回家了。

文法重點3

remember 的用法

當remember 後面接doing 的時候，表達的意思是記得做過某事。例如：

- **I remember seeing this boy.** 我記得看過這男孩。

當remember 後面接to do 的時候，表達的意思是記得去做某事。例如：
- **Please remember to do your homework.** 請記得寫作業。

會話單字懂多少？

讀過前面的內容後，你是不是都懂得這些單字了呢？下列題目中的單字都是與會話及文法相關的單字，測驗看看自己會了多少吧！

( ) ❶ transfer：(A) 變化 (B) 轉接 (C) 傳達

( ) ❷ conversation：(A) 對話 (B) 轉化 (C) 傳播

( ) ❸ trouble：(A) 旅遊 (B) 麻煩 (C) 雙倍

( ) ❹ visit：(A) 簽證 (B) 病毒 (C) 拜訪

( ) ❺ situation：(A) 處理 (B) 情況 (C) 引用

( ) ❻ remember：(A) 醫治 (B) 提醒 (C) 記住

( ) ❼ condition：(A) 編輯 (B) 條件 (C) 傳導

( ) ❽ status：(A) 地位 (B) 雕塑 (C) 條件

( ) ❾ hometown： (A) 城市 (B) 家鄉 (C) 城鎮

( ) ❿ performance： (A) 完美 (B) 威脅 (C) 性能

( ) ⓫ besides： (A) 另外 (B) 主教 (C) 偏袒

( ) ⓬ adopt： (A) 羨慕 (B) 進步 (C) 採用

( ) ⓭ advance： (A) 開始 (B) 先進 (C) 優勢

( ) ⓮ wish： (A) 智慧 (B) 祝願 (C) 魚兒

( ) ⓯ general： (A) 混合 (B) 產生 (C) 一般

答案：1. (B) 2. (A) 3. (B) 4. (C) 5. (B) 6. (C) 7. (B) 8. (A) 9. (B)
10. (C) 11. (A) 12. (C) 13. (B) 14. (B) 15. (C)

I am sure you will be interested in our products, too.

我保證您對我們的產品也會很感興趣的。

職場會話跟著說！ 🎧Track 021

Megan: Hello, this is Megan from Blue Sky Corp. May I speak to Mr. Eric?

梅根：你好，我是藍天公司的梅根。我找艾瑞克先生。

Receptionist: Do you have an appointment with our manager?

櫃台：請問您有和我們經理預約嗎？

Megan: No, I don't. But I am sure he will be interested in my call. Could you help me to get him on the phone? Please!

梅根：沒有。但是我確信他會感興趣的。你能把電話轉給他嗎？麻煩你。

Receptionist: OK. Our manager is available now!

櫃台：好的。現在可以跟經理通話了！

Megan: Thanks! Hello, Mr. Eric?

梅根：謝謝！您好，艾瑞克先生嗎？

Eric: Speaking. The receptionist said you want to talk to me, Miss? What can I do for you?

艾瑞克：是的。櫃台説妳有事情想跟我談，是嗎？

Megan: Yes. I know your company is the third largest independent retailer of electronic products in the world. The retail business thrives under your good administration. I am sure you will be interested in our products, too.

梅根：是的。我瞭解到貴公司是世界第三大獨立經營的電子產品零售商。在您的良好管理下，零售生意蒸蒸日上。我保證您對我們的產品也會很感興趣的。

Eric: I will consider a future cooperation between us.

艾瑞克：我會考慮一下雙方未來的合作。

文法重點看這裡！

學完前面的會話之後，還要懂會話中的文法重點，才能應用在職場！以下補充重要的文法並做詳盡解析，把文法根基打好，讓你無論是出差還是洽商，都用正確英文和外國人打交道！

文法重點1

gain/get/earn 同樣都有「獲得」的意思，該怎麼用呢？

gain 是慢慢地獲得，必須是經由一段時間或是一段努力才得到的，而get 則是泛指「得到」。請利用下面的例句，幫助更熟悉記憶單字的用法：

- **This article gives tips on how to gain weight in a healthy way.**
  這篇文章提供了以健康方式增重的訣竅。
- **Where did you get the book?** 你是從哪裡得到這本書的？
- **He earned the respect of others.** 他獲得了別人的尊敬。

 一般口語中可以用get 來取代gain；earn 主要是指經由努力而得到報酬或是榮譽，例如因為努力工作而得到酬勞或經由努力而獲得別人的肯定與尊敬。

文法重點2

He will be interested to my call. 是錯誤用法

想要說某人對某事感興趣，用be interested 後面要加上介詞in 再接名詞或動名詞。例如：

- **He will be interested in this.** 他會對這個感興趣。

而我們說某事很有趣，則要用interesting 來表示。例如：

- **This joke is very interesting.** 這個玩笑很有趣。

文法重點3

序數詞＋最高級的用法

如果需要在序數詞的後面加上一個表示比較的形容詞，則這個形容詞必須用最高級來表示而不是比較級。例如：

- **The building is the second highest in the area.**
  這棟建築物是這個區域第二高的。
- **Liming is the third tallest in his family.** 利明是他家族裡長得第三高的。

會話單字懂多少？

讀過前面的內容後，你是不是都懂得這些單字了呢？下列題目中的單字都是與會話及文法相關的單字，測驗看看自己會了多少吧！

( ) ❶ appointment： (A) 假設 (B) 安排 (C) 分配

( ) ❷ interested： (A) 容入 (B) 感興趣的 (C) 連貫

( ) ❸ receptionist： (A) 撤退 (B) 接待人員 (C) 負責人

( ) ❹ retailer： (A) 退休 (B) 挽留 (C) 零售商

( ) ❺ provide： (A) 提供 (B) 證明 (C) 省市

( ) ❻ electronic： (A) 電極 (B) 電子的 (C) 電子學

( ) ❼ earn： (A) 耳朵 (B) 堅固 (C) 掙得

( ) ❽ share： (A) 共用 (B) 鯊魚 (C) 塑造

( ) ❾ gain： (A) 獲得 (B) 反對 (C) 基因

( ) ❿ weight： (A) 重量 (B) 運費 (C) 輕盈

( ) ⓫ independent： (A) 決定於 (B) 不獨立 (C) 獨立

( ) ⓬ administration： (A) 管理 (B) 羨慕 (C) 允許

( ) ⓭ professional： (A) 能力 (B) 專業 (C) 教授

( ) ⓮ occupy： (A) 海洋 (B) 發生 (C) 佔有

( ) ⓯ cooperation： (A) 冷卻 (B) 控制 (C) 合作

答案：1. (B) 2. (B) 3. (B) 4. (C) 5. (A) 6. (B) 7. (C) 8. (A) 9. (A)
10. (A) 11. (C) 12. (A) 13. (B) 14. (C) 15. (C)

I have to inform all the employees in time.

我得及時通知各位同仁。

 職場會話跟著說！ 🎧 Track 022

Megan: A piece of bad news! We must have a meeting tomorrow. And he asked me to arrange all the affairs.

梅根：一個壞消息！明天要開會了！他叫我來安排這些事情。

Sarah: Oh, then you have a lot to answer for.

莎拉：噢，那麼妳有一堆事情要做囉。

Megan: Yeah. First, I have to inform all the employees in time. I am afraid not all of them have time to attend. Secondly, I must communicate with the company next to us and persuade them to let us use their big conference room. Thirdly, I have to prepare the equipments.

梅根：是啊！首先，我得及時通知各位同仁。我怕有人沒時間可以參加。第二呢，我得和隔壁公司溝通一下，說服他們讓我用一下他們的大會議室。第三就是我得準備開會用的設備。

Sarah: Don't worry. I think they will agree to let us use their conference room. In the meeting, a projector is a must. Don't forget that.

莎拉：別擔心，他們會同意讓我們用他們的會議室的。投影機是開會必備之物。可別忘了喔！

Megan: Yeah. The boss will show slides in the middle of the meeting. It doesn't matter. I can manage it.

梅根：是啊。老闆要在會議中放映幻燈片呢！沒關係，我能應付過來的。

文法重點看這裡！

學完前面的會話之後，還要懂會話中的文法重點，才能應用在職場！以下補充重要的文法並做詳盡解析，把文法根基打好，讓你無論是出差還是洽商，都用正確英文和外國人打交道！

文法重點1

meet/meeting/party 同樣都有「聚會」的意思，該怎麼用呢？

meet 指競賽型的集會或運動會。meeting 可以指兩個人以上的會面，也可以指一群人為了討論或決定某事而集合在一起。party指為了慶祝某事而舉行的社交性宴會。請利用下面的例句，幫助更熟悉記憶單字的用法：

- **The track meet begins at 3 o'clock.** 田徑賽將於三點舉行。
- **The company called a meeting on Monday.** 公司星期一召開了一次會議。
- **The Greens held a Christmas party last night.** 格林家昨晚舉行了聖誕晚會。

 meeting通常譯成「會議」，指公司行號中各種大小型會議；party通常譯為「派對」。

文法重點2

A bad news! 是錯誤用法

這是一句典型的中式英文，是由「一個壞消息！」直翻過來的。這裡要注意，news 是一個不可數名詞。如果想要說一個壞消息，可以說：

- **A piece of bad news!** 有個壞消息！
- **Bad news!** 壞消息！

文法重點3

All of them not have time to attend. 是錯誤用法

這句的正確說法為：Not all of them have time to attend. not 和all 在一起用的時候表示的是「部份否定」，並非全部否定的意思。使用的時候要多加注意。例如：

- **Not all the students have this book.** 不是所有學生都有這本書。
- **He couldn't answer all of these questions.** 他不能回答這裡所有的問題。

會話單字懂多少？

讀過前面的內容後,你是不是都懂得這些單字了呢?下列題目中的單字都是與會話及文法相關的單字,測驗看看自己會了多少吧!

( ) ❶ god: (A) 金子 (B) 上帝 (C) 女神

( ) ❷ news: (A) 歪斜 (B) 新鮮 (C) 消息

( ) ❸ arrange: (A) 安排 (B) 推理 (C) 範圍

( ) ❹ affair: (A) 影響 (B) 事情 (C) 喜愛

( ) ❺ attend: (A) 注意 (B) 溫柔 (C) 參加

( ) ❻ prepare: (A) 假設 (B) 準備 (C) 進步

( ) ❼ equipment: (A) 均衡 (B) 設備 (C) 繳械

( ) ❽ manage: (A) 人類 (B) 經理 (C) 經營

( ) ❾ track: (A) 陷阱 (B) 卡車 (C) 蹤跡

( ) ❿ piece: (A) 餡餅 (B) 激烈 (C) 碎片

( ) ⓫ communicate: (A) 社區 (B) 交流 (C) 免疫

( ) ⓬ persuade: (A) 觀點 (B) 勸說 (C) 侵略

( ) ⓭ conference: (A) 參考 (B) 會議 (C) 轉化

( ) ⓮ agree: (A) 同意 (B) 貪婪 (C) 惡化

( ) ⓯ projector: (A) 拒絕 (B) 專案 (C) 投影機

答案:1. (B) 2. (C) 3. (A) 4. (B) 5. (C) 6. (B) 7. (B) 8. (C) 9. (C)
10. (C) 11. (B) 12. (B) 13. (B) 14. (A) 15. (C)

Unit 23

We must find the underlying problem in ourselves and its solution.

我們必須找出我們自身隱藏的問題和它的解決辦法。

 職場會話跟著說！ 🎧 Track 023

Ken: Hello, everyone, today I want to talk about our work. Our business is in a mess. The sales in Chinese market is very low recently. I think we can do better than that. Now we must try to change this situation. I hope everyone here can have a discussion.

肯：大家好，今天我想討論一下我們的工作。我們的生意現在很糟糕。最近在中國市場上的銷售量很低。我們可以做得比這更好的。現在我們要儘量改變這種局面。希望大家能一起來討論一下。

Employee A: I believe this must be attributed to the recent economic crisis. The crisis spreads and gives a great blow to consumer confidence, so that they have no desire to purchase.

員工A：我認為這是因為最近的金融危機。經濟危機到處蔓延，打擊了消費者的信心，以至於他們失去了購買慾望。

Ken: Do I make myself clear ? My point is to find our way out. Whatever has happened, we ourselves must be responsible for the result. We must find the underlying problem in ourselves and its solution.

肯：你聽懂我的話了嗎？我的重點是找出解決方法來。不管已經發生了什麼，只有我們自己來承擔後果。我們必須找出我們自身隱藏的問題和它的解決辦法。

Employee B: I think our propaganda work isn't enough. Many consumers even don't know our brand. When they see our products, they don't regard it as a well-known brand. So we can do something in this field.

員工B：我認為是我們的宣傳不夠。很多消費者甚至不知道有我們這個牌子。當他們看到我們的產品，他們都不認為它是名牌產品。因此，我們可以在這個領域改進一下。

文法重點看這裡！

學完前面的會話之後，還要懂會話中的文法重點，才能應用在職場！以下補充重要的文法並做詳盡解析，把文法根基打好，讓你無論是出差還是洽商，都用正確英文和外國人打交道！

文法重點1
enough/adequate/sufficient
同樣都有「足夠」的意思，該怎麼用呢？

adequate指的是數量達到最低標準，符合需求，也有「適當」的意思。enough 和sufficient在多數情況下可以通用，都有「足夠」的意思。請利用下面的例句，幫助更熟悉記憶單字的用法：

- **I have had enough of this nonsense.** 我已經受夠了。
- **To be healthy, one must have an adequate diet.**
  一個人如果想身體健康，則必須有充足的飲食。
- **Have you carried out sufficient investigation?**
  你有沒有進行充分的調查研究？

 enough 比較口語，sufficient 多用於書面。

文法重點2
What we do is no better than that. 是錯誤用法

這句話缺了that引導的子句，故為錯誤。句子的意思是指，主詞所代表的事物，並沒有後面由that 所引導句子的內容好，但正確的用法應為：

- **This boss is no better than the previous one.** 這個老闆沒有比前一個好。
- **What you've done is no better than what he's done.** 你做的沒有比他好。

文法重點3
My important point is to find our way out.
是錯誤用法

這是一句典型的中式英文，是由「我的重點是找出解決方法來。」直翻過來的。如果想要強調自己說話的重點，可以直接說：

- **My point is to stop your investment.** 我的重點是停止你的投資。
- **The key is to understand what he has said.** 重點是要理解他說什麼。
- **My focus is to find a solution.** 我在意的是找出一個解決方式。

會話單字懂多少？

讀過前面的內容後,你是不是都懂得這些單字了呢?下列題目中的單字都是與會話及文法相關的單字,測驗看看自己會了多少吧!

( ) ❶ better： (A) 賭注 (B) 進入 (C) 更好

( ) ❷ economic： (A) 生態的 (B) 經濟的 (C) 經濟學

( ) ❸ crisis： (A) 哭泣 (B) 反抗 (C) 危機

( ) ❹ confidence： (A) 告白 (B) 信心 (C) 機密

( ) ❺ desire： (A) 害怕 (B) 宣言 (C) 欲望

( ) ❻ purchase： (A) 懲罰 (B) 追逐 (C) 購買

( ) ❼ point： (A) 查找 (B) 觀點 (C) 印刷

( ) ❽ underlying： (A) 潛在 (B) 否認 (C) 回復

( ) ❾ solution： (A) 解決 (B) 決心 (C) 幻想

( ) ❿ adequate： (A) 足夠 (B) 著迷 (C) 放棄

( ) ⓫ spread： (A) 傳播 (B) 麵包 (C) 精神

( ) ⓬ clear： (A) 跳蚤 (B) 昂貴 (C) 清晰

( ) ⓭ result： (A) 侮辱 (B) 結果 (C) 尊敬

( ) ⓮ regard： (A) 認為 (B) 花園 (C) 退回

( ) ⓯ suggestion： (A) 糖粉 (B) 消化 (C) 建議

答案：1. (C) 2. (B) 3. (C) 4. (B) 5. (C) 6. (C) 7. (B) 8. (A) 9. (A)
10. (A) 11. (A) 12. (C) 13. (B) 14. (A) 15. (C)

Only by multiplying our efforts can we succeed in difficulties.

只有再加倍努力，我們才能擺脫困境，取得成功。

職場會話跟著說！　Track 024

Employee A: What do you think of this problem? In such a short time, our sales suffer a downturn. A big drop happened so fast in recent sales figures. How can we save the business?

員工A：對這個問題你怎麼想的啊？這麼短的時間裡面，我們的銷售就轉入了低迷期。緊接著最近銷售額很快就大跌。我們怎樣才能挽救生意啊？

Employee B: There are many factors leading to this result. If we had known the economic crisis in advance, we would have avoided this downturn.

員工B：有很多因素促成了這個結果。要是我們事前知道這次經濟危機就好了，就可以避免這次的生意不景氣。

Employee A: Yeah, but the fact is that no one can expect that. It happened without any sign.

員工A：是啊，但是事實上是沒有人可以預料到。它發生的時候沒有任何跡象可尋。

Employee C: Just as our general manager said, I think the most important thing is to take measures to change such a terrible situation.

員工C：正如我們總經理所說的，我認為現在最重要的事情就是採取措施，改變當前糟糕的局面。

Employee B: I agree. Only by multiplying our efforts can we succeed in difficulties.

員工B：我同意。只有再加倍努力，我們才能擺脫困境，取得成功。

文法重點看這裡！

學完前面的會話之後，還要懂會話中的文法重點，才能應用在職場！以下補充重要的文法並做詳盡解析，把文法根基打好，讓你無論是出差還是洽商，都用正確英文和外國人打交道！

文法重點1
fast/quick/soon 同樣都有「快」的意思，該怎麼用呢？

quick 主要是形容在短時間內完成的事情或動作。fast 主要是指人或物體的行動或運動速度快。soon 只能當副詞用，主要是時間方面的「不久」。請利用下面的例句，幫助更熟悉記憶單字的用法：

- **The car runs fast.** 這輛車跑得很快。
- **Let's have a quick review of this lesson.** 讓我們快速複習一下這一課。
- **We will be home soon.** 我們很快就到家了。

文法重點2
對過去虛擬的用法

當我們要表示與過去事實相反的假設，我們就需要用到假設語氣。例如：

- **If she had studied harder, she would have gotten a good mark.**
  如果她之前有認真念書，就能取得優異的成績。
- **If he had come a bit earlier, he would have caught the bus.**
  如果他早一點來，就能趕上公車了。

文法重點3
only by 提前的用法

一般的語句通常是把only by 放在句子的後半部分。但是如果要表示強調的話，only by 也可以提前，放於句首，此時句子需要採用不完全倒裝形式。例如：

- **Only by working harder can he make his dream come true.**
  只有認真工作才能讓他的夢想成真。
- **Only by getting up earlier can the old man earn some money.**
  只有早點起床，那個老男人才能賺到一些錢。

會話單字懂多少？

讀過前面的內容後，你是不是都懂得這些單字了呢？下列題目中的單字都是與會話及文法相關的單字，測驗看看自己會了多少吧！

( )❶ short： (A) 短的 (B) 商店 (C) 缺點

( )❷ drop： (A) 部隊 (B) 旱災 (C) 下跌

( )❸ soon： (A) 很快 (B) 悲傷 (C) 中午

( )❹ figure： (A) 檔 (B) 戰鬥 (C) 圖表

( )❺ avoid： (A) 迎接 (B) 注意 (C) 避免

( )❻ downturn： (A) 下降 (B) 城鎮 (C) 轉向

( )❼ sign： (A) 輕巧 (B) 跡象 (C) 感歎

( )❽ measure： (A) 措施 (B) 機械 (C) 肉類

( )❾ multiply： (A) 乘法 (B) 坎坷 (C) 回覆

( )❿ succeed： (A) 減去 (B) 郊區 (C) 成功

( )⓫ review： (A) 阻止 (B) 溫習 (C) 觀點

( )⓬ suffer： (A) 足夠 (B) 突然 (C) 遭遇

( )⓭ expect： (A) 害蟲 (B) 預料 (C) 裁減

( )⓮ terrible： (A) 很好 (B) 糟糕 (C) 領地

( )⓯ difficulty： (A) 員工 (B) 不同 (C) 困難

答案：1. (A) 2. (C) 3. (A) 4. (C) 5. (C) 6. (A) 7. (B) 8. (A) 9. (A)
10. (C) 11. (B) 12. (C) 13. (B) 14. (B) 15. (C)

I want to adjust my former plan.

我想調整一下我之前的計畫。

 職場會話跟著說！ 🎧 Track 025

Ken: Such being the case, we must spare no effort to reverse the situation. I believe we can accomplish a miracle if we hold together. Do you have the confidence?

肯：既然事以至此，我們必須不遺餘力地扭轉這種局面。我相信我們只要一起努力就可以創造奇蹟。你們有這個信心嗎？

Daniel: Boss, what's your plan? Tell us about it and we can carry it out by all means. We believe we can make it.

丹尼爾：老闆，你有什麼計畫嗎？告訴我們吧！我們會盡一切辦法執行的。我們相信我們一定可以做到。

Ken: Good! I want to adjust my former plan. All the departments have to assign new tasks to their employees. And I hope we can reach a return of one million dollars this year.

肯：好！我想調整一下我之前的計畫。所有部門要重新給員工分配任務。而且，我希望我們可以在今年達到一百萬美元的收入。

Daniel: We can reach this objective only if we can work togther with one heart.

丹尼爾：只有我們同心協力，我們才能達到這個目標。

Ken: Quite right! And if we achieve this goal, a holiday will await you.

肯：很對！要是我們達到了這個目標，你們就可以放一次假了！

Employees: (Cheers!)

員工們：（一陣歡呼聲！）

文法重點看這裡！

學完前面的會話之後，還要懂會話中的文法重點，才能應用在職場！以下補充重要的文法並做詳盡解析，把文法根基打好，讓你無論是出差還是洽商，都用正確英文和外國人打交道！

文法重點1
plan/proposal/program
同樣都有「計畫」的意思，該怎麼用呢？

plan用來泛指「計畫」，可以是臨時的打算，也可以是周詳的計畫。proposal是正式的提出建議，必須是經由別人來接受或拒絕。program是為了做某事而「進行指定的方案」。請利用下面的例句，幫助更熟悉記憶單字的用法：

- **I plan to climb the mountain tomorrow.** 我計畫明天去爬山。
- **His proposal was discussed at the meeting.** 大家在會議上討論了他的提案。
- **It's a training program for new workers.** 這是一份新進人員的培訓方案。

文法重點2
by no means 的用法

by no means 的意思是「無論如何都不」。例如：

- **It's by no means easy to do this.** 無論如何都不能簡單地完成這件事。
- **She is by no means bright.** 她一點也不正向。

by all means 表達的意思則是無論如何都要，盡一切辦法，一定的意思。例如：
- **We'll finish our task by all means this year.**
  我們無論如何都會在今年完成任務。

文法重點3
if only 的用法

if only 的意思是「要是……多好」。例如：

- **If only you can visit me, I will be happy.** 要是你來拜訪我，我會很快樂。
- **If only I had a dog, I wouldn't be lonely.** 要是我有一隻狗，我就不會寂寞了。

會話單字懂多少？

讀過前面的內容後，你是不是都懂得這些單字了呢？下列題目中的單字都是與會話及文法相關的單字，測驗看看自己會了多少吧！

( ) ❶ spare： (A) 蒼白 (B) 火花 (C) 空出

( ) ❷ effort： (A) 提供 (B) 努力 (C) 效果

( ) ❸ reverse： (A) 修改 (B) 扭轉；推翻 (C) 報復

( ) ❹ program： (A) 提議 (B) 項目 (C) 進步

( ) ❺ means： (A)倚靠 (B) 方法 (C) 薄荷

( ) ❻ objective： (A) 積極 (B) 反對 (C) 目標

( ) ❼ heart： (A) 恐懼 (B) 聽見 (C) 心靈

( ) ❽ goal： (A) 目標 (B) 山羊 (C) 金子

( ) ❾ plan： (A) 土地 (B) 計畫 (C) 植物

( ) ❿ climb： (A) 攀爬 (B) 聾的 (C) 瘸腿

( ) ⓫ proposal： (A) 提議 (B) 反對 (C) 專案

( ) ⓬ afford： (A) 斷言 (B) 給予 (C) 富裕

( ) ⓭ adjust： (A) 公正 (B) 管理 (C) 調整

( ) ⓮ await： (A) 阻止 (B) 等候 (C) 清醒

( ) ⓯ cheer： (A) 晶片 (B) 便宜 (C) 歡呼

答案：1. (C) 2. (B) 3. (B) 4. (B) 5. (B) 6. (C) 7. (C) 8. (A) 9. (B)
10. (A) 11. (A) 12. (B) 13. (C) 14. (B) 15. (C)

I will ask you to carry out the market survey first.

我要妳們先進行一次市場調查。

 職場會話跟著說！ 🎧 Track 026

Daniel: According to our general manager's speech, our market department will burden an important task. That is to advertise our products as possible as we can.

丹尼爾：根據總經理剛才的談話，我們市場部將要肩負重擔。那就是盡我們最大的努力進行產品宣傳工作。

Megan: How can we achieve that? Now we have tried lots of ways to improve the situation. But it doesn't work.

梅根：我們要如何才能做到這點呢？現在我們已經嘗試過了很多種方法來改善情況。但是都不能奏效。

Sarah: And also we haven't found out our problems yet. We don't know the direction. How can we carry on our advertising campaign? As we all know, easier said than done.

莎拉：而且，我們還沒找出問題所在。我們都不知道方向。我們該如何進行我們的宣傳活動呢？大家都知道，說起來容易做起來難啊！

Daniel: Yeah, what you guys say is right. Considering these mentioned above, I will ask you to carry out the market survey first, then you will have to connect with advertising media. We must accelerate our advertising. Understand?

丹尼爾：是啊，妳們說的都對。考慮到以上提到的這些問題，我要妳們先進行一次市場調查，然後再聯繫廣告媒體。我們必須加快廣告曝光的速度。明白了嗎？

Megan & Sarah: Yes! We'll try our best!

梅根和莎拉：明白了！我們會加油的！

文法重點看這裡！

學完前面的會話之後，還要懂會話中的文法重點，才能應用在職場！以下補充重要的文法並做詳盡解析，把文法根基打好，讓你無論是出差還是洽商，都用正確英文和外國人打交道！

文法重點1
address/speech/lecture
同樣都有「演說」的意思，該怎麼用呢？

lecture 通常指的是學術演講。address 指的是慎重準備好的正式演說或致辭。speech指的是有準備的講話或臨場即興發言，以表達自己的情感、觀點、意見等。請利用下面的例句，更熟悉記憶單字的用法：

- **He is reading an address of welcome.** 他正在致歡迎辭。
- **The ambassador made a dull speech.** 這位大使發表了一篇枯燥無味的談話。
- **Have you ever attended professor Wang's lectures?**
  你有沒有聽過王教授的演講呢？

文法重點2
media 的用法

media 是medium（媒體）的複數。既然已經是複數了，就不需要在字尾加上s了。例如：

- **Have you connected with advertising media yet?** 你和廣告媒體聯絡了嗎？

文法重點3
accelerate 的用法

accelerate本身就有加快事物速度的意思，因此後面沒有必要加上pace這個詞了，要不然就會犯語意重複的毛病。例如：

- **The runners begin to accelerate when they see the finishing line.**
  跑者看見終點線後開始加速。
- **The car accelerates on the highway.** 汽車在公路上加速。

會話單字懂多少？

讀過前面的內容後，你是不是都懂得這些單字了呢？下列題目中的單字都是與會話及文法相關的單字，測驗看看自己會了多少吧！

( ) ❶ lecture： (A) 羽毛 (B) 離開 (C) 演講

( ) ❷ advertise： (A) 開始 (B) 廣告 (C) 建議

( ) ❸ improve： (A) 重要 (B) 證明 (C) 改進

( ) ❹ consider： (A) 體貼 (B) 考慮 (C) 簡明

( ) ❺ carry： (A) 渡口 (B) 搬動 (C) 貨車

( ) ❻ survey： (A) 紀念品 (B) 生存 (C) 調查

( ) ❼ connect： (A) 阻塞 (B) 聯繫 (C) 征服

( ) ❽ media： (A) 傳媒 (B) 醫藥 (C) 協調

( ) ❾ accelerate： (A) 慶祝 (B) 接受 (C) 加速

( ) ❿ pace： (A) 蒼白 (B) 速度 (C) 粘貼

( ) ⓫ address： (A) 增加 (B) 致辭 (C) 衣著

( ) ⓬ speech： (A) 拼寫 (B) 速度 (C) 講話

( ) ⓭ burden： (A) 荒誕 (B) 擔負 (C) 市區

( ) ⓮ task： (A) 任務 (B) 關稅 (C) 品嚐

( ) ⓯ campaign： (A) 校園 (B) 活動 (C) 照相機

答案：1. (C) 2. (B) 3. (C) 4. (B) 5. (B) 6. (C) 7. (B) 8. (A) 9. (C)
10. (B) 11. (B) 12. (C) 13. (B) 14. (A) 15. (B)

Unit 27

Now please allow me to draw a conclusion to this conference.

現在讓我對這場會議做個總結。

職場會話跟著說！ 🎧 Track 027

Ken: Now please allow me to draw a conclusion to this conference. We now all roughly know of our present sales. All the departments have assigned tasks to your own staff members. I hope I will get a good news soon.

肯：現在讓我對這場會議做個總結。我們對現在的銷售狀況都大致有了瞭解。所有的部門也已經重新給員工分配了他們的任務。我希望不久就會有好消息傳來。

Daniel: We will encourage our employees to work hard. And I do hope in our department there is no one lagging behind in their work.

丹尼爾：我們會鼓勵員工努力工作的。我也強烈希望在我們的部門中，人人都不甘落後。

Ken: That couldn't be better to our company. God helps those who help themselves. Everyone should think they are an essential member of the company.

肯：這對公司而言是再好不過了。自助者天助！每個人都要把自己當作公司不可或缺的一員來看待。

Daniel: Yes! Our company is just like a big family. All of us belong to it.

丹尼爾：會的。我們的公司就像個大家庭一樣。我們都屬於這個大家庭。

Ken: Mm... Now let's call it a day! You can make some preparations for later work. Once you finish your tasks, I will keep my promise. And you can have a holiday.

肯：嗯……今天就讓我們到此為止吧！你們可以先為以後的工作做些準備工作。一旦你們完成任務，我也會兌現我的承諾。你們也就可以享受假期了！

文法重點看這裡！

學完前面的會話之後，還要懂會話中的文法重點，才能應用在職場！以下補充重要的文法並做詳盡解析，把文法根基打好，讓你無論是出差還是洽商，都用正確英文和外國人打交道！

文法重點1
encourage/inspire/support
同樣都是「鼓勵」的意思，該怎麼用呢？

encourage 是鼓勵既定存在的事物，而inspire是激發出新的事物或助長新事物的產生，如inspire an idea（激發點子）。而support 則是較為消極被動的協助，且可以指金錢上的支援。請利用下面的例句，幫助更熟悉記憶單字的用法：

- **She encouraged him to pursue his dreams to be a journalist.**
  她鼓勵他追求他的夢想，成為一名記者。
- **John was inspired to write a book after his amazing adventures in the Amazon forest.** 約翰在亞馬遜叢林驚險之旅後，受到了激發要寫一本書。
- **Her father supported her through college.** 她的父親資助她念大學。

> encourage和inspire都是較為強烈積極地給予心理上的協助，通常是精神層面的支持。encourage 和inspire 通常用在會有後續發展的事物上，而support 則是用在意見上的支持。

文法重點2
couldn't be better 的用法

couldn't be better 表達的意思是「再好不過了」，而couldn't be good 就沒有這層意思，反而表示不好。例如：

- **Things couldn't be better.** 事情再好不過了。
- **It couldn't be better.** 這樣再好不過了。

文法重點3
Let's stop here! 是錯誤的用法

這是一句典型的中式英文，是由「就讓我們到此結束。」直翻過來的。如果想要表達某事到此為止，可以說：

- **Let's call it a day!** 結束這一天吧！
- **That's all for today!** 今天就到此為止！

會話單字懂多少？

讀過前面的內容後，你是不是都懂得這些單字了呢？下列題目中的單字都是與會話及文法相關的單字，測驗看看自己會了多少吧！

( ) ❶ draw： (A) 畫畫 (B) 抽屜 (C) 戲劇

( ) ❷ conclusion： (A) 協議 (B) 結論 (C) 堅硬

( ) ❸ inspire： (A) 安裝 (B) 檢查 (C) 激發

( ) ❹ member： (A) 人類 (B) 記得 (C) 成員

( ) ❺ stop： (A) 停止 (B) 湯料 (C) 頂部

( ) ❻ encourage： (A) 勇氣 (B) 遇見 (C) 鼓勵

( ) ❼ pursue： (A) 追求 (B) 錢包 (C) 目的

( ) ❽ forest： (A) 休息 (B) 森林 (C) 形式

( ) ❾ support： (A) 假設 (B) 支持 (C) 申報

( ) ❿ lag： (A) 腿 (B) 旗子 (C) 落後

( ) ⓫ help： (A) 頭盔 (B) 無助 (C) 幫助

( ) ⓬ essential： (A) 必要的 (B) 精華 (C) 建立

( ) ⓭ belong： (A) 下方 (B) 屬於 (C) 長的

( ) ⓮ preparation： (A) 報告 (B) 裝備 (C) 準備

( ) ⓯ promise： (A) 卓越 (B) 承諾 (C) 升職

答案：1. (A) 2. (B) 3. (C) 4. (C) 5. (A) 6. (C) 7. (A) 8. (B) 9. (B)
10. (C) 11. (C) 12. (A) 13. (B) 14. (C) 15. (B)

Part **4**

工作問題排除

It seems you make mistakes in the order sheet as well as the contract.

好像是訂單及合約出了錯。

 職場會話跟著說！ 🎧Track 028

Sarah: Hi, Megan, Steven just now asked me to tell you that there's something wrong with these documents you sent to the clients last week.

莎拉：嗨，梅根，史蒂芬剛剛叫我跟妳說，妳上周發給客戶的單據出了點錯。

Megan: Really? They shouldn't have any problem for I typed it carefully before mailing. I even put a mark in case of omission.

梅根：不會吧？不該出錯的啊，我在發郵件之前打得很仔細的啊！我甚至還作了標記避免我自己忘記呢！

Sarah: It seems you make mistakes in the order sheet as well as the contract. The sum is wrong, so is the deadline.

莎拉：好像是訂單及合約出了錯。總數不對，最後期限也不對。

Megan: I did revise them. Let me see. But I can't figure out where I went wrong... Oh, I see. Last week, I reinstalled my operation system so that some documents I saved lost. What I sent out are the originals.

梅根：我確實修改了啊。讓我看看。我想不出來哪裡出了問題……噢，記起來了，上個禮拜我的電腦系統重灌了，把一些檔案弄丟了。我把舊的檔案發出去了。

Sarah: Let's make another version.

莎拉：那我們趕快做一份新的吧！

文法重點看這裡！

學完前面的會話之後，還要懂會話中的文法重點，才能應用在職場！以下補充重要的文法並做詳盡解析，把文法根基打好，讓你無論是出差還是洽商，都用正確英文和外國人打交道！

文法重點1
sign/symbol/mark
同樣都有「標示，記號」的意思，該怎麼用呢？

sign 和mark 都可以指印記，壓痕，銘刻等。sign 通常指含有「象徵意義」的符號，但mark 不一定含有象徵意義，例如衣服上的「汗漬」。sign 也可以指書寫以外的其他溝通形式，如sign language（手語）。symbol 也是肉眼可見的形式，通常是其他事物的象徵、符號。請利用下面的例句，幫助更熟悉記憶單字的用法：

Part

4

工
作
問
題
排
除

- **She made a sign with her hand to show that she had finished.**
  她用她的手做出手勢，表示已經完成了。
- **Great Wall is the symbol of China.** 長城是中國的象徵。
- **He made a special mark on his book to differentiate it from others.**
  他在他的書上做了特殊的標記，以別於其他人的。

文法重點2
in case 的用法

in case 後面可以直接接續一個that 引導的子句。例如：

- **We can get up early in case that we are late for school.**
  我們可以早起，以防我們上學遲到。

in case也可以加上介詞of，再接名詞。例如：
- **We can take subway in case of the traffic jam.**
  我們可以坐地鐵，以防堵車。

文法重點3
What I sent out are the old ones. 是錯誤用法

這是一句典型的中式英文，是由「我把舊的檔案發出去了。」直翻過來的。如果想要強調自己發原先的檔案，可以說：

- **What we send out are the originals.** 我們發出的是原件。
- **What we send out is without revising.** 我們發出的檔案是未經修改的。

會話單字懂多少？

讀過前面的內容後，你是不是都懂得這些單字了呢？下列題目中的單字都是與會話及文法相關的單字，測驗看看自己會了多少吧！

( ) ❶ client： (A) 診所 (B) 客戶 (C) 點擊

( ) ❷ type： (A) 疲倦 (B) 輪胎 (C) 類型

( ) ❸ omission： (A) 遺漏 (B) 洩露 (C) 任務

( ) ❹ sum： (A) 太陽 (B) 總數 (C) 拇指

( ) ❺ deadline： (A) 最後期限 (B) 死亡 (C) 死機

( ) ❻ reinstall： (A) 重裝 (B) 反思 (C) 卸載

( ) ❼ operation： (A) 操作者 (B) 操作 (C) 意見

( ) ❽ version： (A) 對抗 (B) 病毒 (C) 版本

( ) ❾ mark： (A) 市場 (B) 雲雀 (C) 標記

( ) ❿ differentiate： (A) 傳遞 (B) 同化 (C) 區別

( ) ⓫ sheet： (A) 貨架 (B) 單子 (C) 全然

( ) ⓬ contract： (A) 聯繫 (B) 合約 (C) 矛盾

( ) ⓭ revise： (A) 旋轉 (B) 復活 (C) 修改

( ) ⓮ figure： (A) 戰鬥 (B) 數目 (C) 火勢

( ) ⓯ save： (A) 調料 (B) 味道 (C) 保存

答案：1. (B) 2. (C) 3. (A) 4. (B) 5. (A) 6. (A) 7. (B) 8. (C) 9. (C)
10. (C) 11. (B) 12. (B) 13. (C) 14. (B) 15. (C)

I will ask Steven for more materials.

我等會就叫史蒂芬給我更多的資料。

 職場會話跟著說！ Track 029

Megan: What should I do? So many documents!

梅根：我該怎麼辦啊？這麼多文件！

Sarah: Don't worry. We'll manage somehow.

莎拉：別著急，我們會有辦法的。

Megan: I must find the way, or I will ruin the whole thing. But I doubt whether I can put it right. I am afraid that our clients have checked the emails and will complain about that.

梅根：我必須找到一個辦法，否則會把整件事情搞砸的。但是，我懷疑我是否能夠處理好。恐怕客戶們已經收到郵件並且開始抱怨了！

Sarah: Don't dwell on that had happened. What we should do is to make the best of a bad job.

莎拉：不要再多想了！我們要做的就是把傷害降到最低。

Megan: You are right. I will ask Steven for more materials. I will collect them and type new ones. I will apologize to the clients on behalf of us and our company when they call back.

梅根：妳說得對。我等會就叫史蒂芬給我更多的資料，並且把它們收集起來，整理出新的文件。當客戶打電話來的時候，我會代表公司以及自己親自向他們致歉。

文法重點看這裡！

學完前面的會話之後，還要懂會話中的文法重點，才能應用在職場！以下補充重要的文法並做詳盡解析，把文法根基打好，讓你無論是出差還是洽商，都用正確英文和外國人打交道！

文法重點1
method/way/manner
同樣都有「方法」的意思，該怎麼用呢？

這三個單字有以下的使用區別，請利用下面的例句，幫助更熟悉記憶單字的用法：

- He used various methods to train his employees.
  他有各種方法來訓練他的員工。
- She finished the task in a professional manner.
  她以專業方式完成了她的任務。
- I am surprised at the way he speaks.
  我對他說話的方式感到驚訝。

文法重點2
doubt 的用法

doubt 後面是不可以接續that 引導的子句的。如果要接續一個子句的話，可以用doubt if 或是doubt whether 來引導。例如：

- I doubt if he will come tonight.
  我懷疑他今晚會不會來。
- Our leader doubts the result of this test.
  我們的領導懷疑這次測試的結果。

文法重點3
I will destroy the whole thing. 是錯誤用法

這覺得是一句典型的中式英文，是由「我把整件事情搞砸了。」直翻過來的，如果想要表達我將搞砸整個事情，可以說：

- I will ruin the whole thing.
  我會毀了整個事情。
- I will make a mess of the whole thing.
  我會把整件事情弄得一團糟。

會話單字懂多少？

讀過前面的內容後，你是不是都懂得這些單字了呢？下列題目中的單字都是與會話及文法相關的單字，測驗看看自己會了多少吧！

( ) ❶ somehow： (A) 怎樣 (B) 以某種方式 (C) 某些

( ) ❷ manner： (A) 方式 (B) 人類 (C) 大廈

( ) ❸ destroy： (A) 目的地 (B) 毀壞 (C) 玩具

( ) ❹ whole： (A) 健康 (B) 整個 (C) 批發

( ) ❺ doubt： (A) 麵團 (B) 懷疑 (C) 逗號

( ) ❻ right： (A) 燈光 (B) 聰明 (C) 正確

( ) ❼ various： (A) 花瓶 (B) 消失 (C) 多樣

( ) ❽ method： (A) 金屬 (B) 方法 (C) 比喻

( ) ❾ surprise： (A) 昂貴 (B) 豪華 (C) 驚訝

( ) ❿ tonight： (A) 嗓音 (B) 今晚 (C) 開心

( ) ⓫ ruin： (A) 破壞 (B) 規則 (C) 尺子

( ) ⓬ dwell on： (A) 水井 (B) 矮人 (C) 一直思索

( ) ⓭ happen： (A) 鋼筆 (B) 快樂 (C) 發生

( ) ⓮ apologize： (A) 道歉 (B) 邏輯 (C) 使徒

( ) ⓯ behalf： (A) 行為 (B) 代表 (C) 開始

答案：1. (B) 2. (A) 3. (B) 4. (B) 5. (B) 6. (C) 7. (C) 8. (B) 9. (C)
10. (B) 11. (A) 12. (C) 13. (C) 14. (A) 15. (B)

Could you do me a favor?

妳能幫我一個忙嗎？

 職場會話跟著說！ 🎧 Track 030

Sarah: Oh, you can consult Jessica. She has worked in our company as an accountant for years. Her work involves various routine book keeping and basic accounting tasks.

莎拉：噢，妳可以去找一下潔西卡。她是我們的會計師，已經在這工作多年了。他的工作就是負責各種簿記與基本會計事項。

Megan: Thanks. I'd better talk to her right now.

梅根：謝謝。我最好現在就去找她談談。

Megan: Hello, Jessica, may I come in?...Could you do me a favor?

梅根：妳好，潔西卡。我可以進來嗎？妳能幫我一個忙嗎？

Jessica: Sure, come in. What happened?

潔西卡：好的，請進。發生了什麼事情嗎？

Megan: There are serious data entry errors in my documents. Sarah told me you have rich experience in verifying data and checking accounting documents, so...

梅根：我的檔案出現了嚴重的資料登錄錯誤。莎拉告訴我，妳在審核資料和查核會計檔案這方面經驗相當豐富，所以……

Jessica: I think what you need are the raw data. There are more than one data source. I just have some of them at hand. I am afraid you have to go to the Export Dapartment.

潔西卡：我覺得目前妳所需要的就是最原始的資料。資料的來源不止一處。我手頭目前只有一些。恐怕妳得到出口部跑一趟了。

Megan: I see. I'll go and get it at once.

梅根：我明白了。我現在馬上過去拿。

文法重點看這裡！

學完前面的會話之後，還要懂會話中的文法重點，才能應用在職場！以下補充重要的文法並做詳盡解析，把文法根基打好，讓你無論是出差還是洽商，都用正確英文和外國人打交道！

文法重點1

mistake/fault/error 都是「錯誤」，該怎麼用呢？

三者解釋成「錯誤」時十分相近，可以通用，但是強調的重點不太一樣。fault 強調過失的責任或不完美的小瑕疵，且犯錯誤的人必須承擔錯誤。mistake 強調的是日常生活中無心造成的錯誤，error強調道德上的錯失或是信仰造成的錯誤。請利用下面的例句，幫助更熟悉記憶單字的用法：

- **There is a mistake in his homework.**
  他的家庭作業裡有個錯誤。
- **It's not my fault; you can't blame me for it.**
  這不是我的錯，你不能歸咎於我。
- **It's the error of my youth.**
  這是我年輕時所犯下的錯。

fault另外也可以指缺點、性格上的弱點。
- **His worst fault was his inconsistency.** 他的最大缺點就是反覆無常。

文法重點2

I'd better 的用法

I'd better 的意思是我最好做些什麼。後面直接接續動詞，而無需加入介詞to。例如：

- **I'd better go to the party.** 我最好去參加聚會。
- **I'd better fetch the basket.** 我最好去拿籃子。

文法重點3

Can you give me a help? 是錯誤用法

這覺得是一句典型的中式英文，是由「你能幫我一下嗎？」直翻過來的。如果想要請求別人的幫助，可以說：

- **Can you give me a hand?** 你能幫我個忙嗎？
- **Could you do me a favor?** 能幫我一下嗎？

會話單字懂多少？

讀過前面的內容後，你是不是都懂得這些單字了呢？下列題目中的單字都是與會話及文法相關的單字，測驗看看自己會了多少吧！

( ) ❶ consult： (A) 消費 (B) 美容 (C) 請教

( ) ❷ accountant： (A) 報賬 (B) 會計師 (C) 堆積

( ) ❸ entry： (A) 輸入 (B) 託付 (C) 嘗試

( ) ❹ fault： (A) 員工 (B) 錯誤 (C) 傳真

( ) ❺ rich： (A) 果園 (B) 達到 (C) 富有

( ) ❻ raw： (A) 光線 (B) 生的 (C) 烏鴉

( ) ❼ export： (A) 出口 (B) 暴露 (C) 專家

( ) ❽ homework： (A) 蜂蜜 (B) 誠實 (C) 家庭作業

( ) ❾ blame： (A) 品牌 (B) 責備 (C) 地毯

( ) ❿ error： (A) 失誤 (B) 噴發 (C) 跑腿

( ) ⓫ youth： (A) 思考 (B) 青春 (C) 呻吟

( ) ⓬ routine： (A) 慣例 (B) 路程 (C) 粗糙

( ) ⓭ favor： (A) 味道 (B) 幫助 (C) 恐懼

( ) ⓮ verify： (A) 核實 (B) 勝利 (C) 邊緣

( ) ⓯ source： (A) 酸的 (B) 來源 (C) 力量

答案：1. (C) 2. (B) 3. (A) 4. (B) 5. (C) 6. (B) 7. (A) 8. (C) 9. (B)
10. (A) 11. (B) 12. (A) 13. (B) 14. (A) 15. (B)

Cross the bridge when you come to it.

船到橋頭自然直。

職場會話跟著說！　🎧 Track 031

Megan: Hello, is Andrew in? Sorry to bother you. Could you give me some raw data about the clients on my list?

梅根：你好，請問安德魯在嗎？抱歉打擾了，你能提供給我名單上客戶們的原始資料嗎？

Andrew: What for? I remember I have given the information to your department last week.

安德魯：為什麼需要這份資料？我記得上個禮拜我已經給過你們部門這份資料了！

Megan: We lost some documents because there is something wrong with the computer. Hardly did I have enough time to react at that moment.

梅根：由於電腦出了點問題。我當時幾乎沒有足夠的時間反應。

Andrew: I see. Luckily we usually backup the files.

安德魯：我明白了。好險我們平常就有把檔案備份起來。

Sarah: You get them? At last, we can see the daylight, and finish the whole task right now.

莎拉：妳拿到檔案了嗎？我們終於可以看見勝利的曙光了，可以馬上完成任務了。

Megan: Cross the bridge when you come to it. That's what I've learned from it. I will never do things by halves.

梅根：我現在終於了解，「船到橋頭自然直。」我以後做事絕不可以半途而廢。

文法重點看這裡！

學完前面的會話之後，還要懂會話中的文法重點，才能應用在職場！以下補充重要的文法並做詳盡解析，把文法根基打好，讓你無論是出差還是洽商，都用正確英文和外國人打交道！

文法重點1
disturb/bother/trouble 都是「打擾」，該怎麼用呢？

disturb 意味著不安或打斷，且強度較trouble 和bother 要強，而後兩者只是指令人感到煩或增加了額外的工作。請利用下面的例句，幫助更熟悉記憶單字的用法：

- **She didn't want anyone to disturb her while she was studying.**
  她在讀書的時候不想要任何人打擾她。
- **She was so lazy that she couldn't even be bothered to take out the garbage.** 她太懶了，甚至不願意麻煩自己把垃圾拿出去。
- **I am sorry to trouble you, but could you tell me the time please?**
  很抱歉打擾你，但你可以告訴我時間嗎？

三者都可以指情緒不安定，disturb 泛指焦慮的感覺，bother 則較強調心煩的感覺，而trouble 也可指焦慮的感覺。

文法重點2
hardly 的用法

hardly 本身就帶有否定的意味，中文意思是「幾乎不」、「幾乎沒有」。所以後面無需再加上表示否定的詞語。例如：

- **I hardly know you.** 我幾乎不認識你。
- **Hardly can I understand your English.** 我幾乎聽不懂你的英語。

文法重點3
Never do things by half. 是錯誤用法

這覺得是一句典型的中式英文，是由「不要做事做一半。」直翻過來的。
如果想要說不要半途而廢，做事做一半就不做了，可以說：

- **Never do things by halves.** 永遠不要半途而廢。
- **Don't give up.** 不要放棄。

會話單字懂多少？

讀過前面的內容後，你是不是都懂得這些單字了呢？下列題目中的單字都是與會話及文法相關的單字，測驗看看自己會了多少吧！

( ) ❶ annoy： (A) 提醒 (B) 打擾 (C) 發表

( ) ❷ hardly： (A) 堅硬 (B) 幾乎不 (C) 艱難

( ) ❸ enough： (A) 巨大 (B) 憤怒 (C) 足夠

( ) ❹ react： (A) 反應 (B) 表演 (C) 到達

( ) ❺ luckily： (A) 幸運 (B) 不幸 (C) 誘惑

( ) ❻ bother： (A) 回來 (B) 後面 (C) 打擾

( ) ❼ copy： (A) 夫妻 (B) 複印 (C) 版權

( ) ❽ learn： (A) 出租 (B) 學習 (C) 漏出

( ) ❾ lazy： (A) 庭院 (B) 領導 (C) 懶惰

( ) ❿ garbage： (A) 垃圾 (B) 花園 (C) 缺口

( ) ⓫ trouble： (A) 通過 (B) 困難 (C) 軍隊

( ) ⓬ backup： (A) 背後 (B) 後上方 (C) 備份

( ) ⓭ file： (A) 找到 (B) 檔案 (C) 良好

( ) ⓮ daylight： (A) 白日夢 (B) 日光 (C) 輕巧

( ) ⓯ bridge： (A) 新娘 (B) 瘋狂 (C) 橋樑

Part

4

工作問題排除

答案：1. (B) 2. (B) 3. (C) 4. (A) 5. (A) 6. (C) 7. (B) 8. (B) 9. (C)
10. (A) 11. (B) 12. (C) 13. (B) 14. (B) 15. (C)

I heard that you performed very well in this program.

我聽說妳在這次的工作項目中表現突出。

職場會話跟著說！　Track 032

Daniel: I heard that you performed very well in this program. You are going to be one pillar of our company in the near future.

丹尼爾：我聽說妳在這次的工作項目中表現突出。不久後妳就會成為公司的主要支柱了！

Megan: It's my duty as an employee to carry it out. I receive help from several departments while the whole matter was on the verge of failure. Most importantly, we didn't lose heart, but believed we could succeed at last.

梅根：這是我作為公司員工應盡的職責。在整件事情瀕臨失敗的情況下，我得到了很多部門的幫助。最重要的是，我們沒有灰心喪氣，而是堅信最後一定可以成功。

Daniel: Never give up, then we can defeat our rivals, no matter how strong they are. Stick to your faith, we can overcome adversity successfully. Good job, Megan!

丹尼爾：永不放棄，我們才能打敗對手，不管他們多麼強大。堅定信仰，我們才能克服逆境。梅根，幹得不錯喔！

Megan: Thanks for your praise. And I will believe in myself as I did this time and keep on my work. Moreover, I realized teamwork is the key to success.

梅根：謝謝你的誇讚。我會像這次一樣相信自己，繼續我的工作。而且，我還明白了，只有發揮團隊的力量才是成功的關鍵。

文法重點看這裡！

學完前面的會話之後，還要懂會話中的文法重點，才能應用在職場！以下補充重要的文法並做詳盡解析，把文法根基打好，讓你無論是出差還是洽商，都用正確英文和外國人打交道！

文法重點1
duty/obligation/responsibility
都有「責任」的意思，該怎麼用呢？

duty 和responsibility用來指工作上必須要完成的任務，而obligation 強調法律或道德層面的責任。請利用下面的例句，幫助更熟悉記憶單字的用法：

- **Her duty included cleaning the house and walking the dog.**
  她的責任包括清掃房子和遛狗。
- **It's her parents' obligation to look after their children.**
  照顧孩子是父母的責任。
- **People should take full responsibility for their actions.**
  人們應該為自己的行為負全責。

文法重點2
believe 的用法

believe表示「相信」、「信以為真」的意思，其後直接跟賓語。例如：

- **Do you believe his report?** 你相信他的報導嗎？

believe in 則表示「信仰」、「信任」的意思。例如：

- **I believe in God.** 我信仰上帝。

文法重點3
We didn't lose our heart to it. 是錯誤用法

這覺得是一句典型的中式英文，是由「我們沒有對它失去信心。」直翻過來的。lose one's heart to sth / sb 在英文裡是表示傾心於某事或愛上了某人的意思。如果想要說明自己對某事沒有失去信心，可以說：

- **We didn't lose heart.** 我們沒有灰心。
- **We didn't give up.** 我們沒有放棄。

會話單字懂多少？

讀過前面的內容後，你是不是都懂得這些單字了呢？下列題目中的單字都是與會話及文法相關的單字，測驗看看自己會了多少吧！

( ) ❶ perform： (A) 香水 (B) 表現 (C) 形成

( ) ❷ obligation： (A) 禮貌 (B) 目標 (C) 義務

( ) ❸ defeat： (A) 打敗 (B) 缺陷 (C) 守衛

( ) ❹ rival： (A) 河流 (B) 對手 (C) 升起

( ) ❺ strong： (A) 長久 (B) 結構 (C) 強壯

( ) ❻ duty： (A) 職責 (B) 塵埃 (C) 經受

( ) ❼ responsibility： (A) 反應 (B) 逃脫 (C) 負責

( ) ❽ action： (A) 行為 (B) 制裁 (C) 表演

( ) ❾ report： (A) 記者 (B) 代表 (C) 報導

( ) ❿ pillar： (A) 藥片 (B) 枕頭 (C) 支柱

( ) ⓫ stick to： (A) 堅持 (B) 棍子 (C) 挑剔

( ) ⓬ faith： (A) 偽造 (B) 信念 (C) 微弱

( ) ⓭ overcome： (A) 克服 (B) 來到 (C) 過期

( ) ⓮ adversity： (A) 廣告 (B) 建議 (C) 逆境

( ) ⓯ teamwork： (A) 團隊合作 (B) 工作 (C) 隊員

答案：1. (B) 2. (C) 3. (A) 4. (B) 5. (C) 6. (A) 7. (C) 8. (A) 9. (C)
10. (C) 11. (A) 12. (B) 13. (A) 14. (C) 15. (A)

Part 5

信件往來

Thank you for your attention and looking forward to your prompt reply.

謝謝您的關注，我們將等待您的回覆。

職場會話跟著說！　Track 033

Dear Mr. Alex,

How are you, Mr. Alex? Long time no see since we had a pleasant cooperation last time. Thanks for your confidence and support. We will be always at your service. Nowadays, we are planning to develop a wholesaling market in China. We will offer your company the most favorable price to buy our new products if you have any need.

In short, any information on investment and on business cooperation will be highly appreciated. And if you have any questions, please feel free to contact us, too.

Thank you for your attention and looking forward to your prompt reply.

Sincerely yours,
Megan

親愛的艾力克斯先生：

艾力克斯先生，您還好嗎？自從上次愉快的合作之後，我們就沒聯繫過了。謝謝您的信任和支持。我們將熱忱地為您服務。近來，我們正在計畫在中國開批發市場。如果您有任何需要購買我們新產品的話，我們將給您提供最實惠的價格。

總之，我們將十分感謝來自您的任何投資和生意合作的消息。如果您有任何問題，也請隨時聯繫我們。

謝謝您的關注，我們將等待您的回覆。

誠摯地，
梅根

文法重點看這裡！

學完前面的會話之後，還要懂會話中的文法重點，才能應用在職場！以下補充重要的文法並做詳盡解析，把文法根基打好，讓你無論是出差還是洽商，都用正確英文和外國人打交道！

文法重點1

need/necessity/necessary
同樣都有「需要」的意思，該怎麼用呢？

necessary 是形容詞，而need 可以作動詞和名詞。necessity 一般有「必需品」的意思，作名詞來用。請利用下面的例句，幫助更熟悉記憶單字的用法：

● **They are in need of food.**
他們需要食物。

● **Daily necessities play a very important role in our life.**
生活必需品在我們的生活中扮演了很重要的角色。

● **It's necessary to be careful about choosing a boyfriend.**
謹慎挑選男朋友是必須的。

> necessary 形容必要性的事情，例如：
> ● **It's necessary to lock the door before you leave the house.**
> 你離開屋子前有必要把門鎖上。
>
> need 可以用在人和事物方面，例如：
> ● **She doesn't need anybody but herself. / She has needs.**
> 她除了自己以外，不需要任何人。／她有需求。

文法重點2

serve 的用法

serve 是個及物動詞，所以後面直接接續名詞。例如：

● **He served his master for many years.**
他侍奉了他的主人多年。

● **Please allow me to serve you, sir.**
請允許我為你服務，先生。

會話單字懂多少？

讀過前面的內容後，你是不是都懂得這些單字了呢？下列題目中的單字都是與會話及文法相關的單字，測驗看看自己會了多少吧！

( ) ❶ serve： (A) 轉彎 (B) 服務 (C) 嚴重

( ) ❷ open： (A) 歌劇 (B) 操作 (C) 打開

( ) ❸ wholesaling： (A) 完整 (B) 航海 (C) 批發

( ) ❹ favorable： (A) 錯誤 (B) 接受 (C) 有利的

( ) ❺ price： (A) 無價 (B) 價格 (C) 獵物

( ) ❻ necessity： (A) 項鏈 (B) 允許 (C) 必要

( ) ❼ investment： (A) 注入 (B) 投資 (C) 裝載

( ) ❽ business： (A) 生意 (B) 公車 (C) 匆忙

( ) ❾ forward： (A) 為了 (B) 向前 (C) 化石

( ) ❿ prompt： (A) 重要 (B) 迅速 (C) 翻越

( ) ⓫ sincerely： (A) 自從 (B) 慶祝 (C) 誠摯地

( ) ⓬ important： (A) 進口 (B) 港口 (C) 重要

( ) ⓭ role： (A) 角色 (B) 小洞 (C) 滾動

( ) ⓮ master： (A) 魔鬼 (B) 主人 (C) 必須

( ) ⓯ explore： (A) 探險 (B) 探險家 (C) 爆炸

答案：1. (B) 2. (C) 3. (C) 4. (C) 5. (B) 6. (C) 7. (B) 8. (A) 9. (B)
10. (B) 11. (C) 12. (C) 13. (A) 14. (B) 15. (A)

Unit 34

If you are interested in any of these items, please contact us.

如果您對其中任何一樣產品感興趣，敬請告知。

職場會話跟著說！ Track 034

Dear sir/madam,

We got your information from the Internet. I am Megan in the Market Department of Blue Sky Corp. We would like to take this opportunity to introduce our company and products, with the hope that we may work with your firm in the future.

We are an American multinational corporation, which specializes in producing electronic products with high performance and technology. We have enclosed our catalog, which introduces our company in detail and covers all our latest products.

If you are interested in any of these items, please inform us. We will send our quotation and specifications to you.

We look forward to hearing from you!

Sincerely,
Megan

敬啟者：

我們從網路上看到您的資訊。我是藍天公司市場部的梅根。我們想藉此機會介紹一下我們公司及產品，希望將來可以合作。

我們是一家美國的跨國公司，專門生產高科技、具備高性能的電子產品。我們已隨函附寄了一份詳細介紹我們公司和所有最新產品的目錄。

如果您對其中任何一樣產品感興趣，敬請告知，我們將把報價和規格寄給您。

期待您的來信！

誠摯地，
梅根

文法重點看這裡！

學完前面的會話之後，還要懂會話中的文法重點，才能應用在職場！以下補充重要的文法並做詳盡解析，把文法根基打好，讓你無論是出差還是洽商，都用正確英文和外國人打交道！

文法重點1
chance/opportunity/occasion
同樣都有「機會」的意思，該怎麼用呢？

chance 和opportunity 都可以指「機遇」， chance強調意外得到的或是偶然發生的機會。opportunity 則較強調人為的因素。不過二者在很多情況下都可以互換。而occasion則是指「時機」，即做某事的適當時機。請利用下面的例句，幫助更熟悉記憶單字的用法：

● **The snow gave us the chance to ski.**
　這場雪讓我們有機會可以滑雪。

● **This is a good opportunity for me to study abroad.**
　對我來說，這是一個出國深造的好機會。

● **There is not an occasion to talk about the scandal.**
　這不是談論那件醜聞的好時機。

文法重點2
look forward to 的用法

look forward 後面接續動詞時，需要用動詞的動名詞形式。例如：

● **I am looking forward to receiving from you.**
　我期待著收到您的來信。

● **My little brother is looking forward to having a holiday.**
　我的弟弟期待著假期。

文法重點3
We have put our catalog in the enclosure.

這是一句典型的中式英文，是由「我們把目錄放在附件裡了。」直翻過來的。如果想要表達隨信附件了，可以說：

● **Enclosed is our catalog.**
　隨信附上我們的目錄。

● **We have enclosed our catalog.**
　我們隨信附上我們的目錄。

會話單字懂多少？

讀過前面的內容後，你是不是都懂得這些單字了呢？下列題目中的單字都是與會話及文法相關的單字，測驗看看自己會了多少吧！

( )❶ internet： (A) 網際網路 (B) 翻譯 (C) 內陸

( )❷ occasion： (A) 職業 (B) 發生 (C) 場合

( )❸ multinational： (A) 國內 (B) 跨國 (C) 多樣化

( )❹ specialize： (A) 專業 (B) 專門 (C) 詳細

( )❺ catalog： (A) 記錄 (B) 合約 (C) 目錄

( )❻ enclosure： (A) 遭遇 (B) 附件 (C) 鼓勵

( )❼ detail： (A) 詳細 (B) 釋放 (C) 偵察

( )❽ cover： (A) 旋轉 (B) 包括 (C) 信用

( )❾ item： (A) 學期 (B) 測試 (C) 物品

( )❿ quotation： (A) 引用 (B) 安靜 (C) 劑量

( )⓫ chance： (A) 大臣 (B) 機會 (C) 改變

( )⓬ ski： (A) 滑雪 (B) 皮膚 (C) 溜冰

( )⓭ abroad： (A) 黑板 (B) 木板 (C) 在國外

( )⓮ scandal： (A) 拖鞋 (B) 醜聞 (C) 掃描

( )⓯ brother： (A) 借 (B) 打擾 (C) 兄弟

答案：1. (A) 2. (C) 3. (B) 4. (B) 5. (C) 6. (B) 7. (A) 8. (B) 9. (C)
10. (A) 11. (B) 12. (A) 13. (C) 14. (B) 15. (C)

But I am afraid that we still need a further discussion.

但是，我想我們還是需要進一步的商談。

職場會話跟著說！ Track 035

Dear Miss Megan,
So glad to have your letter. We are very interested in your latest products. As you know, we are in need of all kinds of merchandise to display in our store window. We have checked that your products are suitable for our local market. Moreover, we make a price comparison between many companies, and the outcome is that your price is affordable and competitive enough for us. So we sincerely hope we can work in collaboration with each other.

But I am afraid that we still need a further discussion. We are looking forward to your reply.

Yours faithfully,
Eric

親愛的梅根小姐，
很高興收到妳的來信。我們對妳們的最新產品很感興趣。正如妳知道的一樣，我們的商店櫥窗陳列需要各種商品。檢驗證明妳們的產品很適合我們當地的市場。而且，我們還進行了各家之間的價格對比，結果發現，妳們的價格既不是很昂貴又具備一定的競爭力。因此，我們真誠的希望雙方能進行合作。

但是，我想我們還是需要進一步的商談。期待妳的回覆。

您忠實的，
艾瑞克

文法重點看這裡！

學完前面的會話之後，還要懂會話中的文法重點，才能應用在職場！以下補充重要的文法並做詳盡解析，把文法根基打好，讓你無論是出差還是洽商，都用正確英文和外國人打交道！

文法重點1
show/display/exhibit
同樣都有「展示」的意思，該怎麼用呢？

三者都有「公開展示物品，以供人欣賞參觀」的意思，因此通常可以互換。請利用下面的例句，幫助更熟悉記憶單字的用法：

● **Please show me your identification to prove you are of age.**
請出示你的身份證以證明你成年了。

● **New cars were exhibited at the exhibition.** 展覽會上展出了新車。

● **Many local artists lack opportunity to display their work.**
很多當地的藝術家沒有機會展出自己的作品。

 中文的「秀」其實就是英文裡的「show」。因此我們常說的「秀給你看」就是 show you。

文法重點2
comparison 的用法

comparison 專指把兩者進行比較或是對比，後面要接續between。例如：

● **There is no comparison between the two dictionaries.**
兩本辭典沒有可比性。

● **Please make a comparison between these fruits.**
請在這些水果之間做個比較。

文法重點3
We are very interest to your latest products.
是錯誤用法

這是一句典型的中式英文，是由「我們對你們的新產品很感興趣。」直翻過來的。如果想要表達對什麼東西很感興趣，可以說：

● **We are very interested in your products.** 我們對你的產品很感興趣。
● **We are of great interest to your products.** 我們對你的產品有很大的興趣。

會話單字懂多少？

讀過前面的內容後，你是不是都懂得這些單字了呢？下列題目中的單字都是與會話及文法相關的單字，測驗看看自己會了多少吧！

( )❶ glad： (A) 逃竄 (B) 少年 (C) 高興

( )❷ merchandise： (A) 商人 (B) 商品 (C) 慈悲

( )❸ parade： (A) 遊行 (B) 驅逐 (C) 發揮

( )❹ suitable： (A) 套房 (B) 合適 (C) 手提箱

( )❺ local： (A) 當地 (B) 上鎖 (C) 位置

( )❻ comparison： (A) 同情 (B) 比較 (C) 指南

( )❼ outcome： (A) 結果 (B) 外出 (C) 爆發

( )❽ affordable： (A) 富裕 (B) 買得起 (C) 同意

( )❾ competitive： (A) 抱怨 (B) 編輯 (C) 競爭力

( )❿ collaboration： (A) 合作 (B) 衣領 (C) 崩潰

( )⓫ discussion： (A) 疾病 (B) 討論 (C) 噁心

( )⓬ identification： (A) 相同 (B) 思想 (C) 身分證

( )⓭ artist： (A) 藝術 (B) 藝術家 (C) 藝術館

( )⓮ display： (A) 陳列 (B) 反對 (C) 玩耍

( )⓯ dictionary： (A) 聽寫 (B) 字典 (C) 獨裁者

答案：1. (C) 2. (B) 3. (A) 4. (B) 5. (A) 6. (B) 7. (A) 8. (B) 9. (C)
10. (A) 11. (B) 12. (C) 13. (B) 14. (A) 15. (B)

Unit 36

We would like to invite you to our anniversary celebration.

我們敬請您屆時參加我們周年慶典。

職場會話跟著說！ Track 036

Dear James,
We would like to invite you to our anniversary celebration.

Blue Sky Crop. is a leading producer in the field of electronic products. Our new models offer superb quality, and their new features endow them with distinct advantages over similar products from other manufacturers. In the meantime, we really appreciate your strenuous effort to promote the sale in the market. We earnestly hope you can spare some time to attend the celebration.

Thank you for taking the time to read this letter. You can reach me by phone or via email. We are looking forward to your reply.

Sincerely yours,
Megan

親愛的詹姆斯先生：
我們敬請您屆時參加我們周年慶典。

藍天公司是電子產品生產領域裡的佼佼者。我們的新產品擁有高品質，它們的新特性也賦予了產品遠高於其他生產商生產的同類產品很多明顯優勢。同時，我們還特別感謝您在市場上對我們產品的全力促銷。我們真誠地希望您能抽出一點時間來參加這次慶典。

謝謝您花費您的寶貴時間來閱讀我們的信件。你可以通過電話或是郵件跟我進行聯繫。期待您的回覆。

您真誠的，
梅根

文法重點看這裡！

學完前面的會話之後，還要懂會話中的文法重點，才能應用在職場！以下補充重要的文法並做詳盡解析，把文法根基打好，讓你無論是出差還是洽商，都用正確英文和外國人打交道！

文法重點1
pattern/model/example
都有「模範」的意思，該怎麼用呢？

model是「依原物比例縮小的模型」或「可供人效仿的模式、系統」，pattern指「服裝的圖樣和縫紉的式樣」等，example則是「舉例說明時的範例」。請利用下面的例句，幫助更熟悉記憶單字的用法：

- **The wallpaper in my room is a pattern of flowers.**
  我屋裡的壁紙是花卉圖案的。
- **This is a model of new ship.** 這是新船的模型。
- **Don't follow your father's bad example.** 不要學你父親的壞榜樣。

文法重點2
bestow 的用法

bestow 的意思是授予，後面接續介系詞on 或者upon。例如：

- **This medal was bestowed upon the winner.** 這枚獎牌授予給勝者。

如果想表達賦予的意思，則要用endow sth/sb with sth。例如：
- **He was endowed with a fortune.** 他被賦予了一筆財富。

文法重點3
Thank you for taking your time to read this letter. **是錯誤用法**

這是一句典型的中式英文，是由「謝謝你花時間來閱讀我們的信件。」直翻過來的。take your time 是不要著急，慢慢來的意思。如果想要表達花費時間，可以說：

- **Thank you for taking the time to read this letter.** 感謝您花時間閱讀這封信。
- **Thank you for spending time on this letter.** 感謝您花時間在這封信上。

會話單字懂多少？

讀過前面的內容後,你是不是都懂得這些單字了呢?下列題目中的單字都是與會話及文法相關的單字,測驗看看自己會了多少吧!

( ) ❶ anniversary: (A) 注釋 (B) 宣告 (C) 週年慶

( ) ❷ celebration: (A) 慶祝 (B) 自由 (C) 名人

( ) ❸ leading: (A) 鉛 (B) 領先 (C) 傳導

( ) ❹ field: (A) 朋友 (B) 領域 (C) 激烈

( ) ❺ pattern: (A) 坐墊 (B) 拍打 (C) 圖案

( ) ❻ superb: (A) 優秀 (B) 超越 (C) 膚淺

( ) ❼ bestow: (A) 賭注 (B) 授予 (C) 背叛

( ) ❽ similar: (A) 相似 (B) 簡單 (C) 激發

( ) ❾ manufacturer: (A) 製造商 (B) 原稿 (C) 人工

( ) ❿ strenuous: (A) 嚴格 (B) 奮發 (C) 壓力

( ) ⓫ promote: (A) 突然 (B) 促進 (C) 迅速

( ) ⓬ via: (A) 通過 (B) 歪斜 (C) 別墅

( ) ⓭ wallpaper: (A) 紙 (B) 壁紙 (C) 牆壁

( ) ⓮ example: (A) 充裕 (B) 例子 (C) 交換

( ) ⓯ medal: (A) 獎章 (B) 媒體 (C) 醫藥

答案:1. (C) 2. (A) 3. (B) 4. (B) 5. (C) 6. (A) 7. (B) 8. (A) 9. (A)
　　　10. (B) 11. (B) 12. (A) 13. (B) 14. (B) 15. (A)

We are so glad to receive your letter.

很高興收到您的來信。

Dear James,

We are so glad to receive your letter. And you asked us about the exact date and place in your reply. Our plan is as follows:

The anniversary celebration will begin from 2 p.m. to 5 p.m. on the morning of March 21st, 2008. It'll be held in the Times Square, DaAn District. Many celebrities, executives and public officers will participate in this celebration. Then this will be followed by an evening party consisting of a dinner and two hours performances at Star Hotel. The main purpose of this activity is to promote both our trade and friendship.

At one time, we went through difficulties together. Now we want to share our joy with you. So you are cordially invited to attend this celebration. See you on March 21st.

Yours sincerely,
Megan

親愛的詹姆斯先生：

很高興收到您的來信。您在回信中問到具體的時間和地點。我們的計畫是這樣的：

周年慶典將在2008年3月21日下午2點開始，5點結束。在大安區的時代廣場舉行。眾多名人、行政人員和政府官員將出席本次慶典。隨後將會在星際飯店舉辦個晚會。晚會包括晚餐和兩個小時的表演。這次活動的主要目的是促進我們的貿易和友誼。

曾經我們共度難關。現在我們也希望與你們共同分享快樂。因此，我們誠摯的歡迎您屆時參加慶典活動。我們3月21日見了。

您真誠的，
梅根

文法重點看這裡！

學完前面的會話之後，還要懂會話中的文法重點，才能應用在職場！以下補充重要的文法並做詳盡解析，把文法根基打好，讓你無論是出差還是洽商，都用正確英文和外國人打交道！

文法重點1
business/trade/commerce
同樣都有「商業」的意思，該怎麼用呢？

business 指的是與買賣相關的工作。trade 的意思與business 相近，但更強調貿易。commerce 多指大規模的買賣或貿易關係，也泛指商業行為或商界。請利用下面的例句，幫助更熟悉記憶單字的用法：

- **She has gone on a business trip; she will be back next Monday.**
  她出差去了，下星期會回來。
- **The book exhibition is held in the Taipei World Trade Center.**
  書展是在臺北世貿中心舉行。
- **In the world of industry and commerce, the competition is intense.**
  在工商界，競爭很激烈。

文法重點2
as follows 的用法

as follows 是個慣用語，表示下文將列舉出眾多要點。例如：

- **The content of this discussion is as follows.** 本次討論的內容如下。
- **The results are as below.** 結果如下。

文法重點3
at a time 的用法

at a time 的意思是「每次；一次」。例如：

- **You can take three pills at a time.** 一次可以吃三粒藥。

at one time 的意思才是「同時；曾經一度」，常用於過去式。例如：
- **At one time we loved each other so deeply.** 我們曾經深愛著對方。

會話單字懂多少？

讀過前面的內容後，你是不是都懂得這些單字了呢？下列題目中的單字都是與會話及文法相關的單字，測驗看看自己會了多少吧！

( ) ❶ exact： (A) 準確 (B) 誇張 (C) 考試

( ) ❷ March： (A) 前進 (B) 三月 (C) 空白

( ) ❸ square： (A) 廣場 (B) 浪費 (C) 敲打

( ) ❹ executive： (A) 行刑 (B) 行政人員 (C) 懲罰

( ) ❺ officer： (A) 後代 (B) 離開 (C) 官員

( ) ❻ participate： (A) 分解 (B) 部分 (C) 參加

( ) ❼ consist： (A) 堅持 (B) 包括；組成 (C) 安慰

( ) ❽ purpose： (A) 目的 (B) 追求 (C) 施加

( ) ❾ activity： (A) 表演 (B) 反映 (C) 活動

( ) ❿ commerce： (A) 任務 (B) 商業 (C) 委員

( ) ⓫ friendship： (A) 友誼 (B) 戰鬥 (C) 友好

( ) ⓬ cordially： (A) 協議 (B) 渴望 (C) 誠摯

( ) ⓭ center： (A) 美分 (B) 中央 (C) 遣送

( ) ⓮ intense： (A) 意圖 (B) 激烈 (C) 嵌入

( ) ⓯ content： (A) 思考 (B) 內容 (C) 污染

答案：1. (A) 2. (B) 3. (A) 4. (B) 5. (C) 6. (C) 7. (B) 8. (A) 9. (C)
10. (B) 11. (A) 12. (C) 13. (B) 14. (B) 15. (B)

Part **6**

簡報製作

I need you to brief me on our new item.

我要妳先向我做個新產品的簡報。

職場會話跟著說！ Track 038

Michelle: Morning, Boss! I'm back from Rome. Max said you're expecting me.

蜜雪：琳西，早安！我從羅馬回來了。邁斯說妳在等我。

Lindsay: Oh, hi, Michelle! Welcome back. But you look exhausted! Are you OK?

琳西：噢，嗨，蜜雪！歡迎回來，但妳看起來累壞了！沒事吧？

Michelle: Don't remind me. I know I look terrible. It was an awfully long flight.

蜜雪：別提了，我知道我的臉色有夠嚇人，坐了那麼久的飛機。

Lindsay: We have work to do, but if you need a day to recover from jet lag, we can start tomorrow.

琳西：我們有工作要進行，但如果妳需要休息一天來調整時差，明天再開始也不遲啊。

Michelle: That's OK. I can start immediately. Fill me in on the task.

蜜雪：沒關係，我可以立即上班。告訴我工作內容吧。

Lindsay: OK. I need you to brief me on our new item PUR038 before we make a presentation to Top Craft Co. The deadline is next Monday. You get to pick your own team.

琳西：好，在向頂力公司進行新產品PUR038 的產品說明會之前，我要妳先向我做個簡報，期限是下個禮拜一。妳可以自己組一個團隊進行。

文法重點看這裡！

學完前面的會話之後，還要懂會話中的文法重點，才能應用在職場！以下補充重要的文法並做詳盡解析，把文法根基打好，讓你無論是出差還是洽商，都用正確英文和外國人打交道！

文法重點1

expect 的用法

expect若要表示「正在等誰」，一定要加上受詞才行。表示「老闆要見你／老闆找你」的幾種說法如下：

- **The boss is expecting you.** 老闆在等你。
- **The boss wants you.** 老闆找你。
- **The boss wants to see you.** 老闆要見你。

文法重點2

Max said you're expecting. You don't?
是錯誤用法

非英文母語者時常會犯「動詞前後不一致」的錯。在這個句子裡，you're expecting 是使用be 動詞，故後面的You don't 必須改成You aren't，即為You aren't expecting 的簡化。英文道不道地，從這裡就可以明顯看出，所以一定要留意。

文法重點3

You're waiting me. 是錯誤用法

「等待某人」的片語為wait for sb.，千萬不要忘了加上介系詞for，這是非常基本的用法，一定要牢牢記住。

wait 的幾種用法如下：
- **That case can wait.** 那件案子可以先擱置一下。
- **Dinner is waiting.** 晚餐煮好了。
- **Don't run so fast. Wait for me!** 別跑那麼快，等等我啊！
- **I'm waiting for the train.** 我正在等火車。

會話單字懂多少？

讀過前面的內容後，你是不是都懂得這些單字了呢？下列題目中的單字都是與會話及文法相關的單字，測驗看看自己會了多少吧！

( )❶ expect： (A) 驚奇 (B) 期待 (C) 懷疑

( )❷ pregnant： (A) 禮物 (B) 懷孕 (C) 簡報

( )❸ embarrass： (A) 開始 (B) 上船 (C) 尷尬

( )❹ rusty： (A) 生疏的 (B) 不鏽鋼 (C) 紅寶石

( )❺ exhausted： (A) 疲累的 (B) 展覽的 (C) 紀念的

( )❻ remind： (A) 提醒 (B) 內心 (C) 背誦

( )❼ awfully： (A) 可怕地 (B) 可愛地 (C) 可憐地

( )❽ flight： (A) 遊行 (B) 飛行 (C) 滑行

( )❾ recover： (A) 度過 (B) 復原 (C) 掩蓋

( )❿ jet lag： (A) 直昇機 (B) 透明絲襪 (C) 時差

( )⓫ immediately： (A) 立刻地 (B) 遲疑地 (C) 強硬地

( )⓬ task： (A) 任性 (B) 任憑 (C) 任務

( )⓭ brief： (A) 短褲 (B) 公事包 (C) 簡報

( )⓮ presentation： (A) 收禮 (B) 介紹；簡報 (C) 友善

( )⓯ deadline： (A) 捐款 (B) 期限 (C) 死巷

答案：1. (B) 2. (B) 3. (C) 4. (A) 5. (A) 6. (A) 7. (A) 8. (B) 9. (B)
10. (C) 11. (A) 12. (C) 13. (C) 14. (B) 15. (B)

Did you work on all the papers and documents we need for tomorrow's brainstorm meeting?

明天集思會議需要的報告和檔案你都弄好了嗎？

 職場會話跟著說！ 🎧Track 039

Dan: Oh, it's quitting time. I'm gonna clock out now. See you, guys.

阿丹：噢，下班時間到了。我先打卡走人囉，拜啦，各位。

Sam: Wait, Dan. Did you work on all the papers and documents we need for tomorrow's brainstorm meeting?

山姆：等等，阿丹。明天集思會議需要的報告和檔案你都弄好了嗎？

Dan: Ugh, not yet. But I can finish those tomorrow.

阿丹：呃，還沒耶，但是我明天會把那些做完。

Sam: No way! We need those materials and numbers first thing in the morning. You got to finish them tonight.

山姆：不行！我們明天一早就要那些資料與數據。你今天晚上一定要完成。

Dan: Ugh, I am through working overtime!

阿丹：哎唷，我受夠不停地加班。

Sam: This is business. We have a deadline to meet. And you won't be the only one under pressure. We've all got to crank out this project tonight.

山姆：這是正事，我們得趕在期限內交差。而且又不是只有你有壓力，我們也都得設法在今天晚上完成手邊的工作。

Dan: Fine, fine. If you say so. I'll do what you just said.

阿丹：好吧、好吧，你都這麼說了。我會照你說的做啦。

Sam: Now you're talking. Keep up the good work, I mean, all of us.

山姆：這樣才對嘛。大家都好好加油吧。

文法重點看這裡！

學完前面的會話之後，還要懂會話中的文法重點，才能應用在職場！以下補充重要的文法並做詳盡解析，把文法根基打好，讓你無論是出差還是洽商，都用正確英文和外國人打交道！

文法重點1

quit 的用法

quit 是表示停止的意思，有關「下班、下課、休息時間」的說法如下：

- **It's quitting time.** 下班（下課、休息）時間到了。
- **I'm getting off work now.** 我要下班了。
- **He just clocked out.** 他已經下班了。
- **She's gone for the day.** 她下班囉。
- **Let's have a drink after work.** 下班後一起喝一杯吧。
- **We are going to the movies after school.** 我們下課後要去看電影。

 quit有另一個常用的意思，即「辭去工作」。因此在使用上一定要特別小心，以避免招來不必要的誤會。

文法重點2

Now you're talking. 的用法

這是英文的俚語，若依字面解釋的「現在你正在說話」來理解的話就是錯誤的，實際上這句俚語指的是「這才對嘛」、「這才像話」的意思，可以用來表達對對方的認同。

文法重點3

That's that. 是錯誤用法

正確來說，要表達「一天結束了」應該用I'm going to call it a day. / I'm going to call it a night. / Time to call it a day. / Time to call it a night 來表示。
而That's that. 是表達「就這樣！什麼都不用說了！」的意思，是措辭非常強烈的語句，絕對不要誤用了，免得招致不必要的誤會。

會話單字懂多少？

讀過前面的內容後，你是不是都懂得這些單字了呢？下列題目中的單字都是與會話及文法相關的單字，測驗看看自己會了多少吧！

( )❶ quit： (A) 開始 (B) 停止 (C) 操作

( )❷ irresponsible： (A) 負責任的 (B) 不負責任的 (C) 責任

( )❸ possible： (A) 值得的 (B) 健全的 (C) 可能的

( )❹ clock： (A) 打卡 (B) 水桶 (C) 板擦

( )❺ usual： (A) 奢侈 (B) 通常 (C) 高利貸

( )❻ confuse： (A) 迷惑 (B) 拒絕 (C) 衝突

( )❼ broken： (A) 破碎的 (B) 凋謝的 (C) 腐爛的

( )❽ papers： (A) 頁數 (B) 文件 (C) 胡椒

( )❾ document： (A) 文件 (B) 報紙 (C) 資料夾

( )❿ brainstorm： (A) 集思廣義 (B) 腦中風 (C) 智慧

( )⓫ material： (A) 材料 (B) 工藝 (C) 程式

( )⓬ overtime： (A) 時間 (B) 過時 (C) 超時

( )⓭ pressure： (A) 壓榨 (B) 壓馬路 (C) 壓力

( )⓮ crank out： (A) 快速生產 (B) 智者 (C) 放慢

( )⓯ project： (A) 企畫 (B) 投影機 (C) 過程

答案：1. (B) 2. (B) 3. (C) 4. (A) 5. (B) 6. (A) 7. (A) 8. (B) 9. (A)
10. (A) 11. (A) 12. (C) 13. (C) 14. (A) 15. (A)

But these figures do not support Max's argument.

但是這些數據並無法支持邁斯的論點。

 職場會話跟著說！ Track **040**

Max: These are just some rough ideas I have. Maybe we can try this out.

邁斯：這些是我初步的想法，也許可以朝這方面試試看。

Michelle: Good points, Max. But we should take a look at the figures Dan got for us. Dan, what are these figures based on? And how solid are they?

蜜雪：邁斯，你的想法很棒。不過我們應該看一下阿丹給我們的數據。阿丹，這些數據是根據什麼得來的？準確度如何呢？

Dan: The figures are based on first quarter's profits. I believe they are very solid.

阿丹：這些數據是根據第一季的獲利得來的。我相信正確度非常高。

Michelle: But these figures do not support Max's argument. And I noticed the numbers didn't add up. Anyway, I want you to go over these numbers once again. We can't use them before they proved to be right.

蜜雪：但是這些數據並無法支持邁斯的論點。而且我注意到這些數字有些不合理。無論如何，我要你再檢查一次這些數字。在證明無誤之前，這些數據不能用。

Dan: Got it. I'll go through all the materials again.

阿丹：知道了。我會再仔細檢查一遍。

Michelle: OK, guys. We've been sitting for 3 hours. We'd better get up and stretch our legs. We'll discuss it further later today.

蜜雪：好了，各位，我們已經坐了三個鐘頭了，該起來伸伸腳了。我們晚點再繼續討論。

文法重點看這裡！

學完前面的會話之後，還要懂會話中的文法重點，才能應用在職場！以下補充重要的文法並做詳盡解析，把文法根基打好，讓你無論是出差還是洽商，都用正確英文和外國人打交道！

文法重點1

Where are these figures come from?
是錯誤用法

這是一句非常常見的錯誤用法，即一個句子裡存在「兩個動詞」。如果要問「什麼人或物是從哪裡來的」，請參考下列正確用法。

- **Where are you from?**
  你是從哪裡來的？（可回答自己的出生國／出生地，或長期居住的地方）
- **Where did these files come from? / Where are these files from?**
  這些檔案是從哪裡來的？
- **Where did you get those pictures?**
  那些照片你是從哪裡拿來的？

文法重點2

Work harder next time. 要看對象使用

想鼓勵別人「work harder」不能隨便亂用！因為這句話有「拜託你努力一點工作好不好、不要偷懶」的負面意思。你可以用在自己身上，或是用在比自己小一輩的人身上，但是千萬不要用在長者或同輩身上，否則會出現火爆場面喔。以下列舉幾種使用情境：

- **Don't be so lazy. You should work harder on your homework.**
  別這麼懶惰，你應該要更努力把回家功課做好。
- **I really need to work harder and stop goofing around.**
  我實在應該要好好努力工作，別再偷懶鬼混了。

> 要對方「加油、繼續保持下去」，正確的用法是「Keep up the good work. / Keep up the great work.」這都是非常正面的鼓勵。而我們常常使用work hard 來表示很用功、很努力，是個正面的用語。

會話單字懂多少？

讀過前面的內容後，你是不是都懂得這些單字了呢？下列題目中的單字都是與會話及文法相關的單字，測驗看看自己會了多少吧！

( ) ❶ reliable： (A) 可通電的 (B) 可移動的 (C) 可信賴的

( ) ❷ Chinglish： (A) 印度英文 (B) 新加坡英文 (C) 中式英文

( ) ❸ rough： (A) 粗略的 (B) 精密的 (C) 普通的

( ) ❹ point： (A) 要點 (B) 平面 (C) 概論

( ) ❺ figures： (A) 數據 (B) 器具 (C) 影像

( ) ❻ quarter： (A) 半年 (B) 兩週 (C) 一季

( ) ❼ profit： (A) 營養 (B) 利潤 (C) 毛重

( ) ❽ support： (A) 支配 (B) 彈性 (C) 支持

( ) ❾ argument： (A) 論點 (B) 和諧 (C) 擁護

( ) ❿ notice： (A) 注意到 (B) 機密 (C) 支票

( ) ⓫ anyway： (A) 盡快 (B) 然而 (C) 無論如何

( ) ⓬ prove： (A) 政府 (B) 證明 (C) 證人

( ) ⓭ stretch： (A) 伸展 (B) 肌肉 (C) 拉傷

( ) ⓮ discuss： (A) 吵架 (B) 討論 (C) 會議

( ) ⓯ further： (A) 羽毛 (B) 精通 (C) 進一步

答案：1. (C) 2. (C) 3. (A) 4. (A) 5. (A) 6. (C) 7. (B) 8. (C) 9. (A)
10. (A) 11. (C) 12. (B) 13. (A) 14. (B) 15. (C)

And I'll make sure all the presentation slides are ready on the computer.

我也會確定電腦上的簡報投影片檔案都準備就緒。

 職場會話跟著說！ 🎧Track **041**

Michelle: Now it's time to prepare for tomorrow's presentation rehearsal.	蜜雪：是時候準備明天的簡報彩排了。
Sam: I think we need to picture the figures and compile a general chart.	山姆：我們覺得需要善用圖表凸顯數據資料，並製作一個總表。
Michelle: Then, Sam, you'll be in charge of creating those charts and graphs. What's next?	蜜雪：那麼，山姆，圖表製作就由你來負責。再來還有什麼？
Renee: We need to book a meeting room. But the meeting rooms are almost booked out. I'm still working on that.	芮妮：我們要預訂明天的會議室。不過目前會議室幾乎被預定光了，我還在努力協調當中。
Michelle: Please try your best to get us a room. You know we cannot reschedule the rehearsal.	蜜雪：請一定要盡全力幫我們弄一間出來，妳知道我們不可能將彩排改期的。
Renee: I will do my best. And I'll make sure all the presentation slides are ready on the computer.	芮妮：我會盡力去協調。我也會確定電腦上的簡報投影片檔案都準備就緒。
Michelle: Good. And don't forget to give me the rundown on the rehearsal.	蜜雪：很好。記得向我詳述一下彩排的流程。
Sam: No problem. Renee and I will see to it.	山姆：沒問題，芮妮和我會照辦。
Michelle: Then that concludes our meeting today. Let's roll.	蜜雪：那麼今天會議就到此結束，大家幹活去吧。

文法重點看這裡！

學完前面的會話之後，還要懂會話中的文法重點，才能應用在職場！以下補充重要的文法並做詳盡解析，把文法根基打好，讓你無論是出差還是洽商，都用正確英文和外國人打交道！

文法重點1

But the meeting rooms are full now.
是錯誤用法

這句話的意思是會議室每間都擠滿了人。如果要表達會議室都被訂光了，要說成「The meeting rooms are all booked out.」才正確。

> 表示「被預定光了、被賣光了」的各種說法如下：
> - **The hotel is booked out.** 旅館已經沒有房間了。
> - **We are sold out tonight.**（產品）都賣光了。
> - **There are no tickets available.** 票都賣光了。
> - **We are out of that item.** 我們目前沒有貨了。
> - **We can back order that item for you.** 我們可以幫你訂貨。

文法重點2

see to sth 的用法

see to sth的意思與「看見」沒有太大的關係，指的是「處理，應付」。see to it後面可以接子句，點出要處理的事。例如：
- **Don't worry. We'll see to it.** 別擔心，我們會處理。
- **I'll see to it that she gets to school early.** 我會確保她早點到學校。

文法重點3

Time is end. 是錯誤用法

若要表示「時間到了」或「是時候～」，可以用「Time's up. / It's about time. / It's time to V~」來表示。類似Time is end. 這種令人傻眼的中式英文，千萬不要拿出來用。

會話單字懂多少?

讀過前面的內容後,你是不是都懂得這些單字了呢?下列題目中的單字都是與會話及文法相關的單字,測驗看看自己會了多少吧!

( ) ❶ prepare: (A) 整頓 (B) 允許 (C) 準備

( ) ❷ rehearsal: (A) 行程 (B) 閉幕 (C) 排練

( ) ❸ book: (A) 雜誌 (B) 預定 (C) 簽約

( ) ❹ lecture: (A) 講台 (B) 講師 (C) 講座

( ) ❺ product: (A) 生產 (B) 產地 (C) 產品

( ) ❻ available: (A) 有空的 (B) 免費的 (C) 付費的

( ) ❼ exactly: (A) 恰好地 (B) 模糊地 (C) 偏差地

( ) ❽ honestly: (A) 不幸地 (B) 老實說 (C) 儘管

( ) ❾ compile: (A) 彙編 (B) 完成 (C) 執行

( ) ❿ general: (A) 大體的 (B) 小眾的 (C) 中堅的

( ) ⓫ chart: (A) 粉筆 (B) 板擦 (C) 圖表

( ) ⓬ create: (A) 創造 (B) 隨興 (C) 拍照

( ) ⓭ graph: (A) 塗鴉 (B) 圖表 (C) 素描

( ) ⓮ slide: (A) 油墨 (B) 檔案 (C) 投影片

( ) ⓯ rundown: (A) 伸展台 (B) 詳述行程 (C) 簡述流程

答案:1. (C) 2. (C) 3. (B) 4. (C) 5. (C) 6. (A) 7. (A) 8. (B) 9. (A)
10. (A) 11. (C) 12. (A) 13. (B) 14. (C) 15. (B)

My presentation contains two main sections: sales and distribution channels.

我的簡報包含兩個主要部分，就是銷售數字和通路。

 職場會話跟著說！ 🎧 Track 042

Max: Before we begin the briefing rehearsal, does anyone have any questions or anything they want to add? If not, then let's start. Michelle, it's all yours.

邁斯：各位，在簡報彩排開始前，有人有問題或是要補充說明的嗎？沒有的話，那我們開始吧。蜜雪，交給妳囉。

Michelle: Thank you, Max. Hello, everyone. My presentation contains two main sections: sales and distribution channels. Let's start with first section.

蜜雪：謝謝妳，邁斯。大家好，我的簡報包含兩個主要部分，就是銷售數字和通路。現在請看第一個部分。

Dan: May I suggest something? I think we should take a look at the local distribution channels before talking about the global market share. It's more convincing that way.

阿丹：我想建議一下：在談論全球市場佔有率之前，應該先談到我們本地的通路配置，這樣比較有說服力。

Renee: But I think we must first impress the customer by our global market share.

芮妮：但是我覺得一開始就必須先用我們的全球市場佔有率讓客戶驚豔。

Sam: OK, let's vote. If you agree with Dan, raise your hand. OK, two votes in favor. And if you agree with Renee, raise your hand…three votes in favor. So let's go with Renee's.

珊珊：我們來表決。同意阿丹的請舉手……好，有兩票。同意芮妮的請舉手……有三票。那就依照芮妮的觀點。

Michelle: Now, where were we? Oh, the global market share. Let's continue.

蜜雪：好了，我們講到哪裡了？喔對了，全球市場佔有率。我們繼續吧。

文法重點看這裡!

學完前面的會話之後,還要懂會話中的文法重點,才能應用在職場!以下補充重要的文法並做詳盡解析,把文法根基打好,讓你無論是出差還是洽商,都用正確英文和外國人打交道!

文法重點1
I'm all yours. 是錯誤用法

其實想說「接下來交給你了」,卻誤說成「我整個人都是你的了」這種充滿愛意(或變態)的句子!這裡正確的說法應該是:It's all yours.(接下來交給你了。)由於這兩句話乍聽(看)之下有點像,所以要小心不要搞混了。

表示「該你了、輪到你了」的說法如下:

- **It's your turn.** 該你了。
- **It's my turn to use the computer.** 輪到我使用電腦了。

文法重點2
before 連接句子可以省略主詞

當before前後連接的子句主詞相同時,before後的子句可以省略主詞,但省略主詞的同時,要再把動詞改為動名詞,也就是加ing。

- **I have dinner before going home.** 我回家前吃了晚餐。
- **She took a shower before going to bed.** 她上床前先洗了澡。
- **He raised his hand before answering the question.** 他回答問題前先舉手。

文法重點3
local distribution channels與
global market share 的用法

distribution channels的意思是「分配渠道」,用在商業就是銷售通路的意思,而local意為「本地的;在地的」,兩者組合起來便可用來說明當地的銷售通路。
market share用在商業就是「市場佔有率」的意思,而global意為「全球的」,兩者組合起來便可用來說明全球市場的佔有率,在跨國企業中應該有不少應用時機!

會話單字懂多少？

讀過前面的內容後，你是不是都懂得這些單字了呢？下列題目中的單字都是與會話及文法相關的單字，測驗看看自己會了多少吧！

( ) ❶ add： (A) 減少 (B) 補充 (C) 除法

( ) ❷ disgusting： (A) 噁心的 (B) 熱愛的 (C) 神氣的

( ) ❸ ashamed： (A) 羞澀的 (B) 羞愧的 (C) 囂張的

( ) ❹ contain： (A) 空地 (B) 桶子 (C) 包括

( ) ❺ main： (A) 次要的 (B) 主要的 (C) 附加的

( ) ❻ distribution： (A) 流動 (B) 冷藏 (C) 分配

( ) ❼ channel： (A) 刺青 (B) 電線 (C) 通路

( ) ❽ suggest： (A) 建議 (B) 建設 (C) 探討

( ) ❾ local： (A) 國外的 (B) 本土的 (C) 偏遠的

( ) ❿ global： (A) 宇宙的 (B) 北半球 (C) 全球的

( ) ⓫ convincing： (A) 不服輸的 (B) 有說服力的 (C) 輕浮的

( ) ⓬ impress： (A) 沒印象 (B) 打動 (C) 印象派

( ) ⓭ vote： (A) 提倡 (B) 宣導 (C) 投票

( ) ⓮ raise： (A) 扛起 (B) 舉起 (C) 放下

( ) ⓯ continue： (A) 繼續 (B) 停止 (C) 暫停

答案：1. (B) 2. (A) 3. (B) 4. (C) 5. (B) 6. (C) 7. (C) 8. (A) 9. (B)
10. (C) 11. (B) 12. (B) 13. (C) 14. (B) 15. (A)

The statistics show that sales could stand out in the third quarter even more.

統計資料顯示，銷售數字在第三季將會有更傑出的表現。

職場會話跟著說！ Track 043

Michelle: Now if you'll take a look at this line graph, you'll see the sales of our new item PUR083 has been going up substantially this quarter. And if you'll refer to the numbers on page ten in your handouts, you'll find out the profits have increase by 25 percent. The statistics show that sales could stand out in the third quarter even more.

蜜雪：請看一下這張曲線圖，妳會發現新產品PUR083的銷售數字在這季大幅提昇。如果妳參照書面資料中第十頁的數字，妳會發現我們的利潤已上升了百分之二十五。統計資料顯示，銷售數字在第三季將會有更傑出的表現。

Lindsay: However, what I'm concerned about is our competitors. They are still out there and even stronger than ever. Do you think we need to pursue an aggressive approach in order to remain competitive in the global market?

琳西：但是，我擔心的是我們的競爭對象。他們像打不死的蟑螂一樣，甚至更強壯。妳覺得我們需要採取更積極的銷售途徑嗎？

Michelle: I don't think so. The price of our product is very competitive on the market. And we are well-known for supplying goods of high quality. I don't believe we should get involved in the cut-throat competition as they do.

蜜雪：我覺得不需要。我們的價格非常具有市場競爭性，而且我們以提供高品質的產品聞名。我不認為我們應該加入對手的價格割喉戰。

Lindsay: I'm impressed by your briefing. Now go and get in touch with Top Craft Co.

琳西：妳的簡報令人印象深刻。現在趕快去跟頂力公司聯繫。

Michelle: Noted. I'll get right on it.

蜜雪：瞭解了，我會立刻去辦。

文法重點看這裡！

學完前面的會話之後，還要懂會話中的文法重點，才能應用在職場！以下補充重要的文法並做詳盡解析，把文法根基打好，讓你無論是出差還是洽商，都用正確英文和外國人打交道！

文法重點1

Thank your compliments. 是錯誤用法

這是很多人開口時會犯的錯。很多你知道的文法、正確用法，在你要開口的那一剎那，通通不知道跑哪裡去了，開口時只剩下中式思維，於是容易講出這樣令人啼笑皆非的中式英文。所以，要好好訓練用英文思考。這句話的正確說法為：

- **Thanks for your compliments. / Thank you for your compliments.**
  謝謝你的讚美（或者簡單說Thank you. / Thank you very much. 就可以了）。

文法重點2

I think we don't need to. 是錯誤用法

這種錯誤實在是太常出現，因此必須提出來提醒各位，千萬記得要把否定的don't 放在think 的前面。這裡的正確說法為：

- **I don't think we need to.** 我覺得我們不需要這麼做。
- **I don't think so.** 我不這麼認為。

文法重點3

I believe we shouldn't... 是錯誤用法

這也是個出現頻繁的錯誤用法，完全是中式英文，因此下次要使用這種句型時，請先在腦中默想一遍：把否定的don't 放在believe 前面，確定無誤之後再說出口。這裡的正確說法為：

- **I don't believe we should...** 我不認為我們應該……

會話單字懂多少？

讀過前面的內容後，你是不是都懂得這些單字了呢？下列題目中的單字都是與會話及文法相關的單字，測驗看看自己會了多少吧！

( ) ❶ proud： (A) 謙虛的 (B) 正直的 (C) 驕傲的

( ) ❷ compliment： (A) 恭維 (B) 補充物 (C) 容器

( ) ❸ concerned： (A) 關心的 (B) 情感的 (C) 惡意的

( ) ❹ pursue： (A) 從事 (B) 皮包 (C) 宣傳

( ) ❺ aggressive： (A) 積極的 (B) 消極的 (C) 中庸的

( ) ❻ approach： (A) 申請 (B) 途徑 (C) 政策

( ) ❼ remain： (A) 評價 (B) 尊敬 (C) 維持

( ) ❽ market： (A) 展覽 (B) 市場 (C) 會館

( ) ❾ capable： (A) 第四台 (B) 能幹的 (C) 行動不便的

( ) ❿ avoid： (A) 接受 (B) 避免 (C) 調查

( ) ⓫ promotion： (A) 規則 (B) 射擊 (C) 晉升

( ) ⓬ substantially： (A) 大幅地 (B) 小幅地 (C) 輕輕地

( ) ⓭ refer： (A) 參照 (B) 參加 (C) 偏好

( ) ⓮ handout： (A) 手抄本 (B) 書面資料 (C) 考卷

( ) ⓯ statistics： (A) 微積分 (B) 統計資料 (C) 電機學

答案：1. (C) 2. (A) 3. (A) 4. (A) 5. (A) 6. (B) 7. (C) 8. (B) 9. (B)
10. (B) 11. (C) 12. (A) 13. (A) 14. (B) 15. (B)

Well, we are going to make a product presentation to Top Craft Co.

我們要向頂力公司做產品簡報。

 職場會話跟著說！ 🎧Track 044

Renee: Congrats, Michelle. I heard the briefing you gave to Lindsay was very successful.

芮妮：恭喜啊，蜜雪。我聽説妳給琳西的產品簡報很成功。

Michelle: Thanks, Renee. But I couldn't do it without you guys. We are a team, remember?

蜜雪：謝啦，芮妮。不過，若是沒有妳們，我可是無法辦到的喔。我們是個團隊，記得嗎？

Renee: It's so nice of you to say that. I'm proud of working with you and delighted to assist all of you in work.

芮妮：妳這樣説真體貼。我很驕傲能與妳共事，也很開心能在工作上協助大家。

Michelle: Well, we are going to make a product presentation to Top Craft Co. I think it's about time for you to be in charge of a case like this.

蜜雪：我們要向頂力公司做產品簡報。我覺得是該讓妳負責這種案子時候了。

Renee: But I don't think I'm qualified yet. I'm not much of a talker.

芮妮：但是我覺得我還不夠資格耶。我不太會講話。

Michelle: I know this might be a rather giant step for you, but you have to grow into this. You don't want to do the chores or run errands for somebody all your life, do you? Think about that.

蜜雪：我知道這對妳來説是個非常巨大的一步，但妳必須要漸漸適應才行。妳總不想一輩子都做一些無關緊要的雜務或幫人跑腿吧？妳仔細想想。

文法重點看這裡！

學完前面的會話之後，還要懂會話中的文法重點，才能應用在職場！以下補充重要的文法並做詳盡解析，把文法根基打好，讓你無論是出差還是洽商，都用正確英文和外國人打交道！

文法重點1

Congratulate your successful briefing.
是錯誤用法

這句完全是從中文直接翻過去的錯誤用法。如果要使用動詞congratulate，請在動詞前面加主詞，動詞後面加受詞，並在值得恭喜的事件前加上on！千萬不要用中文直譯唷。正確的説法如下：

- **I (want to) congratulate you on your successful briefing.**
  恭喜你的簡報辦得很成功。
- **Congratulations on your successful presentation.**
  恭喜你的簡報辦得很成功。
- **Congrats, Eddy. I heard your presentation was very impressive.**
  恭喜你啊，艾迪。聽説你的產品説明會辦得很成功。

文法重點2

You are nice to say that. 是錯誤用法

也許大家會覺得為什麼不能這樣説？這樣説不是很符合我們中文的「你人真好耶」的感覺嗎？別傷腦筋了，因為這是英文，別人的語言，人家不習慣這麼使用，你就別再勉強了，把時間用在學習一般慣用的説法上吧！正確的説法為：

- **It's so nice of you to say that. / It's so sweet of you to say that.**
  你這樣説真體貼。

文法重點3

I'm too proud to be on your team. 是錯誤用法

其實這個句子的文法並沒有錯，但在這裡是誤用了「too... to...」（太……而不能……）這個句型，而導致語意錯誤。要表達正確的語意，應該要説：

- **I'm (very) proud to be on your team.**
  我很驕傲能當你的組員。
- **I'm proud of working with you.**
  能與你共事，我引以為傲。

會話單字懂多少？

讀過前面的內容後，你是不是都懂得這些單字了呢？下列題目中的單字都是與會話及文法相關的單字，測驗看看自己會了多少吧！

( ) ❶ congratulate： (A) 祝賀 (B) 福氣 (C) 幸運

( ) ❷ successful： (A) 失敗的 (B) 成功的 (C) 持平的

( ) ❸ awkward： (A) 尷尬的 (B) 嘲笑的 (C) 激進的

( ) ❹ talented： (A) 世故的 (B) 有才幹的 (C) 平庸的

( ) ❺ assign： (A) 分別 (B) 分派 (C) 安插

( ) ❻ delighted： (A) 愉快的 (B) 輕鬆的 (C) 憤怒的

( ) ❼ assist： (A) 和諧 (B) 協調 (C) 協助

( ) ❽ case： (A) 劃子 (B) 案子 (C) 蓋子

( ) ❾ qualified： (A) 失格的 (B) 夠格的 (C) 品質

( ) ❿ giant： (A) 渺小的 (B) 巨大的 (C) 肥胖的

( ) ⓫ step： (A) 一吋 (B) 一碼 (C) 一步

( ) ⓬ chores： (A) 雜草 (B) 雜事 (C) 雜亂

( ) ⓭ errand： (A) 差事 (B) 差遣 (C) 移交

( ) ⓮ real： (A) 虛偽的 (B) 真實的 (C) 貴重的

( ) ⓯ perfect： (A) 殘缺的 (B) 完美的 (C) 認命的

答案：1. (A) 2. (B) 3. (A) 4. (B) 5. (B) 6. (A) 7. (C) 8. (B) 9. (B) 10. (B) 11. (C) 12. (B) 13. (A) 14. (B) 15. (B)

Honestly, what you mentioned last time will be a real challenge for our company.

老實說，您上次提的方案，對我們公司將會是個很大的挑戰。

 職場會話跟著說！ 🎧Track 045

Renee: Good morning, Mr. Harbour. How are you?

芮妮：早安，賀伯先生，您好嗎？

Harbour: How are you, Renee? Please have a seat. Let's start with where we left off last time.

賀伯：妳好，芮妮，請坐。我們從上次尚未討論完的地方談起吧。

Renee: Honestly, what you mentioned last time will be a real challenge for our company. That's more than a technical issue. Can't we do it our own way? We'll do whatever we can.

芮妮：老實說，您上次提的方案，對我們公司將會是個很大的挑戰。那不僅僅是技術性的問題。不能照著我們的方式走嗎？我們會盡我們所能去做。

Harbour: That's all very interesting, but not good enough. We want something more original and concrete. Any ideas?

賀伯：聽起來很不錯，但還不夠好。我們需要更原創性的、更具體的方案。有其他想法嗎？

Renee: Hmm, I think I got one. But I have to make sure if it is feasible. I'll let you know ASAP.

芮妮：嗯，我想到一個點子了！不過我必須先確認是否可行。我會盡快給您答覆。

Harbour: OK, sounds good to me. I look forward to a favorable result. Now, let's go through the details again. I don't want any last-minute changes, you know.

賀伯：好，聽起來還不錯，我期待有個令人滿意的結果。現在我們來討論一下細節。我可不希望在緊要關頭有什麼變數。

Renee: I understand your concern. We won't let you down.

芮妮：我明白你的擔憂。我們一定不會讓你失望。

文法重點看這裡！

學完前面的會話之後，還要懂會話中的文法重點，才能應用在職場！以下補充重要的文法並做詳盡解析，把文法根基打好，讓你無論是出差還是洽商，都用正確英文和外國人打交道！

文法重點1
Are you OK?

這句話是對方發生一些狀況時，用來詢問對方「還好吧？沒事吧？」的用語，不適合當成一般打招呼的問候語來使用，否則被問的人會一頭霧水喔。

一般打招呼的問候語如下：
- **How are you? / How are you doing?** 你好嗎？
- **How's everything?** 一切都好嗎？
- **How have you been?** 近來好嗎？

文法重點2
ASAP 的用法

ASAP是as soon as possible的縮寫，代表「盡快」，這是一種廣泛運用的商用縮寫，無論是在email或是在公司內部的溝通平台，都很常見到喔！

其他商用縮寫如下：
- **BTW**（**by the way**）順帶一提
- **FAQ**（**frequently asked questions**）常問的問題
- **WFH**（**work from home**）在家辦公
- **CEO**（**chief executive officer**）首席執行長
- **HR**（**human resources**）人資
- **PM**（**project manager**）專案經理
- **PR**（**public relations**）公關
- **R&D**（**research and development**）研發

會話單字懂多少？

讀過前面的內容後，你是不是都懂得這些單字了呢？下列題目中的單字都是與會話及文法相關的單字，測驗看看自己會了多少吧！

( ) **❶ part-time**： (A) 兼職 (B) 全職 (C) 全天候

( ) **❷ full-time**： (A) 兼職 (B) 全職 (C) 全天候

( ) **❸ employer**： (A) 職業 (B) 雇主 (C) 雇員

( ) **❹ mention**： (A) 商量 (B) 佈告 (C) 提到

( ) **❺ challenge**： (A) 機會 (B) 挑戰 (C) 鬥士

( ) **❻ technical**： (A) 實質上 (B) 意識上 (C) 技術上

( ) **❼ issue**： (A) 期刊 (B) 問題 (C) 簽名

( ) **❽ whatever**： (A) 任何 (B) 何時 (C) 到處

( ) **❾ original**： (A) 未來的 (B) 抄襲的 (C) 原創的

( ) **❿ concrete**： (A) 液體的 (B) 具體的 (C) 彈性的

( ) **⓫ feasible**： (A) 移動的 (B) 饗宴 (C) 可行的

( ) **⓬ favorable**： (A) 討人喜歡的 (B) 壞結果的 (C) 虧損的

( ) **⓭ result**： (A) 理由 (B) 條件 (C) 結果

( ) **⓮ detail**： (A) 大綱 (B) 細節 (C) 分類

( ) **⓯ last-minute**： (A) 時針 (B)分針 (C) 臨時的

答案：1. (A) 2. (B) 3. (B) 4. (C) 5. (B) 6. (C) 7. (B) 8. (A) 9. (C)
10. (B) 11. (C) 12. (A) 13. (C) 14. (B) 15. (C)

I'm so honored that you joined me for the presentation.

非常榮幸你們能來參加這場產品說明會。

 職場會話跟著說！ 🎧 Track 046

Renee: Ladies and gentlemen, I'm so honored that you joined me for the presentation. The presentation will last about thirty minutes. Please feel free to stop me with any questions when I go along. Today, I'd like to introduce our new item PUR038. This is our latest model. It's smaller and lighter than the old model. Besides, we've also upgraded the quality.

芮妮：各位先生女士，非常榮幸你們能來參加這場產品說明會。說明會的過程大約持續三十分鐘。中途若有任何問題，請盡量發問。今天我要向各位介紹我們公司的新產品PUR038。這是最新的型號，它比舊型號更輕巧，除此之外，品質也升級了。

Mr. Harbour: I think it's very interesting. Could you explain how it is used?

賀伯先生：這是個很有意思的產品，可以說明一下怎麼使用嗎？

Renee: Sure. Let me demonstrate how to use it. It's very easy to operate and it's adjustable as well. In addition, it comes in three shapes and six sizes.

芮妮：當然。我來為各位示範如何使用。它操作十分簡易，而且是可調式。再來，它有三種造型與六種尺寸。

Ms. Bourne: It looks well-made. How long is it good for?

波恩女士：看起來工非常細，它的使用壽命多久？

Renee: This has the best quality. We dare say that no competitors beat our quality. Normally, it'll be good for six years. But if you clean it often, it'll last even longer.

芮妮：它的品質是最頂級的。我們敢說其他的競爭者不可能超越我們的品質。一般來說，使用壽命為六年，但如果保養得當，可以使用長達六年以上。

文法重點看這裡！

學完前面的會話之後，還要懂會話中的文法重點，才能應用在職場！以下補充重要的文法並做詳盡解析，把文法根基打好，讓你無論是出差還是洽商，都用正確英文和外國人打交道！

文法重點1

I'll make an example of it. 是錯誤用法

這句是「我來為這個產品做個示範。」的直譯，其實這個句子真正的意思是「殺一儆百，以儆效尤」。常常我們背了許多單字、片語、慣用語等等，但如果沒有背熟或瞭解其真正的意思，就胡亂套用的話，真的會很糗！所以一定要避免！正確的說法為：

- **Let me demonstrate how to use it.** 我來為各位示範如何使用。
- **Let me explain how it is used.** 我來為各位解說如何使用。
- **I'll show you how to use it.** 我來教各位如何使用。

文法重點2

This kind owns three shapes and six sizes.
是錯誤用法

這句是「這款擁有三種造型與六種尺寸。」的直譯。其實有時候並不是不知道該怎麼說，而是一下子無法轉換成英文思緒，一不小心就脫口而出了，所以還是一句老話，請多多開口練習。正確的說法為：

- **It comes in three shapes and six sizes.** 它有三種造型與六種尺寸。
- **It is available in three colors.** 它有三種顏色可供選擇。

文法重點3

How long is it good for? 的意思

「be good for + 一段時間」其實是「可以用多久」的意思，而不是在詢問產品好不好，因此若是有人回答「Oh, it is very good.」（噢，這個產品非常好），那就是文不對題，糗大了呢。

會話單字懂多少？

讀過前面的內容後，你是不是都懂得這些單字了呢？下列題目中的單字都是與會話及文法相關的單字，測驗看看自己會了多少吧！

( ) ❶ interesting： (A) 感興趣 (B) 有趣的 (C) 利息

( ) ❷ explain： (A) 示範 (B) 解體 (C) 解説

( ) ❸ example： (A) 例子 (B) 標誌 (C) 實驗

( ) ❹ demonstrate： (A) 展示 (B) 花車 (C) 監察

( ) ❺ operate： (A) 操作 (B) 代考 (C) 購物

( ) ❻ adjustable： (A) 習慣的 (B) 固定的 (C) 可調的

( ) ❼ shape： (A) 狀況 (B) 形狀 (C) 顏色

( ) ❽ size： (A) 尺寸 (B) 抓住 (C) 把握

( ) ❾ honor： (A) 取笑 (B) 光榮 (C) 國歌

( ) ❿ last： (A) 冗長 (B) 持續 (C) 最初

( ) ⓫ introduce： (A) 介入 (B) 介紹 (C) 機能

( ) ⓬ latest： (A) 最舊的 (B) 最廣的 (C) 最新的

( ) ⓭ upgrade： (A) 長高 (B) 變寬 (C) 升級

( ) ⓮ dare： (A) 怕 (B) 敢 (C) 怨

( ) ⓯ normally： (A) 變態地 (B) 穩定地 (C) 正常地

答案：1. (B) 2. (C) 3. (A) 4. (A) 5. (A) 6. (C) 7. (B) 8. (A) 9. (B)
10. (B) 11. (B) 12. (C) 13. (C) 14. (B) 15. (C)

Therefore, this product is just right for your needs.

因此，這個產品完全符合你們的需求。

 職場會話跟著說！ 🎧 Track 047

Renee: Besides, as you can see from this pie chart, our model PUR038 is very competitive on the market. If you'll refer to the figures in your handouts, you'll see that this item is very sought-after and there is a big market for it.

芮妮：除此之外，從這張圓餅圖您們可以看出，我們的新產品 PUR038 非常具有市場競爭性。或者若您們參考書面資料中的數據，可以發現這個產品很受歡迎，市場也很大。

Mr. Harbour: Please give us some good reasons why we should purchase this item.

賀伯先生：為什麼我們應該要購買這個產品，可否給我們幾個好理由？

Renee: One good thing about this item is its high technology. And its high tech leads to durability. It can save time and money, which I know is your company goal. Therefore, this product is just right for your needs. We highly recommend this item for your company.

芮妮：這個產品很大的一個特性是高科技，而高科技又導向耐久性。它能節省時間與金錢，這也是貴公司追求的目標。因此，這個產品完全符合你們的需求，我們也大力推薦。

Mr. Harbour: Your presentation is very impressive. We do have great interest in this item. But we'd like to try it out before we place an order for it.

賀伯先生：妳的產品說明非常令我驚豔。我們的確對妳們的新產品很有興趣。不過我們在下單之前，想先試用看看。

Renee: That's for certain, Mr. Harbour. Here is a sample for your company. And we look forward to receiving your order in the near future.

芮妮：那是一定的，賀伯先生。這個是給貴公司的樣品。期待近期內能接到您的訂單。

文法重點看這裡！

學完前面的會話之後，還要懂會話中的文法重點，才能應用在職場！以下補充重要的文法並做詳盡解析，把文法根基打好，讓你無論是出差還是洽商，都用正確英文和外國人打交道！

文法重點1

Our model PUR038 is very compete on the market. 是錯誤用法

按照中文的語意，compete 是「競爭」沒錯，但它是動詞。依照這個句子的結構，必須要將compete 轉換成competitive「有競爭力的」才對。如果堅持要用compete，則整個句子結構都要換掉。正確的説法為：

- **Our model PUR038 is very competitive in the market.**
  我們的新產品PUR038 在市場上非常具有競爭力。
- **It competes in the marketplace.** 它在市場中有競爭力。

文法重點2

seeked-after 是錯誤用法

請注意，並沒有seeked-after 這個字，正確的拼法為「sought-after」。「sought」是「seek」的過去分詞，因為seek 是不規則動詞。「sought-after」表示「很熱門、很搶手」的意思。這個字的用法如下：

- **She is one of Bollywood's most sought-after actresses.**
  她是寶萊塢最受歡迎的女演員之一。
- **Wii is very sought-after on the market.** Wii 在市場上非常搶手。

文法重點3

I hope you're still interesting in our product. 是錯誤用法

看出這句的問題出在哪裡嗎？是的，這裡應該要是「人be interested in 物」（對～感到興趣）的句型才對，而不能用interesting（有趣的、有意思的）。雖然是很簡單的文法，但説錯、用錯的大有人在，所以用英文時不要急，清楚簡單地表達即可。這句正確的説法應為：I hope you're still interested in our product.（希望你仍然對我們的產品感興趣。）

會話單字懂多少？

讀過前面的內容後，你是不是都懂得這些單字了呢？下列題目中的單字都是與會話及文法相關的單字，測驗看看自己會了多少吧！

( ) ❶ model： (A) 包裝 (B) 型號 (C) 仿造

( ) ❷ compete： (A) 賽跑 (B) 費力 (C) 競爭

( ) ❸ competitive： (A) 有競爭力的 (B) 失利 (C) 對手

( ) ❹ sought-after： (A) 爆香 (B) 搶手 (C) 滯銷

( ) ❺ grammar： (A) 祖母 (B) 奶媽 (C) 文法

( ) ❻ forgive： (A) 失去 (B) 原諒 (C) 記恨

( ) ❼ interested： (A) 感興趣 (B) 有趣 (C) 利息

( ) ❽ effort： (A) 努力 (B) 奴役 (C) 枉費

( ) ❾ chance： (A) 職業 (B) 機會 (C) 零件

( ) ❿ sample： (A) 例句 (B) 樓梯 (C) 樣品

( ) ⓫ receive： (A) 話筒 (B) 收件人 (C) 收到

( ) ⓬ feedback： (A) 餵食 (B) 哺乳 (C) 回饋

( ) ⓭ durability： (A) 不耐 (B) 耐久性 (C) 延長線

( ) ⓮ save： (A) 擁有 (B) 節省 (C) 消費

( ) ⓯ purchase： (A) 合併 (B) 構造 (C) 購買

答案：1. (B) 2. (C) 3. (A) 4. (B) 5. (C) 6. (B) 7. (A) 8. (A) 9. (B)
　　　10. (C) 11. (C) 12. (C) 13. (B) 14. (B) 15. (C)

Part 7

行銷活動

Today we're deciding which items will be the key products that we are going to promote this quarter.

今天我們要決定這季的重點促銷商品。

 職場會話跟著說！ 🎧Track **048**

Lindsay: Is everyone here?

琳西：大家都到齊了嗎？

Michelle: Yes.

蜜雪：是的。

Lindsay: OK. Let's get started. Today we're deciding which items will be the key products that we are going to promote this quarter. Any ideas?

琳西：好，我們開始。今天我們要決定這季的重點促銷商品。各位有什麼想法嗎？

Michelle: I think we can keep promoting our item PUR038. It sells like hot cakes! We can make it hotter in the marketplace.

蜜雪：我覺得我們可以繼續促銷PUR038這個產品，它的銷路好極了。我們可以讓它在市場上越炒越熱。

Max: I don't think that's a good idea. We still have a lot of competitive items on standby. They are good products, too. Since PUR038 sells like hot cakes, it can speak for itself. We can put our effort into other products such as our cutting board series.

邁斯：我覺得這個點子不好。我們仍有許多具競爭力的商品等著我們去行銷。它們也都是好產品。既然PUR038賣得這麼好，就讓它自己推銷自己，我們可以把心力放在其他商品，例如切菜板系列。

Sam: I agree. The cutting boards have been sought-after on the market recently. We are supposed to plan a big promotion for our CB series.

山姆：我贊成。最近切菜板在市面上很搶手。我們應該要幫CB系列大大地推銷一番。

Lindsay: That's a good point, Sam. Any objection? If not, then CB series will be our key items this quarter. That's all for today's meeting.

琳西：說得很好，山姆。各位有任何異議嗎？如果沒有，那就決定CB系列為我們這季的重點行銷產品。今天會議到此結束。

文法重點看這裡！

學完前面的會話之後，還要懂會話中的文法重點，才能應用在職場！以下補充重要的文法並做詳盡解析，把文法根基打好，讓你無論是出差還是洽商，都用正確英文和外國人打交道！

文法重點1
We can keep operating our item PUR038.
是錯誤用法

在這裡用operate這個字來表示「操作產品」並不恰當，因為operate是「操作機器」的意思。這裡直接改成「We can keep promoting our item PUR038.」即可，意思簡單明瞭。

文法重點2
We can let it speak by itself. 是錯誤用法

這句是要表示「讓產品自己說話；讓產品自己推銷自己、為自己說話」，所以應該改成：We can let it speak for itself.（我們可以讓它推銷自己。）
下面的用法也一併記下來：

- **My little sister went to school by herself.** 我的小妹自己一個人去上學。
- **Aunt Susie was beside herself with rage when she heard the news.**
  蘇西阿姨聽到這個消息後，氣得抓狂。
- **I like a sofa to myself when watching TV.**
  看電視時我喜歡一個人獨佔一張沙發。

文法重點3
We suppose to plan a big promotion for our CB series. 是錯誤用法

這裡的suppose（認為應該）要改成被動式，即「be supposed to」=「should」。所以本句應該改成：We are supposed to plan a big promotion for our CB series.（我們應該要幫CB系列大大地推銷一番。）
以下幾個簡單例句供參考：

- **What am I supposed to do? = What should I do?** 我應該怎麼做呢？
- **You're not supposed to smoke in here. = You shouldn't smoke in here.**
  你不應該在這裡抽菸。

會話單字懂多少？

讀過前面的內容後，你是不是都懂得這些單字了呢？下列題目中的單字都是與會話及文法相關的單字，測驗看看自己會了多少吧！

( ) ❶ decide： (A) 決定 (B) 體面 (C) 缺陷

( ) ❷ quarter： (A) 兩季 (B) 一季 (C) 半年

( ) ❸ idea： (A) 主義 (B) 主意 (C) 理想

( ) ❹ promote： (A) 推銷 (B) 專案 (C) 懷孕

( ) ❺ sell： (A) 買進 (B) 賣出 (C) 交易

( ) ❻ hot： (A) 冷的 (B) 熱的 (C) 溫的

( ) ❼ cake： (A) 糖果 (B) 麵粉 (C) 蛋糕

( ) ❽ standby： (A) 待命 (B) 站哨 (C) 崗位

( ) ❾ effort： (A) 提醒 (B) 內心 (C) 努力

( ) ❿ cutting： (A) 減法 (B) 切剁 (C) 造型

( ) ⓫ board： (A) 箱子 (B) 盒子 (C) 板子

( ) ⓬ sought-after： (A) 吃香的 (B) 喝辣的 (C) 追尋

( ) ⓭ recently： (A) 很久 (B) 最近 (C) 好險

( ) ⓮ suppose： (A) 活該 (B) 應該 (C) 應得

( ) ⓯ objection： (A) 造反 (B) 贊成 (C) 異議

答案：1. (A) 2. (B) 3. (B) 4. (A) 5. (B) 6. (B) 7. (C) 8. (A) 9. (C)
10. (B) 11. (C) 12. (A) 13. (B) 14. (B) 15. (C)

Everyone of us will get a new assignment today.

每個組員今天都會分配到新任務。

 職場會話跟著說！ 🎧 Track **049**

Michelle: Hi, guys! We're now discussing the promotion plan on CB series. Everyone of us will get a new assignment today. Before we decide on how to market our product, I want to hear your thoughts about this.

蜜雪：嗨，大夥們！我們要來討論 CB系列的行銷計畫。每個組員今天都會分配到新任務。在決定如何行銷我們的產品之前，我想聽聽你們對此活動的想法。

Dan: We need sponsors. I can look it up on the computer files and find out our previous sponsors. I'll visit them and try to win them around.

阿丹：我們需要贊助商。我可以去查閱電腦資料，找出誰曾經贊助過我們的活動，我會去拜訪他們，說服他們再次贊助我們。

Michelle: Good idea, Dan. Then you will be in charge of this. Any other thoughts?

蜜雪：很棒的想法，阿丹。那們你就負責這個部分。還有其他的想法嗎？

Renee: I volunteer to visit all of our suppliers and see if they are interested to support us. If our promotion succeeds, they will also benefit by it.

芮妮：我自願去拜訪我們所有的廠商，看看他們願不願意資助我們的活動。如果我們促銷活動成功，他們自然也會受益。

Michelle: Great. And this will be your assignment. I'm looking forward to a favorable result. OK. We will be discussing how to market CB series after I get your feedback. Let's roll!

蜜雪：太好了，那妳就負責這個任務，我靜待佳音。好，等我收到你們的回報後，我們再來討論行銷方式。行動吧，各位！

文法重點看這裡！

學完前面的會話之後，還要懂會話中的文法重點，才能應用在職場！以下補充重要的文法並做詳盡解析，把文法根基打好，讓你無論是出差還是洽商，都用正確英文和外國人打交道！

文法重點1

I can look up to the computer files. 是錯誤用法

「look up to ~」是「尊敬某人」的意思，而「look up」是「查閱」的意思，兩個片語長得十分類似。使用時很容易弄錯。本句的正確說法為：I can look it up on the computer files.（我可以查一下電腦檔案。）現在就用以下的例句將兩個片語牢牢記住吧：

- **I look up to my father. He is a great man.** 我很尊敬我父親；他是個偉大的人。
- **I can't find the payment list. I'll look it up on the computer files.**
  我找不到付款清單；我會查閱一下電腦檔案。

文法重點2

I'll visit them and try to win them. 語意錯誤

「win」是「贏、贏得」的意思。例如：I'll win the game.（我會贏得這場比賽。）但是如果是要表示「說服、爭取、贏得某人來幫你」，則要用片語「win round」或「win over」。所以這裡的正確說法為：

- **I'll visit them and try to win them round. / I'll visit them and try to win them over.** 我會去拜訪他們，並爭取他們的贊助。

「win+人」的相關用法：
Win one's support/ trust/ love：贏得贊同／信任／好感
- **Ricky eventually won Ellie's heart.** Ricky最終贏得了Ellie的心。
Win Sb over：說服
- **I'm sure we'll win him over eventually.**
  我很確定我們最後一定能說服他。

會話單字懂多少？

讀過前面的內容後，你是不是都懂得這些單字了呢？下列題目中的單字都是與會話及文法相關的單字，測驗看看自己會了多少吧！

( ) ❶ promotion： (A) 轉動 (B) 運轉 (C) 促銷

( ) ❷ decide： (A) 決定 (B) 定時 (C) 定期

( ) ❸ product： (A) 生產 (B) 產品 (C) 產生

( ) ❹ thought： (A) 辯論 (B) 想法 (C) 條理

( ) ❺ computer： (A) 機器 (B) 主機 (C) 電腦

( ) ❻ file： (A) 檔案 (B) 案子 (C) 報導

( ) ❼ previous： (A) 先前的 (B) 預先的 (C) 預告的

( ) ❽ sponsor： (A) 工廠 (B) 廠商 (C) 贊助商

( ) ❾ visit： (A) 頁數 (B) 文件 (C) 拜訪

( ) ❿ win： (A) 贏得 (B) 風車 (C) 模仿

( ) ⓫ charge： (A) 改變 (B) 責任 (C) 操作

( ) ⓬ volunteer： (A) 主導 (B) 被迫 (C) 義工

( ) ⓭ forward： (A) 向後 (B) 向上 (C) 向前

( ) ⓮ succeed： (A) 失敗 (B) 成功 (C) 平手

( ) ⓯ benefit： (A) 藝人 (B) 受益 (C) 議程

答案：1. (C) 2. (A) 2. (B) 4. (B) 5. (C) 6. (A) 7. (A) 8. (C) 9. (C)
10. (A) 11. (B) 12. (C) 13. (C) 14. (B) 15. (B)

I've sorted out all the materials we need and sifted three great ways of marketing.

我已經整理出所需的資料，並篩選出三種很棒的行銷方式。

 職場會話跟著說！ 🎧 Track 050

Max: I've sorted out all the materials we need and sifted three great ways of marketing from our previous records.	邁斯：我已經整理出所需的資料，並從過去的記錄中篩選出三種很棒的行銷方式。
Sam: Oh, that's good. That way, we can learn from our experience and avoid the same mistakes.	山姆：噢，真不錯。如此一來，我們可以從經驗中學習，並且避免犯下同樣的錯誤。
Max: You've got it. We can discuss them carefully over the meeting and choose the best way to promote our key products.	邁斯：你答對了。我們可以好好在會議中討論，並從中挑選出最棒的方式來推銷我們的主要商品。
Sam: Seems you've got it all planned out. Now I can finally stop worrying and get back to work.	山姆：看來你都把事情規劃好了。現在我終於可以安地心回去工作了。
Max: Why were you worried about my work?	邁斯：你幹嘛擔心我的任務啊？
Sam: Because I was worried about your bad cold affecting your job performance. It seems like I was worried for nothing!	山姆：因為我擔心你的重感冒會影響你的工作表現。看來我是白擔心一場了！

文法重點看這裡！

學完前面的會話之後，還要懂會話中的文法重點，才能應用在職場！以下補充重要的文法並做詳盡解析，把文法根基打好，讓你無論是出差還是洽商，都用正確英文和外國人打交道！

文法重點1

I've cleaned out all the materials we need.
是錯誤用法

想表達「清理出／整理出」許多有用的檔案，直接用中文轉換變成I've cleaned out all the materials we need. 會讓對方誤會把文件都「清掉了／丟掉了」！這句只要把clean out 改成sort out，整個意思就對了。正確說法如下：

- **I've sorted out all the materials we need.**
  我已經將所需的資料整理出來／挑了出來。

  如果要說丟掉或清理，可以用「throw away」或「bin」，如果單用「throw」的話，會有把東西「丟向」某處或「砸向」某處的含意。可以看看以下例句：
  - **I didn't throw them away.** 我並沒有把那些東西丟掉。
  - **I didn't bin them.** 我並沒有把那些東西扔了。

文法重點2

How come were you worried about my work?
是錯誤用法

雖然「how come」等於「why」，但句子的結構完全不同。用「how come」起頭的疑問句，動詞和主詞的位置不需對調，例句如下：

- **How come you were worried about me?**
- **= Why were you worried about me?** 你為何擔心我？

文法重點3

stop 的用法

stop有兩種用法，一種是後面的動詞要變成動名詞的形式。另一種用法是stop to V 的形式，以下用例句說明：

- **I stop shopping.** 我不買東西了。
- **I stop to shop.** 我停下手邊正在做的事，跑去買東西。

會話單字懂多少？

讀過前面的內容後，你是不是都懂得這些單字了呢？下列題目中的單字都是與會話及文法相關的單字，測驗看看自己會了多少吧！

( )❶ series： (A) 連續 (B) 系列 (C) 續集

( )❷ project： (A) 專案 (B) 投影機 (C) 桌布

( )❸ clean： (A) 享受 (B) 體驗 (C) 清理

( )❹ throw： (A) 丟拋 (B) 打架 (C) 重量

( )❺ order： (A) 老人 (B) 年長 (C) 次序

( )❻ useful： (A) 無效的 (B) 有用的 (C) 瑕疵的

( )❼ confusion： (A) 困難 (B) 困頓 (C) 困惑

( )❽ seem： (A) 看見 (B) 肯定 (C) 似乎

( )❾ finally： (A) 簡直 (B) 好在 (C) 終於

( )❿ affect： (A) 影像 (B) 結果 (C) 影響

( )⓫ performance： (A) 表現 (B) 體能 (C) 證書

( )⓬ sift： (A) 菜籃 (B) 篩選 (C) 竹筍

( )⓭ record： (A) 帳單 (B) 卡片 (C) 紀錄

( )⓮ carefully： (A) 仔細地 (B) 粗心地 (C) 大略地

( )⓯ considerate： (A) 考慮 (B) 體貼的 (C) 結論

答案：1. (B) 2. (A) 3. (C) 4. (A) 5. (C) 6. (B) 7. (C) 8. (C) 9. (C)
10. (C) 11. (A) 12. (B) 13. (C) 14. (A) 15. (B)

They've promised to support our plan no matter how we would market our items.

他們已經承諾不管我們的行銷方式為何都會贊助我們。

 職場會話跟著說！ Track 051

Dan: I've won over three sponsors for our promotion plan. They've promised to support our plan no matter how we would market our items. I think I've lucked out!

阿丹：我已經說服三位贊助商來贊助我們的行銷計畫。他們已經承諾不管我們的行銷方式為何都會贊助我們。沒想到我這麼走運！

Renee: Oh, I envy you! I'm out of luck. No suppliers so far would like to support our plan.

芮妮：噢，我真羨慕你！我倒楣透了。目前沒有一個廠商願意贊助我們的計畫。

Dan: How come? What's the problem?

阿丹：為什麼？出了什麼問題呢？

Renee: Beats me. Maybe it's because I'm not much of a talker. I tried so hard to chat with them about anything I could think of, but I just couldn't be enthusiastic about gossiping.

芮妮：這你就問倒我了。也許是因為我太不擅言詞了。我很努力試著和他們大聊特聊，但我對東家長西家短這種事就是熱衷不起來。

Dan: I see what you mean. You used to work with papers and documents. You are not so used to dealing with our suppliers. You've still got a lot to learn about how to be a sales representative.

阿丹：我瞭解妳的意思。你過去都是與文書工作為伍，仍然不習慣跟我們的廠商打交道。關於如何做個業務代表，妳要學的還很多。

文法重點看這裡！

學完前面的會話之後，還要懂會話中的文法重點，才能應用在職場！以下補充重要的文法並做詳盡解析，把文法根基打好，讓你無論是出差還是洽商，都用正確英文和外國人打交道！

文法重點1

Your luck is out. 是錯誤用法

以上這句看似正常，其實不是正確的用法。「運氣不好、好運用盡」時，正確的說法如下：

- **Your luck is running out.** 你的運氣快用完了。
- **You are running out of luck.** 你的運氣已經不多了。
- **You are out of luck.** 你運氣不好。

文法重點2

You beat me. 是錯誤用法

這句是很有趣的錯誤用法。英文有一句慣用語叫「Beats me.」，意思是「這你就問倒我了」、「我不知道」的意思。它省略掉了you 所以就變成「Beats me.」了。雖然使用慣用語會令英文感覺更道地，但用錯了可是很糗的，如果不確定該怎麼說，只要老老實實說一句「I don't know.」或「I have no idea.」就可以清楚表達了。

文法重點3

I misunderstanding you. 是錯誤用法

這是一句常見卻很奇怪的錯誤用法，常常聽到周遭不太常用英文的友人這麼說，其實只要說I misunderstood.（我誤會了。）就可以了。

> 另外的說法有：
> - **I got you wrong.** 我誤會你的話了。
> - **I got it all wrong.** 我完全搞錯了。

會話單字懂多少？

讀過前面的內容後，你是不是都懂得這些單字了呢？下列題目中的單字都是與
會話及文法相關的單字，測驗看看自己會了多少吧！

( ) ❶ luck： (A) 運氣 (B) 算命 (C) 天賦

( ) ❷ lucky： (A) 好運的 (B) 倒楣的 (C) 樂天的

( ) ❸ same： (A) 相異 (B) 相同 (C) 相交

( ) ❹ right： (A) 疑問的 (B) 錯的 (C) 對的

( ) ❺ misunderstand： (A) 瞭解 (B) 誤解 (C) 解釋

( ) ❻ far： (A) 近的 (B) 短的 (C) 遠的

( ) ❼ beat： (A) 鼓棒 (B) 打敗 (C) 蜜蜂

( ) ❽ touch： (A) 觸碰 (B) 手套 (C) 飛踢

( ) ❾ envy： (A) 羨慕 (B) 恨意 (C) 熱情

( ) ❿ chat： (A) 沈默 (B) 聊天 (C) 粉筆

( ) ⓫ enthusiastic： (A) 熱衷 (B) 熟悉 (C) 陌生

( ) ⓬ gossip： (A) 團體 (B) 閒聊 (C) 搜尋網站

( ) ⓭ deal： (A) 行為 (B) 態度 (C) 處理

( ) ⓮ representative： (A) 代表 (B) 表現 (C) 愛現

( ) ⓯ worry： (A) 放心 (B) 生氣 (C) 擔憂

答案：1. (A) 2. (A) 3. (B) 4. (C) 5. (B) 6. (C) 7. (B) 8. (A) 9. (A)
10. (B) 11. (A) 12. (B) 13. (C) 14. (A) 15. (C)

We definitely need to choose internet as a means of marketing.

我們一定要選擇網路作為行銷的工具。

職場會話跟著說！ 🎧 Track 052

Michelle: Thanks so much for your hard work. I'm so impressed by your feedback. We got our sponsors now. We have won over several suppliers supporting us and everything. Good job, everyone.

蜜雪：非常謝謝大家辛苦工作，你們的成果非常驚人。我們現在有贊助商了，也說服了幾家廠商資助我們，還有其他等等。大家做得太好了。

Sam: That's part of our job. We're glad we helped.

山姆：那是我們分內的工作。很高興我們幫上了忙。

Michelle: Good. And it's time to discuss how we should promote our key items. There's plenty of information in your handouts. Now speak your minds.

蜜雪：很好。現在該來討論行銷方式了。你們手中的書面資料有豐富的資訊。現在，大家暢所欲言吧。

Max: We definitely need to choose internet as a means of marketing. It's the current trend.

邁斯：我們一定要選擇網路作為行銷的工具。這是目前的趨勢。

Sam: That's right. We can create a promotion page with attractive banners, and so our company website can stay unchanged but we can still attract buyers.

山姆：沒錯。我們可以設計一個活動網頁與吸引人的點擊圖示，這樣我們不用更動公司網頁就可以吸引買家上門。

Michelle: Then the decisions are made. Let's do that.

蜜雪：那就這麼決定了，我們就照辦吧。

文法重點看這裡！

學完前面的會話之後，還要懂會話中的文法重點，才能應用在職場！以下補充重要的文法並做詳盡解析，把文法根基打好，讓你無論是出差還是洽商，都用正確英文和外國人打交道！

文法重點1

There are many information in your handouts. 是錯誤用法

information是不可屬的單數名詞，所以不能與複數動詞或修飾可數名詞的形容詞連用。正確的説法如下：

- **There is plenty of information in your handouts. / There is a lot of information in your handouts.** 你們手中的書面資料有豐富的資訊。

> 不可數名詞是無法計算的，information（資訊）是其中一項，另外還有一些常見的名詞如money、water、knowledge、beauty、love也都是不可數名詞。
> 這些不可數名詞不能與many搭配使用，要使用much，若要詢問數量的話，也要使用「How much」作為問句開頭。

文法重點2

Talk your minds. 是錯誤用法

雖然talk 與speak 都是「說」的意思，但在這裡，暢所欲言、直言不諱的固定說法為：

- **Speak your mind.** 暢所欲言。
- **Speak out your thoughts.** 毫不保留地説出自己的想法。
- **Just speak out.** 請直言不諱。

文法重點3

means 的用法

mean作為動詞是「意思是；意味著」，但加了個s變成「means」後意思就大不同了！means代表「方法；手段」，因此對話中的「We definitely need to choose internet as a means of marketing.」意思就是「我們一定要選擇網路作為行銷的工具。」

會話單字懂多少？

讀過前面的內容後，你是不是都懂得這些單字了呢？下列題目中的單字都是與會話及文法相關的單字，測驗看看自己會了多少吧！

( ) ❶ sponsor： (A) 贊助商 (B) 廠商 (C) 供應商

( ) ❷ part： (A) 分子 (B) 分母 (C) 部分

( ) ❸ key： (A) 主要的 (B) 連鎖的 (C) 開鎖的

( ) ❹ item： (A) 品項 (B) 頁數 (C) 欄位

( ) ❺ stop： (A) 開始 (B) 停止 (C) 煞車

( ) ❻ tease： (A) 透明 (B) 商展 (C) 逗弄

( ) ❼ weird： (A) 女巫 (B) 巫術 (C) 奇怪

( ) ❽ business： (A) 企業家 (B) 正事 (C) 通路

( ) ❾ means： (A) 建議 (B) 建設 (C) 手段

( ) ❿ marketing： (A) 行銷 (B) 市集 (C) 展覽

( ) ⓫ current： (A) 目前的 (B) 事後的 (C) 未來的

( ) ⓬ trend： (A) 手套 (B) 招式 (C) 趨勢

( ) ⓭ plenty： (A) 極少 (B) 適量 (C) 很多

( ) ⓮ banner： (A) 橫幅 (B) 棒子 (C) 打擊

( ) ⓯ website： (A) 站長 (B) 網路 (C) 網站

答案：1. (A) 2. (C) 3. (A) 4. (A) 5. (B) 6. (C) 7. (C) 8. (B) 9. (C)
10. (A) 11. (A) 12. (C) 13. (C) 14. (A) 15. (C)

Renee, did you talk to our suppliers about our promotion details?

芮妮，妳跟廠商談過促銷細節了嗎？

 職場會話跟著說！ 🎧 Track 053

Michelle: Renee, did you talk to our suppliers about our promotion details?

蜜雪：芮妮，妳跟廠商談過促銷細節了嗎？

Renee: Yes I did. I've asked them to insert fliers into the shipments to our customers. That way the customers who never bought our CB series can also receive the information and know about our promotional products.

芮妮：有，談過了。我要求他們把傳單塞進從他們那裡出給我們客戶的貨裡，這樣沒買過我們CB系列的客戶也能知道我們的促銷商品。

Michelle: Do you need someone to help you send messages to the customers by email?

蜜雪：需要找人幫妳用電子郵件傳送訊息給客戶嗎？

Renee: No, thanks. That's my job. I'm on top of that.

芮妮：不用了，謝謝。這部分的任務是由我負責，我正在處理中。

Michelle: Oh, and did you discuss the exhibitions we talked about last night with our channels?

蜜雪：喔，還有，妳跟通路商談過展覽事宜了嗎？就是我們昨晚談論的那件事。

Renee: Of course I did. And they've promised to help us with that.

芮妮：當然談過囉。而且他們答應要協助我們。

Michelle: Wow, I'm impressed, Renee. You've improved a lot as a sales representative.

蜜雪：哇，妳真令我刮目相看耶，芮妮。身為一個業務代表，妳進步好多啊。

Renee: Thanks, Michelle. Dan trained me well!

芮妮：謝了，蜜雪。一切多虧了阿丹的訓練。

Part 7
行銷活動

179

文法重點看這裡！

學完前面的會話之後，還要懂會話中的文法重點，才能應用在職場！以下補充重要的文法並做詳盡解析，把文法根基打好，讓你無論是出差還是洽商，都用正確英文和外國人打交道！

文法重點1
plug 與 insert 的不同

plug是「塞住」的意思，例如把插頭塞進插座裡，整個插座被插頭塞住、堵住了。而insert除了塞住的意思，還有把信放入信封，把書籤夾入書中的那種「夾帶」的感覺，不一定要把空間塞滿。

這裡要把傳單塞進（夾帶進）貨箱裡，如果用plug 就好像把所以縫隙通通用相同傳單塞滿似的，但其實並不是這樣，一個貨箱裡只需要幾張傳單就可以讓客戶接收到訊息了。所以I've asked them to insert fliers into the shipments to our customers. 比較合適。

文法重點2
It's none of your business. 盡量不要使用

這句話的意思為「這不關你的事」，是措辭非常強烈的句子，帶有強烈的負面意味，所以千萬不要隨便使用。

如果想表達不需要工作上幫手，只需要說：No, thanks. It's my job. I'll take care of that. 就可以清楚表達了。

有些慣用語我們常聽到，但如果對在什麼場合使用沒有確實的把握，就請不要使用，只要利用簡單的英文表達自己的想法即可，否則要是不小心說出「None of your business.」這類的話，可能會導致嚴重的後果喔。

文法重點3
train 的用法

train在不同詞性的時候，有不同的用法，如作為名詞使用時，就代表「火車」。作為動詞的時候，就是「訓練；培訓；鍛鍊」的意思。可以參考例句，試著分辨二者的不同：

- **I went to Taipei by train.** 我搭火車去台北。
- **He trained his dog to shake hands.** 他訓練他的狗握手。

會話單字懂多少?

讀過前面的內容後,你是不是都懂得這些單字了呢?下列題目中的單字都是與會話及文法相關的單字,測驗看看自己會了多少吧!

( ) ❶ supplier: (A) 供應商 (B) 器具 (C) 補充

( ) ❷ plug: (A) 塞住 (B) 丟入 (C) 耳機

( ) ❸ flier: (A) 蒼蠅 (B) 傳單 (C) 飛機

( ) ❹ customer: (A) 海關 (B) 恭維 (C) 顧客

( ) ❺ shipment: (A) 運輸 (B) 油輪 (C) 母艦

( ) ❻ insert: (A) 插入 (B) 手術刀 (C) 經典

( ) ❼ strange: (A) 奇怪的 (B) 神奇的 (C) 奇妙的

( ) ❽ send: (A) 寄送 (B) 採購 (C) 政策

( ) ❾ language: (A) 語音 (B) 語言 (C) 歌詞

( ) ❿ wrong: (A) 準確的 (B) 偏差的 (C) 錯誤的

( ) ⓫ offend: (A) 冒犯 (B) 傲慢 (C) 偏見

( ) ⓬ phrase: (A) 措辭 (B) 階段 (C) 字典

( ) ⓭ improve: (A) 善良 (B) 改善 (C) 證明

( ) ⓮ representative: (A) 表情 (B) 代表 (C) 主席

( ) ⓯ train: (A) 柔軟 (B) 體操 (C) 訓練

答案: 1. (A) 2. (A) 3. (B) 4. (C) 5. (A) 6. (A) 7. (A) 8. (A) 9. (B)
10. (C) 11. (A) 12. (A) 13. (B) 14. (B) 15. (C)

What are we gonna do with the prices?

我們要如何決定價格呢？

 職場會話跟著說！ Track 054

Renee: What are we gonna do with the prices? There must be a discount or how can we compete in the marketplace?

芮妮：我們要如何決定價格呢？一定要有折扣才行，不然我們怎麼在市場上競爭呢？

Dan: I got an idea. We can use e-coupons.

阿丹：我想到了，我們可以用電子折價券。

Michelle: Please explain your idea, Dan.

蜜雪：請解說一下，阿丹。

Dan: Here's what I thought: We spread out the news that we got e-coupons on our promotion page. Buyers using e-coupons through the Internet can buy three get one free. Mix & Match is acceptable.

阿丹：我的想法是這樣：我們把消息散播出去，讓大家知道我們活動網頁上有電子折價券。買家利用電子折價券在網上購買，則可以買三送一，可任意搭配各種顏色、尺寸、樣式。

Renee: Ooh, that's a major selling point. I'm willing to buy more if I can Mix & Match things. People might buy them for themselves or as gifts.

芮妮：哦，那是很大的賣點。如果可以混搭購買，我也願意多買一點，因為送禮自用兩相宜。

Dan: But if they buy through our distribution channels, we don't offer "buy three get one free" because the prices are comparatively lower already.

阿丹：但若在我們其他的通路購買則沒有買三送一的優惠，因為通路的價格本已相對便宜了。

Michelle: Fair enough. So we all agree to this plan, right? Then it's finalized.

蜜雪：有道理。大家都同意這個方案了喔？那麼就照這樣定案了。

文法重點看這裡！

學完前面的會話之後，還要懂會話中的文法重點，才能應用在職場！以下補充重要的文法並做詳盡解析，把文法根基打好，讓你無論是出差還是洽商，都用正確英文和外國人打交道！

文法重點1

Clear yourself. 語意錯誤

「clear oneself」是為自己辯駁，洗刷冤情的意思，要表達「解釋清楚」，正確的表達方式應該是：

- **Please explain your idea.** 請解釋你的想法。
- **Please explain yourself.** 請再說清楚一點。

文法重點2

sell point 是錯誤用法

賣點的英文為「selling point」。雖然你說sell point 一般人還是可以意會出來，但還是先把正確的用法學起來比較實在。

- **"Buy one get one free" is a major selling point.**
  「買一送一」是個很大的賣點。
- **We must create a unique selling point.** 我們一定要創造出一個獨特的賣點。

   若要辦促銷活動，可以參考以下用法：
   - **on sale** 特價拍賣
   - **anniversary sale** 周年慶
   - **clearance sale** 清倉大拍賣
   - **flash sale** 限時拍賣

文法重點3

fair enough 的用法

如果依照字面意義將fair enough解讀為「足夠公平」，那可能會在與母語人士溝通時遇到困難喔！fair enough常常用在口語上，意思為「有道理」，通常會使用在「雖然一開始不太認同對方，但在聽了解釋後，可以接受對方的行為或論點」這種情境中。

會話單字懂多少？

讀過前面的內容後，你是不是都懂得這些單字了呢？下列題目中的單字都是與會話及文法相關的單字，測驗看看自己會了多少吧！

( ) ❶ lower： (A) 降低 (B) 蹲下 (C) 窪地

( ) ❷ coupon： (A) 彩券 (B) 折價券 (C) 月票

( ) ❸ clear： (A) 澄清 (B) 半透明 (C) 混濁

( ) ❹ explain： (A) 解釋 (B) 分解 (C) 實驗

( ) ❺ laugh： (A) 輕視 (B) 笑 (C) 感動

( ) ❻ discount： (A) 折損 (B) 索賠 (C) 折扣

( ) ❼ spread： (A) 分贓 (B) 散佈 (C) 眼線

( ) ❽ Internet： (A) 國際 (B) 外部 (C) 網路

( ) ❾ acceptable： (A) 可安插 (B) 可分配 (C) 可接受

( ) ❿ major： (A) 重要的 (B) 輕鬆的 (C) 次要的

( ) ⓫ willing： (A) 有意願的 (B) 勉強的 (C) 脅迫的

( ) ⓬ gift： (A) 任務 (B) 手段 (C) 禮物

( ) ⓭ comparatively： (A) 對比地 (B) 對應地 (C) 爭奪地

( ) ⓮ fair： (A) 刀子 (B) 歧視 (C) 公平

( ) ⓯ finalize： (A) 結束 (B) 開始 (C) 停頓

答案：1. (A) 2. (B) 3. (A) 4. (A) 5. (B) 6. (C) 7. (B) 8. (C) 9. (C)
10. (A) 11. (A) 12. (C) 13. (A) 14. (C) 15. (A)

I'm calling again to discuss the exhibitions with Mr. Martin.

我又打來想跟馬丁先生討論展示會的事。

 職場會話跟著說！ 🎧Track 055

Renee: Hello, this is Renee Chang calling from Alpha Co. Please get me the extension 41.

芮妮：您好，我是艾法公司的張芮妮，請幫我接分機41。

Martin's Secretary: Mr. Martin's office. May I help you?

馬丁的秘書：馬丁先生辦公室，有什麼可以為您效勞的嗎？

Renee: Oh, hi, Miss Wood. This is Renee. How are you? I'm calling again to discuss the exhibitions with Mr. Martin. Is he available?

芮妮：噢，嗨，伍德小姐，我是芮妮，妳好嗎？我又打來想跟馬丁先生討論展示會的事。他有空接電話嗎？

Martin's Secretary: Sorry, Renee. Mr. Martin can't come to the phone. He's all tied up in staff meeting. But he said he would be free tomorrow morning and you two could discuss it over brunch. What do you say?

馬丁的秘書：抱歉，芮妮，馬丁先生沒辦法接電話，他正忙著開幹部會議呢。不過他說他明天上午有空，你們可以一邊吃早午餐一邊討論。妳覺得呢？

Renee: Perfect! Thanks so much for your help. I owe you one. Let's do lunch sometime. My treat.

芮妮：太好了！非常謝謝妳的幫忙，我欠妳一個人情。我們找個時間吃午餐，我請客。

Martin's Secretary: That's great. We'll talk later then.

馬丁的秘書：真棒，那晚點再聊囉。

Renee: OK. Call me!

芮妮：嗯，記得打給我喔！

文法重點看這裡！

學完前面的會話之後，還要懂會話中的文法重點，才能應用在職場！以下補充重要的文法並做詳盡解析，把文法根基打好，讓你無論是出差還是洽商，都用正確英文和外國人打交道！

文法重點1

Hello, I'm Renee Chang. Please turn extension 41 for me. 是錯誤用法

不要笑喔，很多人確實不知道電話英語中不使用「I'm XXX」這種説法！正確説法請參考例句：

* **This is Jenny Wu (calling from ABC Co).** 我是（ABC公司的）吳珍妮。

> 想要「轉」接分機，可不是用turn 這個字喔，外國人可是會聽得一頭霧水的。
> * **Please get me the extension 41.** 請幫我轉接分機41。
> * **Please connect me with extension 18.** 請幫我轉接分機18。
> * **Extension 15, please.** 請接分機15。

文法重點2

I want to find Mr. Martin. Is he able to speak? 是錯誤用法

在電話英語中，找某人聽電話不可以用「find」，正確用法如下：

* **May I speak to Mr. Martin, please?** 我可以和馬丁先生通話嗎？
* **Could I speak to Mr. Martin, please?** 請問可以和馬丁先生通話嗎？
* **Could you put me through to Mr. Martin, please?**
  請幫我轉接馬丁先生好嗎？
* **I'd like to speak to Mr. Martin, please.** 請讓我和馬丁先生談談。

文法重點3

I'm calling to order date time. 是錯誤用法

order 是訂購的意思，date 這個自大多指的是男女之間的約會，若誤用了可是會招來不必要的誤會的。表達「預約會面時間」的用法如下：

* **I'm calling to make an appointment with Mr. Wang.**
  我打來跟王先生約見面的時間。
* **I have an appointment with my dentist.** 我跟牙醫約好看牙齒。

會話單字懂多少？

讀過前面的內容後，你是不是都懂得這些單字了呢？下列題目中的單字都是與會話及文法相關的單字，測驗看看自己會了多少吧！

( )❶ extension： (A) 橡皮筋 (B) 橡膠 (C) 分機

( )❷ dumb： (A) 聾的 (B) 啞的 (C) 盲的

( )❸ purpose： (A) 目的 (B) 格調 (C) 機會

( )❹ order： (A) 階級 (B) 取消 (C) 訂購

( )❺ date： (A) 約會 (B) 失約 (C) 赴約

( )❻ colleague： (A) 同伴 (B) 同事 (C) 同儕

( )❼ office： (A) 倉庫 (B) 辦公室 (C) 會議廳

( )❽ discussion： (A) 討論 (B) 公佈 (C) 執行

( )❾ exhibition： (A) 開發 (B) 銷路 (C) 展覽

( )❿ available： (A) 無效的 (B) 有空的 (C) 免費的

( )⓫ staff： (A) 職員 (B) 核心 (C) 合作

( )⓬ brunch： (A) 午餐 (B) 午晚餐 (C) 早午餐

( )⓭ perfect： (A) 瑕疵的 (B) 一般的 (C) 完美的

( )⓮ owe： (A) 擁抱 (B) 貓頭鷹 (C) 欠債

( )⓯ treat： (A) 步道 (B) 請客 (C) 訓練

答案：1. (C) 2. (B) 3. (A) 4. (C) 5. (A) 6. (B) 7. (B) 8. (A) 9. (C)
10. (B) 11. (A) 12. (C) 13. (C) 14. (C) 15. (B)

Not selling like hot cakes. They are selling like crazy!

何止賣得非常好，簡直是賣翻了！

 職場會話跟著說！ Track 056

Lindsay: How did we do? I heard our CB series are selling like hot cakes.

琳西：目前的銷售如何？我聽說我們的CB系列賣得非常好。

Michelle: Not selling like hot cakes. They are selling like crazy! Look at these sales figures!

蜜雪：何止賣得非常好，簡直是賣翻了！您看看這些銷售數字！

Lindsay: Very good. I'm glad that CB series have taken off so well. Thanks, Michelle.

琳西：太好了。我非常高興我們的CB系列能有這麼好的成績。謝謝妳，蜜雪。

Michelle: It was a group effort. I couldn't have done this without my team.

蜜雪：這是團體的功勞。沒有我的組員我絕對無法做到這樣的成果。

Lindsay: All of you are a great asset to our company. I'm so proud of you all.

琳西：妳們都是公司重要的資產，我為妳們感到驕傲。

Michelle: Thank you, Boss!

蜜雪：謝謝妳，老闆。

Lindsay: By the way, do you think sales will keep going up like this?

琳西：對了，妳覺得銷售會一直像這樣衝高嗎？

Michelle: The quality of our product is superior to others and our prices are very competitive. So it looks promising. But we still need to keep an eye on the market saturation factor.

蜜雪：我們的品質優於別人，價格也非常具有競爭力，所以後勢依然看俏，但仍須密切注意市場需求是否飽和。

文法重點看這裡！

學完前面的會話之後，還要懂會話中的文法重點，才能應用在職場！以下補充重要的文法並做詳盡解析，把文法根基打好，讓你無論是出差還是洽商，都用正確英文和外國人打交道！

文法重點1
They are selling like maniac! 不是常見用法

這句話應該是「狂賣」的直譯。雖然這個句子的文法不能說有錯，但語言這種東西，其實就是一種習慣，有其慣用的方式。外國人講「狂賣」時，一般會說「sell like crazy」而不會用「maniac」這個字，雖然都有瘋狂的意思，還是不要太顛覆一般的說法比較好喔。

表達「暢銷」的用語有：
- **The CD is selling like hot cakes.** 這張CD銷路非常好。
- **The book is selling like crazy.** 這本書賣翻了。
- **These jeans are selling so well.** 這些牛仔褲真的很暢銷。

文法重點2
I can't do this without my team. 不是適當用法

單就這句來看，文法沒有錯誤。但如果放在文中，應該以過去式或過去完成式來表達比較貼切，因為「事情是發生在過去」。因此改成I couldn't have done this without my team. 比較適切。

文法重點3
大幅飆升可以這樣說

在英文中，如果要說銷售成績或價格大幅飆升，可以考慮使用skyrocket或是soar，兩者都有竄上高空的含意在。使用方式如下：

- **Sales will keep skyrocket like this.** 銷售會持續大幅攀升。
- **The price of flour keeps soaring.** 麵粉的價格不斷飆升。

會話單字懂多少？

讀過前面的內容後，你是不是都懂得這些單字了呢？下列題目中的單字都是與會話及文法相關的單字，測驗看看自己會了多少吧！

( ) ❶ maniac： (A) 發餉的 (B) 發狂的 (C) 發願的

( ) ❷ crazy： (A) 瘋狂的 (B) 平靜的 (C) 顫抖的

( ) ❸ group： (A) 團體 (B) 筷子 (C) 容器

( ) ❹ skyscraper： (A) 公寓 (B) 平房 (C) 摩天樓

( ) ❺ skyrocket： (A) 火箭 (B) 猛漲 (C) 火災

( ) ❻ joke： (A) 名言 (B) 笑話 (C) 短文

( ) ❼ funny： (A) 好吃 (B) 好看 (C) 有趣

( ) ❽ crack： (A) 背誦 (B) 聽寫 (C) 裂開

( ) ❾ asset： (A) 階級 (B) 資產 (C) 帳目

( ) ❿ proud： (A) 驕傲的 (B) 同情的 (C) 敬佩的

( ) ⓫ superior： (A) 劣於 (B) 標準 (C) 優於

( ) ⓬ price： (A) 標籤 (B) 價格 (C) 報表

( ) ⓭ promising： (A) 有希望的 (B) 無希望的 (C) 承諾

( ) ⓮ saturation： (A) 飢餓 (B)飽和 (C) 升級

( ) ⓯ factor： (A) 工廠 (B) 卡車 (C) 因素

答案：1. (B) 2. (A) 3. (A) 4. (C) 5. (B) 6. (B) 7. (C) 8. (C) 9. (B)
10. (A) 11. (C) 12. (B) 13. (A) 14. (B) 15. (C)

Dan, did you inform APR Co. that we are having a promotion for CB series?

阿丹，你有通知APR公司我們現在CB系列有優惠的訊息嗎？

職場會話跟著說！　　Track **057**

Michelle: Dan, did you inform APR Co. that we are having a promotion for CB series?

蜜雪：阿丹，你有通知APR公司我們現在CB系列有優惠的訊息嗎？

Dan: Not yet, but I'm working on it right now. I'm organizing a complete price list with pictures so that they can get all the information and specifications at a time.

阿丹：還沒，但我正在處理當中。我正在弄一張完整的價目表並附上圖片，這樣他們一次就可以收到所有的資訊及產品規格。

Michelle: OK, that is a good thought. But please finish it ASAP. Time is ticking away.

蜜雪：好，這個想法很好，但是你要盡快完成。時間一分一秒地過去了喔。

Dan: Sure, I'll finish the list and send it to APR Co. by today.

阿丹：我今天以前會完成價格表並寄給APR公司。

Michelle: Good. Keep me posted.

蜜雪：很好，讓我知道最新狀況。

Dan: Noted. I'll let you know if I have any information.

阿丹：知道了。有什麼事我一定會讓妳知道。

Michelle: Oh, by the way, do let them know that we quote them the best price.

蜜雪：喔，對了，一定要讓他們知道我們報給他們的價格是最好的價格。

Dan: That's for certain. I'll take care of that. You can count on me.

阿丹：那是一定要的。我會處理好的，妳儘管放心。

文法重點看這裡！

學完前面的會話之後，還要懂會話中的文法重點，才能應用在職場！以下補充重要的文法並做詳盡解析，把文法根基打好，讓你無論是出差還是洽商，都用正確英文和外國人打交道！

文法重點1
Price list is a good think. 是錯誤用法

這裡的think 是動詞，不能接在冠詞及形容詞後面，應該要改成名詞thought，故正確的說法為：My price list is a good thought.

> thought 這個字延伸出了一些實用的字彙，列舉如下：
> thought-provoking 引人深思的，發人深省的
> ● **This is a thought-provoking movie.** 這是一部發人深省的電影
> thoughtful 考慮周到的，體貼的
> ● **My brother is always thoughtful of me.** 我弟弟一直對我很體貼。

文法重點2
Time fly. 是錯誤用法

中文的「時光飛逝」，英文也是用「time」+「fly」，但是請留意動詞的變化，字尾必須去y 加ies，變成第三人稱單數的動詞，因為時間是不可數的單數名詞。
正確的寫法為：
● **Time flies.** 時光飛逝。

文法重點3
Keep me posted 的用法

如果聽到上司說「Keep me posted」，可不是叫你把他貼在討論區什麼之類的，也不要想到郵局寄信或郵票之類的。「post」是「使熟悉、使瞭解」的意思，故「Keep me posted」就是讓我知道、讓我熟悉，即「隨時通知我最新狀況」的意思。

會話單字懂多少？

讀過前面的內容後,你是不是都懂得這些單字了呢?下列題目中的單字都是與會話及文法相關的單字,測驗看看自己會了多少吧!

( ) ❶ inform: (A) 通知 (B) 擁護 (C) 採購

( ) ❷ organize: (A) 機會 (B) 組織 (C) 機構

( ) ❸ complete: (A) 一半的 (B) 殘缺的 (C) 完整的

( ) ❹ picture: (A) 照片 (B) 油畫 (C) 水彩畫

( ) ❺ use: (A) 使勁 (B) 用途 (C) 因素

( ) ❻ useless: (A) 沒勁 (B) 沒用 (C) 沒條理

( ) ❼ wonder: (A) 驚悚 (B) 驚奇 (C) 驚喜

( ) ❽ fly: (A) 飛機 (B) 飛行 (C) 傳單

( ) ❾ count: (A) 計算 (B) 折價券 (C) 除法

( ) ❿ specification: (A) 規矩 (B) 規定 (C) 規格

( ) ⓫ tick: (A) 滴答聲 (B) 轟隆聲 (C) 風聲

( ) ⓬ post: (A) 使瞭解 (B) 使走運 (C) 使勤奮

( ) ⓭ quote: (A) 扣款 (B) 報價 (C) 記誦

( ) ⓮ certain: (A) 無疑的 (B) 無害的 (C) 無菌的

( ) ⓯ care: (A) 照料 (B) 粗心 (C) 良心

答案:1. (A) 2. (B) 3. (C) 4. (A) 5. (B) 6. (B) 7. (B) 8. (B) 9. (A)
10. (C) 11. (A) 12. (A) 13. (B) 14. (A) 15. (A)

Part

7

行銷活動

Part 8

報價與協調

She wants us to provide pricing and samples for their approval ASAP.

她要我們盡快提供報價和樣品讓她們審核。

 職場會話跟著說！  Track 058

Lindsay: Kate just called and left a message. She wanted to know whether we received her e-mail.

琳西：凱特剛才打電話過來並且留了言。她想知道我們有沒有收到她寄的電子郵件。

Michelle: I just received her e-mail ten minutes ago. Due to their current factory discontinuing item GSL, she wants to know whether we have a source that can produce this item.

蜜雪：我是在十分鐘前收到她的電子郵件。由於她們的工廠目前已停產GSL，她想知道我們有沒有廠商可以生產這個產品。

Lindsay: We do have a source who can produce this item, don't we?

琳西：我們的確有可以生產這個產品的廠商，不是嗎？

Michelle: Right. She wants us to provide pricing and samples for their approval ASAP.

蜜雪：沒錯。她要我們盡快提供報價和樣品讓她們審核。

Lindsay: Does she mention what size and color she requires?

琳西：她有提到她要什麼尺寸和顏色嗎？

Michelle: Yes. She requires size "10" x "12" x "1" inches in blue, red and brown.

蜜雪：有。她要「10」x「12」x「1」的尺寸和藍、紅、棕三色。

Lindsay: Send her our pricing today and tell her we can send samples no later than this Friday.

琳西：今天就寄報價給她，告訴她我們禮拜五前會寄出樣品。

Michelle: Got it. I'll do it right away.

蜜雪：知道了，我馬上去辦。

文法重點看這裡！

學完前面的會話之後，還要懂會話中的文法重點，才能應用在職場！以下補充重要的文法並做詳盡解析，把文法根基打好，讓你無論是出差還是洽商，都用正確英文和外國人打交道！

文法重點1

Due to their current factory discontinue item GSL... 是錯誤用法

因為英文不是我們的母語，所以在使用上常會忘了文法的動詞變化。這句的正確說法有兩種：「Due to their current factory discontinuing item GSL...」或者「Due to the fact that their current factory discontinued item GSL...」。其實瞭解文法最好的方法就是依照例句造出自己的句子，這樣不但印象深刻好記誦，更可以活用於日常生活中。例如：

● **Due to the fact that my cat becomes ill, I have to take a day off to take care of her.**

  = Due to my cat becoming ill, I have to take a day off to take care of her.
  因為我家的貓咪生病了，我必須請假一天照顧牠。

文法重點2

for their approve 是錯誤用法

這又是另一個詞類變化的問題。在這裡approve 這個動詞要改成名詞，變成approval 才是正確的。所以正確的說法是「for their approval」（供他們審核）。

- for your approval（動詞：approve）
- for your reference（動詞：refer）
- for your information（動詞：inform）

文法重點3

right away和right now 的用法

right away意思是「立刻；馬上」，而right now則是指「現在」。後者有強調當下時空的意涵在，前者在強調「馬上去做」時，與right now通用，但若沒有強調當下發生的話，則不能通用。例如：

● **When you see Tom tomorrow, tell him to call me right away.**
  你明天看到湯姆時，告訴他立刻打電話給我。

會話單字懂多少？

讀過前面的內容後，你是不是都懂得這些單字了呢？下列題目中的單字都是與會話及文法相關的單字，測驗看看自己會了多少吧！

( ) ❶ whether： (A) 絕對 (B) 幾乎不 (C) 是否

( ) ❷ ago： (A) 在～之前 (B) 在～之下 (C) 在～之後

( ) ❸ factory： (A) 因素 (B) 工廠 (C) 工作坊

( ) ❹ discontinue： (A) 量產 (B) 生產 (C) 停產

( ) ❺ sauce： (A) 來源 (B) 醬料 (C) 石油

( ) ❻ source： (A) 來源 (B) 醬料 (C) 石油

( ) ❼ professional： (A) 業餘的 (B) 兼差的 (C) 專業的

( ) ❽ confuse： (A) 釐清 (B) 搞混 (C) 懷疑

( ) ❾ pricing： (A) 報價 (B) 王子 (C) 公主

( ) ❿ approve： (A) 核准 (B) 推進 (C) 證明

( ) ⓫ ASAP： (A) 慢慢來 (B) 盡快 (C) 隨意

( ) ⓬ require： (A) 需要 (B) 應該 (C) 可能

( ) ⓭ approval： (A) 核准 (B) 拒絕 (C) 異議

( ) ⓮ mention： (A) 嗅覺 (B) 提到 (C) 講座

( ) ⓯ later： (A) 較晚地 (B) 較近的 (C) 較早地

答案：1. (C) 2. (A) 3. (B) 4. (C) 5. (B) 6. (A) 7. (C) 8. (B) 9. (A)
　　　10. (A) 11. (B) 12. (A) 13. (A) 14. (B) 15. (A)

She thinks both our pricing and minimum order quantity are too high.

她說我們報的價格和最低訂購量都太高了。

職場會話跟著說！ 🎧Track 059

Lindsay: Did you receive any feedback from Kate about pricing and samples we sent last week?

琳西：關於我們上星期給的報價和樣品，妳有收到凱特的回應嗎？

Michelle: Yes, we just talked on the phone. She has received our samples and she thinks they look good. But...

蜜雪：有，我們剛才通過電話了。她已經收到我們寄的樣品，樣品看起來很不錯，但是……

Lindsay: But what? What's her concern?

琳西：但是什麼？她的顧慮是什麼？

Michelle: She thinks both our pricing and minimum order quantity are too high. She needs to know if we can requote the price.

蜜雪：她說我們報的價格和最低訂購量都太高了。她想確認我們是不是可以重新報價。

Lindsay: If we could requote the price, could she accept the current MOQ?

琳西：如果我們可以重新報價，她能接受目前的最低訂購量嗎？

Michelle: She didn't confirm, but she said she would try her best to convince her boss.

蜜雪：她尚未確認，但她說她會盡力說服她的老闆。

Lindsay: OK, fair enough. Tell her we'll send out the revised pricing by today.

琳西：好，很合理。告訴她我們今天就會傳新的報價過去。

Michelle: Got it. And I'll update you as soon as I have any news.

蜜雪：知道了。一旦有任何最新消息，我會向妳報告。

Part

8

報價與協調

199

文法重點看這裡！

學完前面的會話之後，還要懂會話中的文法重點，才能應用在職場！以下補充重要的文法並做詳盡解析，把文法根基打好，讓你無論是出差還是洽商，都用正確英文和外國人打交道！

We just called on the phone. 是錯誤用法

這句英文很明顯是從中文直翻過去。既然已經on the phone（透過電話、在電話上）了，就不必再用call（打電話），直接說「We just talked on the phone.」即可。

> 以下是跟電話有關的片語：
> - **answer the phone** 接電話
> - **hang up the phone** 掛斷電話
> - **pick up the phone** 接起電話

文法重點2
mini order quantity 還是 minimum order quantity?

mini 是「袖珍的、迷你的」的意思，跟minimum「最小的、最低的」意思完全不同，mini 並不是minimum 的縮寫或簡稱。正確的說法是「minimum order quantity」（最低訂購量）。如果平常懶得講這麼長，可以直接說MOQ 就好了。

文法重點3
conform 和confirm 大不同

這兩個字不僅長得很像，發音也有點類似。「conform」是「遵照、遵從」；「confirm」是「確認、核准」。請用以下例句熟悉這兩個字的用法：

- **Please confirm the purchase order so we can proceed with production.**
  請確認這份訂單，然後我們才能進行生產。
- **If you don't conform to our sales contract, we will end our business relationship with you.**
  如果你不遵照合約上的規定，我們將終止與你們生意上的往來。

會話單字懂多少？

讀過前面的內容後，你是不是都懂得這些單字了呢？下列題目中的單字都是與會話及文法相關的單字，測驗看看自己會了多少吧！

( )❶ reply： (A) 復原 (B) 答覆 (C) 快轉

( )❷ concern： (A) 演唱會 (B) 關心 (C) 水泥

( )❸ mini： (A) 麥克風 (B) 袖珍的 (C) 侏儒

( )❹ quantity： (A) 品質 (B) 數量 (C) 品管

( )❺ requote： (A) 重生 (B) 重新規劃 (C) 重新報價

( )❻ MOQ： (A) 最低訂購量 (B) 最長銷售期 (C) 最高報酬

( )❼ conform： (A) 尊敬 (B) 遵照 (C) 崇拜

( )❽ confirm： (A) 忽略 (B) 駁回 (C) 確認

( )❾ feedback： (A) 回應 (B) 反芻 (C) 吃飽

( )❿ minimum： (A) 最小的 (B) 極限的 (C) 迷你裙

( )⓫ accept： (A) 除外 (B) 接近 (C) 接受

( )⓬ convince： (A) 挑釁 (B) 說服 (C) 證實

( )⓭ enough： (A) 不足 (B) 充滿 (C) 足夠

( )⓮ revise： (A) 修改 (B) 詩歌 (C) 散文

( )⓯ update： (A) 更新 (B) 修正 (C) 改變

答案：1. (B) 2. (B) 3. (B) 4. (B) 5. (C) 6. (A) 7. (B) 8. (C) 9. (A)
10. (A) 11. (C) 12. (B) 13. (C) 14. (A) 15. (A)

However, our supplier insists on increasing MOQ to 1000 dozen.

但是，我們的廠商堅持一定要將最低訂購量調到1000打。

職場會話跟著說！ 🎧 Track 060

Max: Nice to see you, Ms. Reiner. I'm here to talk to you about your new purchase order.

邁斯：很高興見到妳，萊諾小姐。我來是要跟妳談談妳最近下的新訂單。

Ms. Reiner: Nice to see you, too, Max. What seems to be the problem?

萊諾小姐：你好，邁斯。發生什麼問題嗎？

Max: As you know, there is a global shortage of plastic raw martial. We have tried our best to offer the best price for you. However, our supplier insists on increasing MOQ to 1000 dozen or they will have problem processing your order.

邁斯：如妳所知道的，全球塑膠原料嚴重短缺，我們已盡我們所能幫貴公司維持住最好的價格，但是，我們的廠商堅持一定要將最低訂購量調到1000打，不然他們很可能無法接妳們的單子。

Ms. Reiner: 1000 dozen? That's a large order. I don't think we can accept this.

萊諾小姐：1000打？這訂單太大了，我想我們無法接受。

Max: Please understand that we offer you the very best price. And, we are willing to separate the whole batch into three shipments to benefit your company.

邁斯：請瞭解我們給妳的是最低的價格。而且，我們願意分三批出貨以利貴公司。

文法重點看這裡！

學完前面的會話之後，還要懂會話中的文法重點，才能應用在職場！以下補充重要的文法並做詳盡解析，把文法根基打好，讓你無論是出差還是洽商，都用正確英文和外國人打交道！

文法重點1
globe shortage of~ 是錯誤用法

這句錯在直接從中文的「全球～短缺」翻過去，卻忘了詞性必須變化。這句的globe「球體」必須改成形容詞global「全球的」才對。所以正確的說法是「a global shortage of ~」，例如：

- **There is a global shortage of food.** 全球食物短缺。
- **There is a global shortage of petroleum.** 全球石油短缺。

文法重點2
Our supplier insists to increase MOQ to 1000 dozen. 是錯誤用法

這句是文法上的錯誤。要特別留意insist的特別用法，在insist 後面接介系詞on再加V-ing。例如：

- **I insist on having lunch with you.** 我一定要跟你吃午餐。

文法重點3
We are willing to cut the merchandise into three parts. 語意錯誤

其實這句文法沒錯，但這樣說會讓對方誤會你要把一個商品切成三等分，因此有時候不能直接這樣中翻英。若要比表達「願意把貨分成三批出貨」，你可以這樣說：

- **We are willing to separate the goods into three shipments.**
  我們願意將貨物分成三批出貨。
- **We are willing to split the goods in three shipments.**
  我們願意將貨物分成三批出貨。

會話單字懂多少？

讀過前面的內容後，你是不是都懂得這些單字了呢？下列題目中的單字都是與會話及文法相關的單字，測驗看看自己會了多少吧！

( ) ❶ purchase： (A) 採購 (B) 屋況 (C) 單據

( ) ❷ globe： (A) 球狀物 (B) 正方形 (C) 橢圓形

( ) ❸ shortage： (A) 矮小 (B) 短缺 (C) 超過

( ) ❹ plastic： (A) 價格 (B) 油料 (C) 塑膠

( ) ❺ raw： (A) 一排 (B) 生的 (C) 乾的

( ) ❻ insist： (A) 插入 (B) 無知 (C) 堅持

( ) ❼ dozen： (A) 鼓棒 (B) 半箱 (C) 一打

( ) ❽ process： (A) 處理 (B) 進步 (C) 熱情

( ) ❾ merchandise： (A) 商業 (B) 商品 (C) 商機

( ) ❿ separately： (A) 分開地 (B) 結合地 (C) 一體地

( ) ⓫ damage： (A) 保存 (B) 熟悉 (C) 損壞

( ) ⓬ split： (A) 團體 (B) 團結 (C) 劃分

( ) ⓭ express： (A) 表現 (B) 表達 (C) 表裡

( ) ⓮ proposal： (A) 訂婚 (B) 目的 (C) 提議

( ) ⓯ batch： (A) 海灘 (B) 一批 (C) 一支

答案：1. (A) 2. (A) 3. (B) 4. (C) 5. (B) 6. (C) 7. (C) 8. (A) 9. (B)
10. (A) 11. (C) 12. (C) 13. (B) 14. (C) 15. (B)

Will we make any money on this order if we agree to her price?

如果我們接受她的價格，我們還有利潤嗎？

職場會話跟著說！ Track 061

Max: Ms. Reiner said she will accept 1000 dozen on the condition that we lower the price to $15.00 per dozen.

邁斯：萊諾小姐說如果我們把價格降至每打15美元，她就接受我們新的最低訂購量。

Michelle: She's driving a hard bargain. How much per dozen now?

蜜雪：她還真會殺價。目前一打的價格是多少？

Max: The current price is $18.00 per dozen.

邁斯：目前是一打18美元。

Michelle: Will we make any money on this order if we agree to her price?

蜜雪：如果我們接受她的價格，我們還有利潤嗎？

Max: Definitely. Not a large profit, though.

邁斯：絕對有的，只是不多而已。

Michelle: What do you think we should do?

蜜雪：你覺得我們應該怎麼做呢？

Max: I think we should make it $15.00. After all, she is one of our best customers and she's been loyal to us all these years.

邁斯：我覺得我們應該降到15美元。畢竟她是我們最好的客戶之一，長久以來也很忠於我們公司。

Michelle: OK. Make it to $15.00. The price is for Ms. Reiner only. Go fill her in on the good news.

蜜雪：好吧，降到15美元吧。這個價格只適用於萊諾小姐的訂單。去告訴她這個好消息吧。

文法重點看這裡！

學完前面的會話之後，還要懂會話中的文法重點，才能應用在職場！以下補充重要的文法並做詳盡解析，把文法根基打好，讓你無論是出差還是洽商，都用正確英文和外國人打交道！

文法重點1
She's riding a hard bargain. 是錯誤用法

這個慣用語正確的說法應為「drive a hard bargain」，即「很會殺價、價錢殺得很低」的意思。當學習一個新用語時，一定要先瞭解其意義，不要囫圇吞棗，心想反正「ride」跟「drive」都差不多嘛！這樣不行喔！

> 其他有關「如何殺價」的句子如下：
> - **Can I get this cheaper? / Can you make it cheaper?**
>   可以算我便宜一點嗎？
> - **What if I buy two?** 如果我一次帶兩件呢？
> - **Can you give me a discount?** 可以給幫我打折嗎？

文法重點2
Go fill her in the good news. 是錯誤用法

「fill sb. in」是慣用語，亦為「告訴某人」，也等於「tell sb.」的意思。但如果後面要加上要告知的「資訊、內容」時，一定不要忘記在前面加上介系詞「on」，即「fill sb. in on sth.」。所以，這句要改成：Go fill her in on the good news.（去告訴她這個好消息吧。）

> 要通知別人好消息時，有以下幾種開頭可以參考：
> - **We are delighted to tell you that...** 我們很高興能告訴您……
> - **We are pleased to learn that...** 我們很高興得知……
> - **We agree with you on...** 我們同意您……

會話單字懂多少？

讀過前面的內容後，你是不是都懂得這些單字了呢？下列題目中的單字都是與會話及文法相關的單字，測驗看看自己會了多少吧！

( ) ❶ condition： (A) 調整 (B) 條件 (C) 地點

( ) ❷ lower： (A) 降低 (B) 趴下 (C) 平躺下

( ) ❸ dozen： (A) 兩打 (B) 十二個 (C) 二十四個

( ) ❹ believe： (A) 疑惑 (B) 首肯 (C) 相信

( ) ❺ phrase： (A) 措辭 (B) 階段 (C) 讚美

( ) ❻ mistake： (A) 正確 (B) 錯誤 (C) 改善

( ) ❼ agree： (A) 同儕 (B) 同意 (C) 同事

( ) ❽ definitely： (A) 當然地 (B) 當然不 (C) 幾乎不

( ) ❾ large： (A) 瘦的 (B) 長的 (C) 大的

( ) ❿ profit： (A) 資本 (B) 通路 (C) 利潤

( ) ⓫ customer： (A) 客戶 (B) 商人 (C) 雇主

( ) ⓬ loyal： (A) 熱衷的 (B) 忠誠的 (C) 美味的

( ) ⓭ news： (A) 消息 (B) 通告 (C) 報紙

( ) ⓮ current： (A) 目前的 (B) 事後的 (C) 未來的

( ) ⓯ price： (A) 標誌 (B) 市場 (C) 價格

答案：1. (B) 2. (A) 3. (B) 4. (C) 5. (A) 6. (B) 7. (B) 8. (A) 9. (C)
10. (C) 11. (A) 12. (B) 13. (A) 14. (A) 15. (C)

After negotiating with our supplier, we now can offer you $15.00 per dozen.

在跟廠商協商之後，現在我們可以提供妳一打15美元的價格。

職場會話跟著說！ 🎧 Track 062

Max: Hello. This is Max Huang from Alpha Co. May I speak to Ms. Reiner, please?	邁斯：您好，我是艾法公司的黃邁斯。麻煩請萊諾小姐聽電話。
Receptionist: Please hold. I'll put you through.	接待員：請稍後，我幫您轉接。
Ms. Reiner: This is Reiner speaking.	萊諾小姐：我是萊諾。
Max: Good afternoon, Ms. Reiner. I'm calling to tell you the good news.	邁斯：午安，萊諾小姐。我打來告訴妳一個好消息。
Ms. Reiner: Oh, is this regarding the price?	萊諾小姐：噢，是有關價格的事嗎？
Max: You're right. After negotiating with our supplier, we now can offer you $15.00 per dozen.	邁斯：妳說對了。在跟廠商協商之後，現在我們可以提供妳一打15美元的價格。
Ms. Reiner: That's perfectly wonderful! Thanks for trying so hard. Please increase the quantity to meet the requested MOQ, which I believe is 1000 dozen.	萊諾小姐：這實在太棒了！謝謝你努力幫我們降價。請把我的訂單數量增加到你們要求的最低數量，是1000打沒錯吧。
Max: I'll get on it immediately. Thank you for your long-standing support.	邁斯：我馬上就去處理。也謝謝妳對我們長期的支持。

文法重點看這裡！

學完前面的會話之後，還要懂會話中的文法重點，才能應用在職場！以下補充重要的文法並做詳盡解析，把文法根基打好，讓你無論是出差還是洽商，都用正確英文和外國人打交道！

文法重點1
You can say that again. 要注意使用時機

是一句很常用的俚語，其延伸的意思為「妳說對了。」但是，對客戶或沒那麼熟的人，還是少用俚語為妙，免得節外生枝，引起不愉快。

> 另外的類似用語：
> • **You said it.** 沒錯，妳說對了。
> • **You've got it.** 你答對了。

文法重點2
Oh, after negotiate with our supplier, ~
是錯誤用法

注意介系詞「after」後面的動詞要變成「V-ing」（動名詞），所以這句要改成：「After negotiating with our supplier, ~」（在跟廠商協商之後～）。使用英文時，要記得留意介系詞後面的動詞變化。

文法重點3
meet 的用法

meet不只有「見面」的意思，也有「滿足、達到、完成」的意思，例如：

• **The house doesn't meet our need.**
  這棟房子沒有滿足我們的要求。

• **Can you meet the target before the deadline?**
  你能在期限到來前完成目標嗎？

會話單字懂多少？

讀過前面的內容後，你是不是都懂得這些單字了呢？下列題目中的單字都是與會話及文法相關的單字，測驗看看自己會了多少吧！

( ) ❶ regarding： (A) 尊敬 (B) 關於 (C) 補充

( ) ❷ again： (A) 一次 (B) 兩次 (C) 再一次

( ) ❸ ask： (A) 詢問 (B) 辯論 (C) 同意

( ) ❹ twice： (A) 兩次 (B) 再一次 (C) 一次

( ) ❺ actually： (A) 其實 (B) 一般 (C) 幾乎

( ) ❻ polite： (A) 放肆的 (B) 禮貌的 (C) 野蠻的

( ) ❼ slang： (A) 標幟 (B) 俚語 (C) 成語

( ) ❽ German： (A) 瑞士人 (B) 挪威人 (C) 德國人

( ) ❾ apology： (A) 道歉 (B) 謊言 (C) 實話

( ) ❿ perfectly： (A) 完美地 (B) 瑕疵地 (C) 塗鴉地

( ) ⓫ try： (A) 嘗試 (B) 用力 (C) 實驗

( ) ⓬ meet： (A) 達到 (B) 果糖 (C) 糖漿

( ) ⓭ requested： (A) 要求的 (B) 入門的 (C) 進階的

( ) ⓮ immediately： (A) 拖延地 (B) 立刻地 (C) 隔天地

( ) ⓯ long-standing： (A) 長年的 (B) 久站的 (C) 藕斷絲連的

答案：1. (B) 2. (C) 3. (A) 4. (A) 5. (A) 6. (B) 7. (B) 8. (C) 9. (A)
10. (A) 11. (A) 12. (A) 13. (A) 14. (B) 15. (A)

I'd like to know what would be your production lead time for a new order of 10K forks.

我想知道10萬支叉子從下單到出貨要多少時間。

 職場會話跟著說！　🎧Track 063

Mr. Moore: Hello. This is Bob Moore from RMC Co. I'd like to speak to Mr. Sam Lin, please.	摩爾先生：你好。我是RMC公司的鮑伯摩爾，我想請林山姆先生聽電話。
Sam: Speaking. Hi, Mr. Moore. How may I help you today?	山姆：我就是。你好，摩爾先生，今天有什麼可以為你效勞的？
Mr. Moore: Hello, Sam. I'd like to know what would be your production lead time for a new order of 10K forks.	摩爾先生：你好，山姆。我想知道10萬支叉子從下單到出貨要多少時間。
Sam: We can prepare 10K forks for you in 2 weeks.	山姆：我們兩個星期就可以幫您出10萬支叉子的貨。
Mr. Moore: Could you please check if you can ship earlier? This is top urgent. This order is for one of our customers.	摩爾先生：可以麻煩你查查看能否更早出貨？這張訂單非常急，貨是我們的一個客戶要的。
Sam: Let me check the production schedule... I believe we can ship the goods by air freight in 10 days if we work overtime three days in a row.	山姆：讓我查一下生產排程……我想我們如果一連加三天的班，就可以在十天內空運出貨。
Mr. Moore: That would be great! I will be sending you a new purchase order in no time.	摩爾先生：那太好了！我會立刻寄新訂單過來給你。
Sam: Thank you. We will proceed with your order as soon as we receive it.	山姆：謝謝你。一收到你的訂單我們就會馬上處理。

文法重點看這裡！

學完前面的會話之後，還要懂會話中的文法重點，才能應用在職場！以下補充重要的文法並做詳盡解析，把文法根基打好，讓你無論是出差還是洽商，都用正確英文和外國人打交道！

文法重點1
I am Sam Lin. 注意使用時機

一般在電話中，我們介紹自己時不講「I am +人名」，而是説「This is +人名」。而在文中這個情況，如果接電話的人剛好是對方要找的人，就可以直接説：This is 人名.（我就是。）或者直接説「Speaking.」（我就是。）就可以了。

文法重點2
freight 與 fright 的混用

又是一對超像的雙胞胎單字！所以使用上要特別小心。「fright」是「恐怖、可怕」的意思；「freight」有「貨物、貨運或運費」的意思。兩者的用法如下：

- **Martha gave me a fright by bursting out screaming!**
  瑪莎忽然尖叫起來，把我嚇壞了！
- **Take off your witch costumes! You look a fright.**
  脱掉那身巫婆裝扮！妳看起來很可笑耶。
- **Please ship the goods by air freight.** 貨物請用空運運送。
- **We will take care of the air freight.** 空運費我們會負責。

文法重點3
in a row 的用法

in a row是固定的説法，為「連續」的意思。如果不清楚慣用語，直接説「...if we work overtime for three days.」就好了，簡單明瞭。

> row本身有「一排；一行；一列」的意思，如：
> - **a row of houses** 一排房子
> - **a row of seats** 一排座位
> - **a row of people** 一列人

會話單字懂多少？

讀過前面的內容後，你是不是都懂得這些單字了呢？下列題目中的單字都是與會話及文法相關的單字，測驗看看自己會了多少吧！

( ) ❶ fork： (A) 叉子 (B) 刀子 (C) 湯匙

( ) ❷ prepare： (A) 預習 (B) 準備 (C) 複習

( ) ❸ check： (A) 查看 (B) 骨折 (C) 事前

( ) ❹ ship： (A) 運送 (B) 娛樂 (C) 驗證

( ) ❺ top： (A) 等級 (B) 最重要的 (C) 分類

( ) ❻ urgent： (A) 隨遇而安 (B) 輕緩的 (C) 急迫的

( ) ❼ schedule： (A) 彩券 (B) 機票 (C) 日程

( ) ❽ fright： (A) 恐怖 (B) 輕鬆 (C) 歡笑

( ) ❾ overtime： (A) 超時地 (B) 超強的 (C) 過份的

( ) ❿ line： (A) 一包 (B) 一欄 (C) 一行

( ) ⓫ row： (A) 一排 (B) 一箱 (C) 一噸

( ) ⓬ proceed： (A) 激進 (B) 進步 (C) 進行

( ) ⓭ soon： (A) 慢地 (B) 快地 (C) 不疾不徐地

( ) ⓮ receive： (A) 話筒 (B) 耳機 (C) 收到

( ) ⓯ freight： (A) 貨運 (B) 塔臺 (C) 母船

答案：1. (A) 2. (B) 3. (A) 4. (A) 5. (B) 6. (C) 7. (C) 8. (A) 9. (A)
　　　10. (C) 11. (A) 12. (C) 13. (B) 14. (C) 15. (A)

We will send the signed contract over and proceed with your order in no time.

我們馬上會簽好合約寄過去，然後立刻處理您的訂單。

 職場會話跟著說！ Track 064

Mr. Moore: Hi, Sam. Did you receive my purchase order? I sent it by fax a minute ago.

摩爾先生：嗨，山姆。妳有收到我的訂單嗎？我剛剛傳真過去了。

Sam: Yes, Mr. Moore. The fax came in just now. We got both your order and sales contract.

山姆：有的，摩爾先生。傳真剛剛進來了，我收到你的訂單和銷貨合約。

Mr. Moore: Good. Please confirm my order of 10K forks and sign the contract by return.

摩爾先生：好，請確認我一萬叉子的訂單，並且將合約簽好回傳。

Sam: Before we sign the contract, I'd like to reconfirm a few things.

山姆：在我們簽銷貨合約之前，我們想再次確認一些細節。

Mr. Moore: Sure. Go ahead.

摩爾先生：沒問題，請說。

Sam: Stop me if I'm wrong. The goods should be shipped to L.A. by air. The freight term is FOB CKS airport. The payment will be made by T/T. No barcode required.

山姆：如果我說錯了請告訴我。這批貨要空運至洛杉磯，運費條款是FOB 中正機場，會利用電匯付款，產品不需要貼電腦條碼。

Mr. Moore: Correct. We will made the payment as soon as we receive the goods. Please process our order immediately.

摩爾先生：正確。一收到貨我們就會立刻付款。請馬上處理我們的訂單。

Sam: Sure. We will send the signed contract over and proceed with your order in no time.

山姆：沒問題。我們馬上會簽好合約寄過去，然後立刻處理您的訂單。

文法重點看這裡！

學完前面的會話之後，還要懂會話中的文法重點，才能應用在職場！以下補充重要的文法並做詳盡解析，把文法根基打好，讓你無論是出差還是洽商，都用正確英文和外國人打交道！

文法重點1
The fax comes in just now. 是錯誤用法

這個句子的問題出在，「just now」這個詞，必須和「過去式」連用。「just now」表示「剛剛、現在正～」的意思。當妳看到「傳真」時，就表示它已經進來了，所以這句要改成「The fax came in just now.」才正確。其他例句如下：

- **John came by me just now.** 約翰剛才從我旁邊走過去。
- **We talked on the phone just now.** 我們剛才在講電話。

文法重點2
stop 的用法

stop有兩種重要用法，其一是動詞要變成動名詞的形式，代表「停下某件事」。另外還有一種用法，即stop to V 的形式，代表「停下手邊的事，改為做另一件事」。以下用例句說明：

- **I stop shopping.** 我不買東西了。
- **I stop to shop.** 我停下手邊正在做的事，跑去買東西。

文法重點3
in no time 的用法

in no time不能照字面解釋為沒有時間，而是指「立刻；馬上」，跟soon的含意相當接近。例如：

- **I'll be there in no time.** 我快到了。

> at no time則是真的擁有否定的意味，意思為「從來不會；絕對不會」。例如：
> - **At no time should you commit a crime.** 在任何時候你都不應犯罪。

會話單字懂多少？

讀過前面的內容後,你是不是都懂得這些單字了呢?下列題目中的單字都是與會話及文法相關的單字,測驗看看自己會了多少吧!

( )❶ fax: (A) 列印 (B) 影印 (C) 傳真

( )❷ minute: (A) 秒鐘 (B) 分鐘 (C) 時鐘

( )❸ sales: (A) 銷售 (B) 清空 (C) 買進

( )❹ contract: (A) 合群 (B) 合作 (C) 合約

( )❺ sign: (A) 簽名 (B) 書籤 (C) 公證

( )❻ recomfirm: (A) 再次約定 (B) 再次確認 (C) 再次赴約

( )❼ term: (A) 暫時 (B) 條款 (C) 展覽

( )❽ airport: (A) 機場 (B) 機師 (C) 空服員

( )❾ payment: (A) 明細 (B) 細項 (C) 款項

( )❿ T/T: (A) 發票 (B) 電匯 (C) 收據

( )⓫ barcode: (A) 條碼 (B) 條件 (C) 空調

( )⓬ repeat: (A) 約定 (B) 聽寫 (C) 重述

( )⓭ similar: (A) 無效的 (B) 熟悉的 (C) 相似的

( )⓮ familiar: (A) 無效的 (B) 熟悉的 (C) 相似的

( )⓯ return: (A) 轉向 (B) 回覆 (C) 瑕疵

答案:1. (C) 2. (B) 3. (A) 4. (C) 5. (A) 6. (B) 7. (B) 8. (A) 9. (C)
10. (B) 11. (A) 12. (C) 13. (C) 14. (B) 15. (B)

It's a bit late since it's supposed be made a month ago.

這筆款項有點遲了，應該一個月以前就要付了。

職場會話跟著說！　🎧Track 065

Max: Sorry to bother you, but I'd like to know when we can receive your payment. It's a bit late since it's supposed to be made a month ago.

邁斯：很抱歉打擾妳，但是我想知道我們什麼時候可以收到您的款項。這筆款項有點遲了，應該一個月以前就要付了。

Ms. Reiner: I'm sorry about the delay. This simple job gets complicated because we are switching bank accounts. We've got tons of paperwork to work on and need another ten days to finish all procedures.

萊諾小姐：很抱歉延誤了。由於我們公司正在轉換帳戶，本來很簡單的付款動作變得很複雜，我們還需要10天的時間完成所有的書面手續。

Max: Is it possible that you pay it earlier by the end of this month?

邁斯：有沒有可能提早到這個月底以前付款呢？

Ms. Reiner: The next payment run we're doing will be ten days later. This is when the invoice will be paid, not earlier. Please understand.

萊諾小姐：我們公司下一次的款項核發日是10天後，到那時才能付款，無法提早。請體諒。

Max: We understand. But still, please expedite the payment as soon as possible. Thank you.

邁斯：我們瞭解，但是還是請妳們盡可能地加速付款動作。謝謝妳。

Part

8

報價與協調

文法重點看這裡！

學完前面的會話之後，還要懂會話中的文法重點，才能應用在職場！以下補充重要的文法並做詳盡解析，把文法根基打好，讓你無論是出差還是洽商，都用正確英文和外國人打交道！

文法重點1

I'd like to know when can we receive your payment? 是錯誤用法

以上的句子，如果只有後面的部分，即「When can we receive your payment?」，就是一個正確無誤的疑問句。但是這裡在前面加上了「I'd like to know～」，使得這個句子不再是疑問句，而是一句「直述句」。因此這個句子要改成「I'd like to know when we can receive your payment.」才對；主詞與助動詞不需對調，句末改為句點。

文法重點2

We've got many paperworks to work on and need ten days again to finish all the procedure. 是錯誤用法

「paperwork」（文書作業）是「不可數」名詞，所以不能寫成paperworks，也不能用many 來修飾。故前半句要改成「We've got a lot of paperwork to work on」。
若要表示「需要再～天的時間」的說法為「need another ~ days」或「need ~ more days」，故後半句要改成「and need another ten days to finish all the procedure.」或「and need ten more days to finish all the procedure.」。

文法重點3

This is when the invoice will pay. 是錯誤用法

「invoice」（發票）是要由人去付款，故這句要改成「This is when the invoice will be paid.」
在國際貿易上，一般都要先將「出貨檔（包括發票）」先寄給客人去提貨，款項之後才會付。除非是信用不良的客戶，必須先收到款項才出貨，不然一般都會通融先給客戶檔去清關提貨。

218

會話單字懂多少？

讀過前面的內容後，你是不是都懂得這些單字了呢？下列題目中的單字都是與會話及文法相關的單字，測驗看看自己會了多少吧！

( ) ❶ bother： (A) 超前 (B) 打擾 (C) 兄弟

( ) ❷ late： (A) 遲的 (B) 早的 (C) 舊的

( ) ❸ delay： (A) 延遲 (B) 加速 (C) 細節

( ) ❹ simple： (A) 複合的 (B) 繁複的 (C) 簡單的

( ) ❺ complicated：(A) 複合的 (B) 繁複的 (C) 簡單的

( ) ❻ switch： (A) 傳送 (B) 轉換 (C) 通勤

( ) ❼ account： (A) 印章 (B) 銀行 (C) 戶頭

( ) ❽ paperwork： (A) 日程表 (B) 程式 (C) 文書作業

( ) ❾ procedure：(A) 生產 (B) 程序 (C) 文書作業

( ) ❿ possible： (A) 可能的 (B) 無情的 (C) 機率的

( ) ⓫ month： (A) 季 (B) 週 (C) 月

( ) ⓬ invoice： (A) 報表 (B) 發票 (C) 收據

( ) ⓭ situation： (A) 情況 (B) 冷靜 (C) 承諾

( ) ⓮ expedite： (A) 減速 (B) 加速 (C) 煞車

( ) ⓯ ton： (A) 許多 (B) 不多 (C) 很少

答案：1. (B) 2. (A) 3. (A) 4. (C) 5. (B) 6. (B) 7. (C) 8. (C) 9. (B)
10. (A) 11. (C) 12. (B) 13. (A) 14. (B) 15. (A)

I'm sorry for the defective goods.

對於瑕疵品我們深感抱歉。

職場會話跟著說！ Track 066

Mr. Moore: Sam, we recently received a complaint from a customer about the spoons.

摩爾先生：山姆，我的一個客戶向我們抱怨湯匙出了問題。

Sam: Oh, what's the problem?

山姆：噢，是出了什麼問題呢？

Mr. Moore: It's about the poor plating. Can you replace them? Or they'll hand inspect and remove the defective ones and charge you back.

摩爾先生：湯匙的電鍍品質很差。你們可以換一批給他們嗎？否則他們要請工人整批檢查找出瑕疵的數量，然後向你們索賠。

Sam: I'm sorry for the defective goods. The replacement will be prepared and shipped by sea in three days.

山姆：對於瑕疵品我們深感抱歉。三天內我們會把替換的貨準備好並用海運寄出。

Mr. Moore: This is not acceptable. They need the goods very urgently. You got to airfreight them.

摩爾先生：這樣不行。他們急需這批貨。你們必須用空運寄出。

Sam: But the airfreight would be too expensive to afford. After all, we're making little money on this item in order to support your customer.

山姆：可是空運費太高我們負擔不起。畢竟為了照顧你的客戶，這個產品幾乎以成本價賣出。

Mr. Moore: I understand. Air-ship the replacement, anyway. I'll ask them to share the cost.

摩爾先生：我瞭解。無論如何還是用空運寄出。我會要求客戶分擔空運費。

Sam: Thank you. We will proceed immediately. And sorry again for all the trouble.

山姆：謝謝你，我們會馬上進行。也要為造成的麻煩再次跟你說聲抱歉。

文法重點看這裡！

學完前面的會話之後，還要懂會話中的文法重點，才能應用在職場！以下補充重要的文法並做詳盡解析，把文法根基打好，讓你無論是出差還是洽商，都用正確英文和外國人打交道！

文法重點1
My apologize for the defective goods.
是錯誤用法

道歉的名詞為「apology」，動詞為「apologize」，故這句應該改成下列任一種說法：

- **My apologies for the defective goods.** 對於瑕疵品，我向您致歉。
- **I apologize for the defective goods.** 對於瑕疵貨品我感到很抱歉。

文法重點2
equivalent 與replacement

一般在買賣貿易上，如果原本售出的商品有瑕疵，且非買主造成的，一般都會再寄另一批貨去替換，而替換的貨一般都用「replacement」這個字，幾乎沒有人會用「equivalent」（等值的）。

 equivalent 給人一種不一定是同樣的貨，但價值一樣的感覺。請各位記住最道地的用法吧。

文法重點3
I'll manage. 是錯誤用法

雖然「I'll manage.」字面上翻起來是「我會處理」，但其實這句話帶有點「不耐」的意味，有一種我會應付啦，你別囉唆或管太多的感覺。
所以如果要向客戶表達我會「試著去做」或「盡力去做」，可以用以下的短句：

- **I'll try.** 我會試著去做。
- **I'll try my best. / I'll do my best.** 我會盡力去做。

會話單字懂多少？

讀過前面的內容後，你是不是都懂得這些單字了呢？下列題目中的單字都是與會話及文法相關的單字，測驗看看自己會了多少吧！

( )❶ complaint： (A) 賠償 (B) 抱怨 (C) 嘲弄

( )❷ plating： (A) 電鍍 (B) 油漆 (C) 幣紙

( )❸ replace： (A) 替換 (B) 兼職 (C) 掌握

( )❹ apologize： (A) 憤怒 (B) 喜樂 (C) 道歉

( )❺ defective： (A) 完全的 (B) 瑕疵的 (C) 傾斜的

( )❻ equivalent： (A) 同音字 (B) 等價物 (C) 反義字

( )❼ replacement： (A) 承諾 (B) 匯兌 (C) 替換

( )❽ interchangeable： (A) 可兌現 (B) 可抽成 (C) 可互換

( )❾ manage： (A) 認真 (B) 應付 (C) 惡劣

( )❿ attitude： (A) 態度 (B) 希望 (C) 表現

( )⓫ dismiss： (A) 集會 (B) 罷工 (C) 解散

( )⓬ inspect： (A) 聽力 (B) 檢查 (C) 原料

( )⓭ remove： (A) 移除 (B) 跳動 (C) 跳高

( )⓮ airfreight： (A) 海運 (B) 空運 (C) 陸運

( )⓯ cost： (A) 利潤 (B) 毛利 (C) 成本

答案：1. (B) 2. (A) 3. (A) 4. (C) 5. (B) 6. (B) 7. (C) 8. (C) 9. (B)
10. (A) 11. (C) 12. (B) 13. (A) 14. (B) 15. (C)

Part **9**

展覽

You will be responsible for the exhibition this year.

妳將負責今年的展覽事宜。

 職場會話跟著說！ 🎧Track 067

Michelle: We missed the fair last year. Are we going to participate in the fair this year?

蜜雪：公司去年錯過了展覽。我們今年打算參展設攤位嗎？

Lindsay: Definitely. We are very satisfied with our several latest lines of products, and we want to promote them into the global market.

琳西：當然了。最新的幾條產品線讓我們非常滿意，我們想將它們推進全球市場。

Michelle: Just thinking about it makes me excited.

蜜雪：只要一想到要將新產品推進國際市場就讓我感到非常興奮。

Lindsay: You would be more excited if you knew who would be assigned to attend the fair.

琳西：妳要是知道公司準備派誰去參展，妳會更興奮。

Michelle: Oh, my goodness! Are you serious? Do you mean it?

蜜雪：噢，老天！妳是認真的嗎？妳是說真的嗎？

Lindsay: Of course I mean it! You will be responsible for the exhibition this year. You've been working so hard trying to promote the new lines. And you did great. You deserve this.

琳西：我當然是認真的！妳將負責今年的展覽事宜。妳一直很努力推展我們的新產品，而且妳做得很好。這是妳應得的。

文法重點看這裡！

學完前面的會話之後，還要懂會話中的文法重點，才能應用在職場！以下補充重要的文法並做詳盡解析，把文法根基打好，讓你無論是出差還是洽商，都用正確英文和外國人打交道！

文法重點1

Are we going to participate the fair this year? 是錯誤用法

「participate」是參加的意思，其為不及物動詞，因此後面有一個介系詞「in」，千萬不要漏掉。這句正確的說法為：

* **Are we going to participate in the fair this year?**
  我們今年打算參展嗎？

「參加」的其他的同義字如下：
* **take part in** 參加
* **join in** 參加

文法重點2

Just think about it makes me excited. 是錯誤用法

這句的的前半段是當自主詞，即makes 之前的部分是一個主詞，所以think 要由動詞改為動名詞，故整句的正確說法為：

* **Just thinking about it makes me excited.**
  光想到這件事就讓我感到興奮。

文法重點3

Are you sincere? 是錯誤用法

如果要詢問對方是說真的嗎？是認真的嗎？不能說Are you sincere?（你是正直的嗎？）正確的說法應該是：

* **Are you serious?** 你是認真的嗎？
* **Do you mean it?** 你是說真的嗎？

會話單字懂多少？

讀過前面的內容後,你是不是都懂得這些單字了呢?下列題目中的單字都是與會話及文法相關的單字,測驗看看自己會了多少吧!

( ) ❶ annual: (A) 一年兩次 (B) 兩年一次 (C) 一年一次

( ) ❷ fair: (A) 展覽 (B) 工廠 (C) 來源

( ) ❸ hold: (A) 量產 (B) 舉辦 (C) 考量

( ) ❹ Boston: (A) 旁氏 (B) 威靈頓 (C) 波士頓

( ) ❺ miss: (A) 核准 (B) 錯過 (C) 停產

( ) ❻ participate: (A) 參加 (B) 加入 (C) 會員

( ) ❼ satisfied: (A) 興奮的 (B) 失望的 (C) 滿意的

( ) ❽ several: (A) 幾乎不 (B) 幾個 (C) 很多

( ) ❾ assign: (A) 分派 (B) 搞混 (C) 懷疑

( ) ❿ price: (A) 報價 (B) 王子 (C) 公主

( ) ⓫ sincere: (A) 邪惡的 (B) 正直的 (C) 聰明的

( ) ⓬ serious: (A) 認真的 (B) 痛苦的 (C) 隨意的

( ) ⓭ responsible: (A) 負責 (B) 拒絕 (C) 異議

( ) ⓮ deserve: (A) 提到 (B) 應得 (C) 演講

( ) ⓯ wonder: (A) 奇蹟 (B) 願望 (C) 其實

答案:1. (C) 2. (A) 3. (B) 4. (C) 5. (B) 6. (A) 7. (C) 8. (B) 9. (A)
10. (A) 11. (B) 12. (A) 13. (A) 14. (B) 15. (A)

Unit 68

Dan and I will work on the design of our booth.

阿丹和我會負責設計我們的攤位。

 職場會話跟著說！ Track 068

Michelle: Guys, we are going to participate in the Home Product Fair in Boston. And I will be responsible for the exhibition this year.

蜜雪：大夥們，公司今年要參加波士頓的居家用品展。而今年由我負責展覽事宜。

Sam: Oh, that's wonderful! Congratulations, Michelle! We are so happy for you.

山姆：那真是太棒了！恭喜妳，蜜雪！我們都為妳感到高興。

Michelle: Thanks, everyone. Today each of you will get a new assignment. Any volunteers?

蜜雪：謝謝了，各位。今天每個人都會被分派新的任務。有人自願嗎？

Max: I'll get in contact with the show management and collect all the application forms and papers we need. I'll also check the daily event schedule of the show.

邁斯：我會聯絡主辦單位，收集所有需要的參展表格及文件。我也會查詢展場的每日活動表。

Sam: I'll have the catalogue of our products ready and will prepare fliers for the show.

山姆：我會將產品目錄準備好，也會準備可以在展場發的傳單。

Renee: Dan and I will work on the design of our booth.

芮妮：阿丹和我會負責設計我們的攤位。

Michelle: Great! You guys are excellent. Oh, I forgot to mention that one of you will be going to Boston with me. I'll let you know my decision next week. Now that's all for today. Let's roll.

蜜雪：很好！你們真的太優秀了。喔，我忘了提，你們其中一個會跟我一起到波士頓參展。下禮拜我會揭曉答案。今天就到此結束。大家行動吧。

文法重點看這裡！

學完前面的會話之後，還要懂會話中的文法重點，才能應用在職場！以下補充重要的文法並做詳盡解析，把文法根基打好，讓你無論是出差還是洽商，都用正確英文和外國人打交道！

文法重點1

We are going to attend to the Home Product Fair in Boston. 是錯誤用法

「attend」是「參加」的意思，後面可直接接受詞，不需要加上介系詞。如果是「attend to」，則有照料、專心、致力於的意思，與對話內容不相符，因此本句應該改成：

● **We are going to attend the Home Product Fair in Boston.**
  我們要參加波士頓的居家用品展。

文法重點2

Congratulation, Michelle! 是錯誤用法

「congratulation」的確是恭喜的意思，但記得，使用時一定要變成複數，即「Congratulations!」。學英文時，除了大方向要抓好，更要留意小地方，讓你的英文道地。其他例句如下：

● **Congratulations on your baby boy.**
  恭喜妳生了小寶寶。

● **We congratulate on your promotion.**
  我們恭喜你獲得升遷。

文法重點3

flier和flies 分清楚

錯別字也是是用英文時很大的致命傷。「flies」是「飛」的第三人稱單數，也是「蒼蠅」的複數，但是，文中真正要說的是「傳單」這個字。傳單的英文是「flier」，複數「fliers」。所以要特別留意容易誤用的字。

會話單字懂多少？

讀過前面的內容後，你是不是都懂得這些單字了呢？下列題目中的單字都是與會話及文法相關的單字，測驗看看自己會了多少吧！

( ) ❶ correct： (A) 糾正 (B) 擁護 (C) 採購

( ) ❷ exhibition： (A) 機會 (B) 展示 (C) 機構

( ) ❸ volunteer： (A) 遲疑 (B) 逼迫 (C) 自願者

( ) ❹ contact： (A) 聯絡 (B) 報價 (C) 因素

( ) ❺ show： (A) 使記誦 (B) 展示會 (C) 規格

( ) ❻ management： (A) 扣款 (B) 管理 (C) 條理

( ) ❼ collect： (A) 驚悚 (B) 收集 (C) 驚嘆

( ) ❽ application： (A) 飛行 (B) 申請 (C) 傳單

( ) ❾ form： (A) 表格 (B) 折券價 (C) 乘法

( ) ❿ catalogue： (A) 規矩 (B) 彩圖 (C) 目錄

( ) ⓫ design： (A) 設計 (B) 設計師 (C) 勤奮

( ) ⓬ booth： (A) 攤位 (B) 靴子 (C) 兩者都

( ) ⓭ mention： (A) 照料 (B) 提到 (C) 看管

( ) ⓮ daily： (A) 每日 (B) 每月 (C) 每年

( ) ⓯ event： (A) 事件 (B) 粗心 (C) 願望

答案：1. (A) 2. (B) 3. (C) 4. (A) 5. (B) 6. (B) 7. (B) 8. (B) 9. (A)
　　　10. (C) 11. (A) 12. (A) 13. (B) 14. (A) 15. (A)

I've also got the information about move-in and move-out hours and the show hours.

我手上也有進出場時間及展示時間的資料。

 職場會話跟著說！ Track **069**

Max: I have got in contact with the show management and received the application form for the fair participants. I'm going to send the application form over by today if possible.

邁斯：我已經聯絡主辦單位，也收到了參展廠商的申請表。可能的話，我今天就會把表格寄過去。

Michelle: Good. Anything else?

蜜雪：很好。其他呢？

Max: I've also got the information about move-in and move-out hours and the show hours.

邁斯：我手上也有進出場時間及展示時間的資料。

Michelle: What about the exhibition space? Do we know where to set up our booth?

蜜雪：那關於展場空間呢？我們知道要在哪裡設攤位嗎？

Max: According to John, you know, our temp sales representative in Boston, the exhibition space is very spacious. And Renee and Dan have completed the design of the booth. They will keep you updated.

邁斯：根據約翰的說法，就是我們臨時派駐在波士頓的業務代表，他說展場空間很寬敞。而且芮妮和阿丹已經設計好我們的攤位了，他們隨時會跟妳報告。

Michelle: Great. Anything else I need to know?

蜜雪：很好。還有什麼我需要知道的嗎？

Max: Oh, I'm trying to say hello to some of the co-organizers of the show. I see some familiar names on the list. You know, just in case.

邁斯：對了，我在協辦名單上看到一些熟人，我試著跟他們打聲招呼，妳知道的，只是以防萬一。

文法重點看這裡！

學完前面的會話之後，還要懂會話中的文法重點，才能應用在職場！以下補充重要的文法並做詳盡解析，把文法根基打好，讓你無論是出差還是洽商，都用正確英文和外國人打交道！

文法重點1
I have contact the show management.
是錯誤用法

聯絡的英文為「contact」。以上這句錯誤的地方在於，使用完成式時，contact 忘記變化成過去分詞。所以本句應該改成：
• I have contacted the show management. /
  I have got in contact with the show management.
  我已經聯絡展示會的主辦單位了。

文法重點2
apply form 是錯誤用法

基本上，沒有apply form 這種用法，雖然中文直接翻譯為「申請表」，但是請記得把動詞apply 的詞性改成名詞application才是正確的。所以申請書的正確說法是「application form」。

各種文書單據的用字如下：
• **form** 表格
• **sheet** 單子（紙張）
• **spreadsheet** 試算表（類似的格式）

文法重點3
They will keep you update. 是錯誤用法

使某人了解最新進度，update 要改成updated 才是正確的。所以本句的正確說法為：

• **They will keep you updated.**
  他們隨時會向你更新進度。

• **They will keep you posted.**
  他們隨時會向你報告最新情況。

會話單字懂多少？

讀過前面的內容後，你是不是都懂得這些單字了呢？下列題目中的單字都是與會話及文法相關的單字，測驗看看自己會了多少吧！

( ) ❶ receive： (A) 復原 (B) 接到 (C) 迴避

( ) ❷ apply： (A) 答覆 (B) 申請 (C) 快轉

( ) ❸ participant： (A) 演唱 (B) 參加 (C) 合作

( ) ❹ possible： (A) 無疑的 (B) 可能的 (C) 確認的

( ) ❺ anything： (A) 無論如何 (B) 到處 (C) 任何事

( ) ❻ information： (A) 資訊 (B) 關心 (C) 品管

( ) ❼ space： (A) 廣闊 (B) 空間 (C) 品質

( ) ❽ set： (A) 建築 (B) 數量 (C) 設立

( ) ❾ according： (A) 根據 (B) 規劃 (C) 重新

( ) ❿ temp： (A) 暫時的 (B) 銷售 (C) 報酬

( ) ⓫ representative： (A) 演唱 (B) 關心 (C) 代表

( ) ⓬ spacious： (A) 尊敬 (B) 寬廣 (C) 崇拜

( ) ⓭ complete： (A) 祭拜 (B) 遵照 (C) 完成

( ) ⓮ co-organizer： (A) 協辦者 (B) 飭回 (C) 營業

( ) ⓯ familiar： (A) 熟悉的 (B) 反對的 (C) 理解的

答案：1. (B) 2. (B) 3. (B) 4. (B) 5. (C) 6. (A) 7. (B) 8. (C) 9. (A)
10. (A) 11. (C) 12. (B) 13. (C) 14. (A) 15. (A)

By the way, when is the application deadline?

對了，參展報名截止是什麼時候？

Sam: I've prepared five cartons of our catalogues and fliers ready for the show.

山姆：我已經準備了五箱目錄和傳單供展場使用。

Michelle: I believed you've made sure that all four lines of products are printed on the catalogues and fliers, right?

蜜雪：我相信你已經確認四個產品種類都在目錄和傳單上了，對吧？

Sam: Of course. You can count on me!

山姆：那當然，我做事妳放心。

Michelle: Thank you, Sam. By the way, when is the application deadline? Max said he'd like to send out the form as soon as possible.

蜜雪：謝謝你，山姆。對了，參展報名截止是什麼時候？邁斯說他想盡快寄出申請表。

Sam: The deadline is this Friday. I've filled him in on the product lines and exhibition cost as well. He can send the application form anytime now if you okay it.

山姆：截止期限是這個星期五。我已經告訴他哪些產品要參展，也告訴他參展費用了。只要妳允許，他隨時可以寄出申請。

Michelle: Good. Tell him to proceed immediately. Let me know if he needs copies of my I.D.

蜜雪：很好，你請他盡快進行吧。如果他需要我的證件影本，再告訴我。

Sam: Oh, one more thing, the fair attendants should wear the badge. And our banners and signs can only be displayed in and around our own booth, not in aisles.

山姆：喔，還有一件事。參展人員必須配戴名牌。我們的旗幟或招牌只能放在我們的攤位裡面或旁邊，不能放在走道上。

文法重點看這裡！

學完前面的會話之後，還要懂會話中的文法重點，才能應用在職場！以下補充重要的文法並做詳盡解析，把文法根基打好，讓你無論是出差還是洽商，都用正確英文和外國人打交道！

文法重點1

production line 與 lines of products 的不同

「production line」是生產線的意思，可以想像在生產線上工作的作業員或技師那樣的情景。而「lines of products」則是指不同種類的「商品」，例如：

● **This skirt is one of our latest lines.** 這條裙子是我們最新的產品之一。

文法重點2

When is the application limit? 是錯誤用法

截止日期的英文為「deadline」，故這句應改為「When is the application deadline?」。要小心不要直接把中文翻成英文。

> 列舉一些常用日期的說法：
> ● **closing date** 結關日
> ● **ETD (estimated time of departure)** 預計出貨日
> ● **ETA (estimated time of arrival)** 預計到貨日

文法重點3

He can send the application form anytime now if you okay. 是錯誤用法

這句只有一個地方出了問題，就是「okay」後面忘了接受詞。「okay」當作「同意」時，是及物動詞，後面一定要接同意的事情。

> 表達「同意、允許行動」實用用語：
> ● **We green light the shipment.** 我們同意出貨。
> ● **We confirm the order. Please proceed.** 我們確認訂單。請進行。

讀過前面的內容後，你是不是都懂得這些單字了呢？下列題目中的單字都是與會話及文法相關的單字，測驗看看自己會了多少吧！

( ) ❶ prepare： (A) 準備 (B) 採排 (C) 了解

( ) ❷ carton： (A) 紙箱 (B) 方形 (C) 橢圓

( ) ❸ flier： (A) 垃圾 (B) 傳單 (C) 超過

( ) ❹ production： (A) 價格 (B) 油料 (C) 生產

( ) ❺ print： (A)排隊 (B) 聽從 (C) 印刷

( ) ❻ limit： (A) 插入 (B) 無知 (C) 限制

( ) ❼ deadline： (A) 終場休息 (B) 終場休息 (C) 截止日

( ) ❽ anytime： (A) 隨時 (B) 任何人 (C) 隨處

( ) ❾ okay： (A) 保存 (B) 熟悉 (C) 同意

( ) ❿ proceed： (A) 處理 (B) 進步 (C) 熱情

( ) ⓫ immediately： (A) 稍後 (B) 立即 (C) 商機

( ) ⓬ copy： (A) 團保 (B) 團結 (C) 影本

( ) ⓭ badge： (A) 蝙蝠 (B) 名牌 (C) 棒子

( ) ⓮ sign： (A) 訂婚 (B) 招牌 (C) 提議

( ) ⓯ aisle： (A) 大廳 (B) 走道 (C) 房間

答案：1. (A) 2. (A) 3. (B) 4. (C) 5. (C) 6. (C) 7. (C) 8. (A) 9. (C)
10. (A) 11. (B) 12. (C) 13. (B) 14. (B) 15. (B)

Actually, we went online and collected lots of fair related materials.

其實，我們上網收集了很多展覽相關資料。

 職場會話跟著說！ Track 071

Michelle: Designers, how are the booth design going?

蜜雪：設計師們，我們的攤位設計得如何了？

Renee: Oh, Michelle! Don't call me a designer. You've making me blush.

芮妮：噢，蜜雪！不要叫我設計師啦！我臉都紅了。

Dan: But I like that title. You can call me a designer, Michelle.

阿丹：可是我喜歡這個頭銜耶。妳可以這麼叫我，蜜雪。

Michelle: Haha. OK, joking aside, how are the things going?

蜜雪：哈……好了，說正經的，事情進行得怎麼樣了？

Renee: We've designed the booth in three sizes because we're not sure how large our space will be. Here you are.

芮妮：我們設計了三種不同尺寸的攤位，因為我們不知道分配到的範圍有多大。

Dan: Actually, we went online and collected lots of fair related materials. We also referred to some photos of previous exhibitions on the computer.

阿丹：其實，我們上網收集了很多展覽相關資料。我們也在電腦裡找到一些過去參展的照片作參考。

Michelle: Thanks for your hard work. We'll choose one of the booths for the show in the meeting.

蜜雪：謝謝，辛苦你們了。我們會在開會時選出最合適的展場攤位。

文法重點看這裡！

學完前面的會話之後，還要懂會話中的文法重點，才能應用在職場！以下補充重要的文法並做詳盡解析，把文法根基打好，讓你無論是出差還是洽商，都用正確英文和外國人打交道！

文法重點1
both、booth、boot、boost 分清楚

以上四個字相互誤用的是錯誤率極高，一般都是在粗心的情況下，沒有好好理解清楚而誤用。因此，一定要多加小心，不要讓錯別字影響你的英文實力。

- **both** 兩者都～
- **booth** 攤位
- **boot** 靴子
- **boost** 促進

文法重點2
joking beside 是錯誤用法

要表達「不說笑了，說正經的」時，正確的說法是「joking aside」，而不是 joking beside。很多時候，差一個字就差很多，請千萬要把正在學習的英文用語了解清楚，不要誤用了。

文法重點3
We'll choice one of the booths for the show.
是錯誤用法

「choice」是選擇的意思，照中文翻譯好像沒錯。但是不要忘了，一個句子一定要有動詞，因為choice 是「選擇」的名詞，所以要改成選擇的動詞，即「choose」才正確。因此，本句的正確說法為：

- **We'll choose one of the booths for the show.**
  我們會選出一個展示用的攤位。

會話單字懂多少？

讀過前面的內容後，你是不是都懂得這些單字了呢？下列題目中的單字都是與會話及文法相關的單字，測驗看看自己會了多少吧！

（　）❶ designer： (A) 設計 (B) 設計師 (C) 地點

（　）❷ design： (A) 設計 (B) 設計師 (C) 地點

（　）❸ blush： (A) 蒼白 (B) 臉紅 (C) 沖水

（　）❹ title： (A) 名單 (B) 首肯 (C) 頭銜

（　）❺ joke： (A) 開玩笑 (B) 騎士 (C) 唱機

（　）❻ beside： (A) 在～上面 (B) 在～旁邊 (C) 在～下方

（　）❼ aside： (A) 丟掉 (B) 放一旁 (C) 絞碎

（　）❽ welcome： (A) 歡迎 (B) 當然 (C) 幾乎

（　）❾ large： (A) 瘦的 (B) 長的 (C) 大的

（　）❿ excellent： (A) 資本 (B) 通路 (C) 優秀

（　）⓫ actually： (A) 其實 (B) 終於 (C) 否則

（　）⓬ online： (A) 購物 (B) 上網 (C) 美味

（　）⓭ related： (A) 相關的 (B) 通告 (C) 宣傳

（　）⓮ choice： (A) 選擇 (B) 事件 (C) 未來

（　）⓯ refer： (A) 標誌 (B) 提議 (C) 參考

答案：1. (B) 2. (A) 3. (B) 4. (C) 5. (A) 6. (B) 7. (B) 8. (A) 9. (C)
10. (C) 11. (A) 12. (B) 13. (A) 14. (A) 15. (C)

Unit 72

The main point of our show is to promote our latest products into the global market.

我們展覽的重點就是要把最新的產品推到國際市場。

 職場會話跟著說！ 🎧 Track 072

Michelle: Today we'll discuss how we should highlight our exhibition and decide on the focus of our show. Any ideas?

蜜雪：今天我們要討論如何強調我們這次的展覽，要決定什麼是這次展覽的重點。有什麼想法嗎？

Max: The main point of our show is to promote our latest products into the global market. So I think the demonstration is the most important part of our show.

邁斯：我們展覽的重點就是要把最新的產品推到國際市場。因此，我覺得產品展示說明是最重要的部分。

Renee: I agree with Max. I'm convinced that our products will sell pretty well if we can draw buyers' attention to our demonstrations. They will be amazed at what they see.

芮妮：我同意邁斯的看法。我很肯定，只要我們的產品解說展示能把買家的目光吸引過來，我們的產品一定會大賣。我們的產品一定會令大家大為驚奇。

Sam: After all, our products are the result of the latest technology. They are high-tech items.

山姆：畢竟我們的產品是最新科技的結晶，是高科技產品。

Michelle: Then demonstrations will be the highlight of our show. By the way, Dan, I'll confirm our daily schedule during the fair later today. And you need to book our flights first thing in the morning.

蜜雪：那就決定產品展示說明為我們展覽的重點。對了，阿丹，我今天晚點會確認展場那幾天的行程。你明天一早就要先預定好機票。

文法重點看這裡！

學完前面的會話之後，還要懂會話中的文法重點，才能應用在職場！以下補充重要的文法並做詳盡解析，把文法根基打好，讓你無論是出差還是洽商，都用正確英文和外國人打交道！

文法重點1
pull buyers' attention 是錯誤用法

這句是「將買家的注意力拉過來」的直譯，但實際上並不是這樣講。「吸引某人的注意」應該說成「draw someone's attention to~」，因此正確說法為：

• **...if we can draw buyers' attention to our demonstrations.** 如果我們可以將買家的注意力吸引到我們的產品展示說明上。

文法重點2
They will be amazing at what they see.
是錯誤用法

「amazing」是「令人驚奇的」；「amazed」是「感到驚奇的」。因此，這句應該改成「They will be amazed at what they see.」（他們將會驚嘆自己所看到的。）

> 常用的類似的用法還有：
> • **interesting** 有意思的
> • **interested** 感到有興趣的
> • **impressing** 令人印象深刻的
> • **impressed** 感到印象深刻的

文法重點3
By the way 的用法

「By the way」是片語，意思是「順帶一提」，常常會簡寫成「BTW」。在對話中使用「By the way」時，通常是要提到與當下對話相關性不高的話題。

會話單字懂多少？

9

展覽

讀過前面的內容後，你是不是都懂得這些單字了呢？下列題目中的單字都是與會話及文法相關的單字，測驗看看自己會了多少吧！

( )❶ highlight：(A) 高山 (B) 強調 (C) 補充

( )❷ convinced：(A) 確實的 (B) 強行的 (C) 確信的

( )❸ pull：(A) 拉 (B) 推 (C) 彈

( )❹ buyer：(A) 買家 (B) 賣家 (C) 買賣

( )❺ attention：(A) 注意力 (B) 公信力 (C) 魄力

( )❻ attract：(A) 放肆 (B) 吸引 (C) 說服

( )❼ draw：(A) 花費 (B) 吸引 (C) 承諾

( )❽ memory：(A) 背誦 (B) 磁碟 (C) 回憶

( )❾ phrase：(A) 用語 (B) 謊言 (C) 實話

( )❿ memorize：(A) 記憶 (B) 瑕疵 (C) 塗鴉

( )⓫ focus：(A) 焦點 (B) 雷射 (C) 實驗

( )⓬ latest：(A) 最新的 (B) 最舊的 (C) 最棒的

( )⓭ result：(A) 結果 (B) 入門的 (C) 進階的

( )⓮ technology：(A) 結果 (B) 科技 (C) 類比

( )⓯ book：(A) 預訂 (B) 雜誌 (C) 大詞典

答案：1. (B) 2. (C) 3. (A) 4. (A) 5. (A) 6. (B) 7. (B) 8. (C) 9. (A)
10. (A) 11. (A) 12. (A) 13. (A) 14. (B) 15. (A)

We are not far from the fair.

我們離展場並不遠。

職場會話跟著說！ 🎧Track **073**

Michelle: The show is tomorrow. But today we need to check our booth and make sure all our products are in good condition.

蜜雪：展覽明天才開始，但是今天我們要先檢查一下攤位，確認所有產品的狀況都良好。

Dan: Yes, Ma'am. Let's go. Maybe we can grab a bite on the way to the fair. I'm hungry.

阿丹：好的，小姐。我們走吧，看能不能順便在路上吃點東西，我肚子餓了。

Michelle: What are you hungry for?

蜜雪：你想吃什麼？

Dan: A hot dog, the works, would be great.

阿丹：一份熱狗，什麼醬料都加，就再好不過了。

Michelle: Ah, here comes the shuttle bus. Come on, let's move.

蜜雪：啊，接駁車來了，快點，我們走了。

Dan: We are not far from the fair. The map says it's the first turning on the right after the library.

阿丹：我們離展場並不遠，地圖是標示著過了圖書館右邊第一個左轉。

Michelle: OK. We're here. Let's get off the bus.

蜜雪：好了，我們到了。下車吧。

文法重點看這裡！

學完前面的會話之後，還要懂會話中的文法重點，才能應用在職場！以下補充重要的文法並做詳盡解析，把文法根基打好，讓你無論是出差還是洽商，都用正確英文和外國人打交道！

文法重點1

in good situation　是錯誤用法

要表達「狀況良好」應該說「in good condition」。雖然situation 與condition 都有「情況」的意思，但這裡不能用situation替代condition。故正確的說法為「in good condition」。

由「condition」組成的其他用法如下：
- **on the condition that~** 在～條件之下
- **in dreadful conditions** 在惡劣的環境下

文法重點2

grip a bite　是錯誤用法

雖然「grip」和「grab」都有抓取的意思，這裡不能說成grip a bite，而要說成「grab a bite」（隨意買點東西吃），因為「grab」有「匆匆吃什麼東西」的意思。
關於「grip」這個單字，以下這個慣用語很好用，請務必記下來：
- **get a grip** 冷靜一點

文法重點3

Let's get down the bus.　是錯誤用法

這句的正確說法為「get down from the bus」（從車上下來／下車）

相關用法為：
- **get on the bus** 上公車
- **get off the bus** 下公車
- **get in the car** 坐上汽車
- **get out of the car** 下（汽）車

會話單字懂多少？

讀過前面的內容後，你是不是都懂得這些單字了呢？下列題目中的單字都是與會話及文法相關的單字，測驗看看自己會了多少吧！

( ) ❶ situation： (A) 情況 (B) 相處 (C) 湯匙

( ) ❷ grip： (A) 搔 (B) 抓 (C) 踢

( ) ❸ bite： (A) 便餐 (B) 骨折 (C) 受傷

( ) ❹ hungry： (A) 餓了 (B) 睏了 (C) 倦了

( ) ❺ grab： (A) 匆忙趕著 (B) 慢慢做事 (C) 速戰速決

( ) ❻ embarrassing： (A) 感到尷尬 (B) 害羞 (C) 令人尷尬

( ) ❼ shuttle： (A) 穿梭 (B) 太空梭 (C) 關上

( ) ❽ move： (A) 移動 (B) 跳躍 (C) 蹲下

( ) ❾ far： (A) 遠的 (B) 近的 (C) 熱鬧的

( ) ❿ map： (A) 座標 (B) 指南針 (C) 地圖

( ) ⓫ turning： (A) 轉角 (B) 回憶 (C) 尺規

( ) ⓬ library： (A) 閱讀 (B) 欄位 (C) 圖書館

( ) ⓭ close： (A) 上面 (B) 靠近 (C) 斜角

( ) ⓮ next： (A) 上一個 (B) 中間 (C) 下一個

( ) ⓯ block： (A) 街口 (B) 大道 (C) 公園

答案：1. (A) 2. (B) 3. (A) 4. (A) 5. (A) 6. (C) 7. (A) 8. (A) 9. (A)
10. (C) 11. (A) 12. (C) 13. (B) 14. (C) 15. (A)

Unit 74

Dan, what do you think of our exhibition so far?

阿丹，你覺得到目前為止我們展覽辦得如何？

 職場會話跟著說！ Track 074

Michelle: Dan, what do you think of our exhibition so far? I need to take some notes and I need your opinion.

蜜雪：阿丹，你覺得到目前為止我們展覽辦得如何？我得做些記錄，需要你的觀點。

Dan: I think no one can match us as far as quality is concerned.

阿丹：我覺得就品質來說，沒有別的產品比得上我們。

Michelle: What do you think about TG Co. next to our booth?

蜜雪：你覺得我們隔壁攤的TG公司怎麼樣？

Dan: I must say I'm quite impressed by their approach to business.

阿丹：我得承認他們做生意的方法讓我印象深刻。

Michelle: I feel the same way. Their way of doing business is quite aggressive.

蜜雪：我也有同感。他們做生意的手段很激進。

Dan: But I don't think they'll go very far if they don't improve the quality of their products.

阿丹：但是我不認為他們生意能做得長久，如果他們不改善產品品質的話。

Michelle: So the bottom line is quality.

蜜雪：所以重點是品質。

文法重點看這裡！

學完前面的會話之後，還要懂會話中的文法重點，才能應用在職場！以下補充重要的文法並做詳盡解析，把文法根基打好，讓你無論是出差還是洽商，都用正確英文和外國人打交道！

文法重點1
What do you think our exhibition so far?
是錯誤用法

這句是從中文直接翻過來的，缺了介系詞of所以不正確，正確的說法為「What do you think of our exhibition so far?」（你覺得到目前為止我們的展覽辦得如何？）千萬不要忘記介系詞！

文法重點2
I'm quite impressing by their approach to business. 是錯誤用法

「impressing」是「令人印象深刻的」；「impressed」是「感到印象深刻」。因此，這句應該改成「I'm quite impressed by their approach to business.」（他們做生意的方法讓我印象深刻。）

常用的類似的用法還有：
- **confusing** 令人困惑的
- **confused** 感到困惑的
- **embarrassing** 令人尷尬的
- **embarrassed** 感到尷尬的

文法重點3
button 與 bottom 大不同

「button」指按鈕，「bottom」則指底部，這兩個字發音很容易被搞混！他們最大的不同在於「bottom」說完嘴巴要閉上，而「button」說完嘴巴不必闔上。如果能把尾音發清楚，就成功了一半囉！

會話單字懂多少？

讀過前面的內容後，你是不是都懂得這些單字了呢？下列題目中的單字都是與會話及文法相關的單字，測驗看看自己會了多少吧！

( ) ❶ match：(A) 摔角 (B) 攻擊 (C) 匹敵

( ) ❷ concern：(A) 服務 (B) 涉及 (C) 傷心

( ) ❸ edge：(A) 優勢 (B) 清空 (C) 退化

( ) ❹ quite：(A) 超過 (B) 合作 (C) 相當

( ) ❺ approach：(A) 方法 (B) 書籤 (C) 公證

( ) ❻ aggressive：(A) 激進的 (B) 偷懶的 (C) 開放的

( ) ❼ improve：(A) 暫時 (B) 改善 (C) 雕刻

( ) ❽ button：(A) 按鈕 (B) 底線 (C) 飛安

( ) ❾ main：(A) 次要 (B) 旁支 (C) 主要

( ) ❿ point：(A) 發票 (B) 要點 (C) 收據

( ) ⓫ conclusion：(A) 結論 (B) 條件 (C) 支票

( ) ⓬ pronunciation：(A) 約定 (B) 聽寫 (C) 發音

( ) ⓭ bottom：(A) 按鈕 (B) 底線 (C) 飛安

( ) ⓮ note：(A) 記性 (B) 記下 (C) 記得

( ) ⓯ opinion：(A) 合作 (B) 觀點 (C) 瑕疵

答案：1. (C) 2. (B) 3. (A) 4. (C) 5. (A) 6. (A) 7. (B) 8. (A) 9. (C)
10. (B) 11. (A) 12. (C) 13. (B) 14. (B) 15. (B)

Maybe we should buy some creative products for our RD team.

也許我們該幫研發團隊帶些有創意的產品回去。

 職場會話跟著說！ Track 075

Salesperson: Hello, ma'am. Would you like to take a look at our products? They are high-tech items.

業務員：女士，您好。您要不要參考一下我們的產品？我們賣的都是高科技產品。

Michelle: Hmm, they look interesting. Can I have a copy of your brochure?

蜜雪：嗯，你們的產品看起來蠻有意思的。可以給我一本介紹手冊嗎？

Salesperson: Sure, do you have a minute? Why don't you have a seat and let me show you how to operate this item?

業務員：沒問題。可以打擾一分鐘嗎？您要不要請坐，我可以示範怎麼操作這個產品給您看。

Michelle: OK. Go ahead.

蜜雪：好啊，你開始操作吧。

Salesperson: You see, if you press this red button, the helmet becomes an umbrella. And it's not heavy at all. You can try it yourself.

業務員：妳瞧，如果妳按下這個紅色按鈕，這頂安全帽就變成一支雨傘，而且一點也不重。妳可以自己試試看。

Michelle: It is very light. How amazing!

蜜雪：真的很輕耶。真神奇！

Dan: Michelle, here you are. What are you doing here?

阿丹：蜜雪，原來妳在這裡。妳在這裡幹嘛？

Michelle: I found something very interesting. Maybe we should buy some creative products for our RD team.

蜜雪：我發現很有意思的東西。也許我們該幫研發團隊帶些有創意的產品回去。

文法重點看這裡！

學完前面的會話之後，還要懂會話中的文法重點，才能應用在職場！以下補充重要的文法並做詳盡解析，把文法根基打好，讓你無論是出差還是洽商，都用正確英文和外國人打交道！

文法重點1

Do you have the time? 使用要注意

「Do you have the time?」是「請問現在幾點？」的意思。

另外一句看起來很像的句子「Do you have time?」（你有空嗎？）如果這句用在陌生人身上，會給人感覺有點輕浮。建議如果要搭訕，可以請問對方「Do you have the time?」（請問現在幾點？）也可以達到開啟話題的功效。

文法重點2

have a sit 是錯誤用法

要人家請坐的說法是「have a seat」。國人發sit（短音）和seat（長音）時，常常發得都一樣，沒有區別，因此要特別注意發音上的問題。

文法重點3

And it's not weight at all. 是錯誤用法

這句是從中文直譯過去的，但正確的說法應該是「And it's not heavy at all.」（它一點也不重。）請一定要先留意詞性的變化，再套入句子中。

表達「重的、龐大的」說法有：
- **weighty** 沈重的、有心事的
- **hefty** 重的、肌肉發達的
- **bulky** 笨重的

會話單字懂多少？

讀過前面的內容後，你是不是都懂得這些單字了呢？下列題目中的單字都是與會話及文法相關的單字，測驗看看自己會了多少吧！

( ) ❶ ma'am：(A) 阿姨 (B) 女士 (C) 爵士

( ) ❷ high-tech：(A) 高科技 (B) 草創 (C) 落後

( ) ❸ brochure：(A) 小冊子 (B) 參考書 (C) 劇本

( ) ❹ operate：(A) 延遲 (B) 加速 (C) 操作

( ) ❺ ahead：(A) 向後 (B) 向前 (C) 向下

( ) ❻ press：(A) 揪 (B) 按 (C) 摔

( ) ❼ helmet：(A) 棒球帽 (B) 貝雷帽 (C) 頭盔

( ) ❽ umbrella：(A) 雨衣 (B) 雨帽 (C) 雨傘

( ) ❾ weight：(A) 容量 (B) 重量 (C) 長度

( ) ❿ light：(A) 輕的 (B) 重的 (C) 沉的

( ) ⓫ heavy：(A) 輕的 (B) 薄的 (C) 重的

( ) ⓬ amazing：(A) 很差 (B) 很棒 (C) 很恐怖

( ) ⓭ creative：(A) 創意 (B) 抄襲 (C) 專注

( ) ⓮ RD：(A) 研發 (B) 人力資源 (C) 業務

( ) ⓯ team：(A) 團隊 (B) 加速 (C) 歡呼

答案：1. (B) 2. (A) 3. (A) 4. (C) 5. (B) 6. (B) 7. (C) 8. (C) 9. (B)
10. (A) 11. (C) 12. (B) 13. (A) 14. (A) 15. (A)

Unit 76

We will inform you of the shipping details before we ship the goods.

我們出貨前還會再通知妳出貨明細。

職場會話跟著說！ 🎧 Track 076

Dan: Please fill out this order sheet. And don't forget to write down your name, address and telephone number.

阿丹：麻煩填寫這張訂購單。別忘了填上妳的大名、地址和電話。

Customer: When will I receive the goods?

客戶：我什麼時候可以收到貨？

Dan: Normally our lead time is 14 days.

阿丹：一般我們的交貨期是14天。

Customer: Can you ship it any sooner? Can the goods arrive no later than this month?

客戶：能快一點出貨嗎？貨物可以在月底前到達嗎？

Dan: We'll do our best. We'll proceed with your order first thing in the morning.

阿丹：我們會盡量趕。我們明天一早就會先處理妳的訂單。

Customer: Thank you, young man.

客戶：謝了，年輕人。

Dan: No problem. We will inform you of the shipping details before we ship the goods. Thank you for your order, ma'am.

阿丹：不客氣。我們出貨前還會再通知妳出貨明細。謝謝妳的訂單，女士。

Customer: I've been looking for a product like this, and now I found it at last. Hope we will have a good and long-tern business relationship.

客戶：我一直在尋找你們生產的這種產品，現在終於被我找到了。希望我們能有一個美好、長久的合作關係。

文法重點看這裡！

學完前面的會話之後，還要懂會話中的文法重點，才能應用在職場！以下補充重要的文法並做詳盡解析，把文法根基打好，讓你無論是出差還是洽商，都用正確英文和外國人打交道！

文法重點1

Please fill this order sheet. 是錯誤用法

要表達「填寫表格」時，英文要用「fill out」或「fill in」這兩個片語。所以本句的正確說法為「Please fill out this order sheet.」或「Please fill in this order sheet.」（請填寫這張訂購單。）

> 另外一些相關用法為：
> - **write down** 寫下
> - **note down** 記錄下來
> - **keep a diary (keep a journal)** 寫日記

文法重點2

Can the goods be arrived no later than this month? 是錯誤用法

這裡有個很重要的地方，「arrive」這個字很妙，無論主詞是人或物，他都是使用「主動式」，所以這個句子應該改成「Can the goods arrive no later than this month?」（貨可以在這個月前送到嗎？）再舉一些實用例句：

- **The magazine I ordered will arrive in two days.** 我訂的雜誌兩天後會送到。
- **We arrived in Hong Kong last night.** 我們昨天晚上抵達香港。
- **The baby girl arrived yesterday morning.** 這名女嬰是昨天早上出生的。

文法重點3

We will inform you the shipping details. 是錯誤用法

「通知某人事情」時，要用「inform sb. of sth.」這個片語，記得這裡的介系詞是「of」喔。所以這句正確的說法為「We will inform you of the shipping details.」（我們會通知你出貨明細。）

「inform sb. of sth.」是個任何考試都會出現的片語，請一定要想辦法記下來喔。

會話單字懂多少？

讀過前面的內容後，你是不是都懂得這些單字了呢？下列題目中的單字都是與會話及文法相關的單字，測驗看看自己會了多少吧！

（　）❶ fill： (A) 賠償 (B) 填滿 (C) 丟棄

（　）❷ sheet： (A) 單子 (B) 零錢 (C) 幣紙

（　）❸ forget： (A) 忘記 (B) 記得 (C) 掌握

（　）❹ write： (A) 唱 (B) 寫 (C) 畫

（　）❺ address： (A) 門牌 (B) 信箱 (C) 地址

（　）❻ telephone： (A) 手機 (B) 電話 (C) 電郵

（　）❼ goods： (A) 很好 (B) 抽屜 (C) 貨物

（　）❽ normally： (A) 同音的 (B) 變態的 (C) 正常的

（　）❾ sooner： (A) 最快 (B) 較快 (C) 較慢

（　）❿ arrive： (A) 到達 (B) 離開 (C) 互換

（　）⓫ month： (A) 嘴巴 (B) 老鼠 (C) 月份

（　）⓬ proceed： (A) 憤怒 (B) 進行 (C) 道歉

（　）⓭ inform： (A) 通知 (B) 應付 (C) 平等

（　）⓮ long-term： (A) 短期 (B) 長期 (C) 暫時

（　）⓯ relationship： (A) 婚姻 (B) 親戚 (C) 關係

答案：1. (B) 2. (A) 3. (A) 4. (B) 5. (C) 6. (B) 7. (C) 8. (C) 9. (B)
　　　10. (A) 11. (C) 12. (B) 13. (A) 14. (B) 15. (C)

NOTE

原來如此 系列 E259

這本口說最實用！英文職場高手，76篇情境會話從此擺脫中式英文

職場情境對話╳文法解析╳單字測驗，學會最正確、最道地的英文！

作　　者　張慈庭、許澄瑄◎合著
顧　　問　曾文旭
社　　長　王毓芳
編輯統籌　耿文國、黃璽宇
主　　編　吳靜宜
執行主編　潘妍潔
執行編輯　吳芸蓁、吳欣蓉
美術編輯　王桂芳、張嘉容
法律顧問　北辰著作權事務所　蕭雄淋律師、幸秋妙律師

初　　版　2022年07月
出　　版　捷徑文化出版事業有限公司
電　　話　（02）2752-5618
傳　　真　（02）2752-5619

定　　價　新台幣350元／港幣117元
產品內容　一書

總 經 銷　采舍國際有限公司
地　　址　235新北市中和區中山路二段366巷10號3樓
電　　話　（02）8245-8786
傳　　真　（02）8245-8718

港澳地區總經銷　和平圖書有限公司
地　　址　香港柴灣嘉業街12號百樂門大廈17樓
電　　話　（852）2804-6687
傳　　真　（852）2804-6409

▶本書部分圖片由 freepik 圖庫提供。

捷徑 Book站

現在就上臉書（FACEBOOK）「捷徑BOOK站」並按讚加入粉絲團，
就可享每月不定期新書資訊和粉絲專享小禮物喔！
http://www.facebook.com/royalroadbooks
讀者來函：royalroadbooks@gmail.com

本書如有缺頁、破損或倒裝，
請聯絡捷徑文化出版社。

【版權所有　翻印必究】

國家圖書館出版品預行編目資料

這本口說最實用！英文職場高手，76篇情境會話
從此擺脫中式英文／張慈庭、許澄瑄合著.
-- 初版. -- [臺北市]：捷徑文化出版事業有限公司,
2022.07
　面；　公分. -- (原來如此：E259)
ISBN 978-626-7116-11-1(平裝)
1. CST: 英語　2. CST: 讀本
805.18　　　　　　　　　　　　　111008184